1919 A Land Fit For Heroes

'This captivating book....described with colour and panache. Hutton is a gifted storyteller, which makes for stimulating reading.'
(Who Do You Think You Are Magazine)

The Vice Captain

'Fascinating details of Soho from a completely different angle. It made me nostalgic to visit the watering holes of my youth… I can thoroughly recommend this book (on) London's naughty square mile. It's beautifully written.'
(George Melly)

'So easy to read – so hard to put down.'
(Colin Dexter)

The Story of Soho: The Windmill Years 1932–64

'Hutton has an engaging style and the story races along.'
(Theatre Magazine)

'This is a lively memoir, uncovering tales of villains and tarts and the birth of the sex industry… fascinating stories, well told.'
(Books Monthly)

FULL CIRCLE

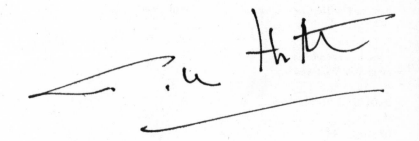

Full Circle

Published by The Conrad Press Ltd. in the United Kingdom 2022

Tel: +44(0)1227 472 874
www.theconradpress.com
info@theconradpress.com

ISBN 978-1-914913-42-6

Printed and bound in Great Britain by Clays Ltd, Elcograf S.p.A

Typesetting and cover design by The Book Typesetters
www.thebooktypesetters.com

The Conrad Press logo was designed by Maria Priestley.

FULL CIRCLE

A story of love, fame and despair

MIKE HUTTON

Acknowledgements

For my daughter Chloe, who persuaded me to write this book.

And for Joan Beretta, for her invaluable help.

Prologue

Much has been written about my grandfather, the artist Sir Alexander Brett, and the internationally acclaimed entertainer Gloria Bird, but little about their long term relationship. This took place over a period of almost sixty years and was intense yet complex. Their meetings were often months, sometimes years apart, depending on their commitments. Despite both of them marrying and seeking love elsewhere, the bond between them remained. Originally based on passion it changed and deepened. Their professional successes were frequently balanced by hostile criticism and personal tragedies.

An extensive archive of material including photographs, interviews, correspondence and film footage allows their unique story to be told set amidst a backdrop of many of the most important events of the 20th century.

Rex Brett
Oxfordshire
August 2025

Chapter 1

June 1976

Standing on the steps of Burlington House, he stared rather apprehensively at the crowds milling around in the grand courtyard. Snapped at that moment by an agency photographer, the picture appeared the following week in the Tatler as part of their coverage of the summer exhibition at the Royal Academy. A casual observer may have concluded that Sir Alexander Brett was a former colonial officer, or perhaps a military man rather than Britain's foremost artist. His white linen suit is well cut and his brogues have been buffed to a glossy sheen.

He even sports a regimental tie and his white hair is cut short. Not at all our perceived perception of a Bohemian painter. Strangely it is in the dark months of winter when he assumes this role. He is featured regularly in the press wearing a wide brimmed fedora and flamboyant cloak.

Stepping into the crowd, he walks stiffly with the aid of a black Malacca cane, which he taps impatiently trying to navigate a route through the throng. His smart appearance has not been helped by a battered old panama hat that is needed for protection from the searing heat. For two weeks London has sweltered under cloudless skies, with humidity levels more associated with the middle east. Britons spend much of the year complaining about the climate and longing for some sunshine, but within days of a heatwave they crave rain. What is enjoyed on foreign beaches becomes a trial, particularly in urban areas. People become tetchy and aggressive.

Just outside the entrance to the exhibition a car has broken down causing a massive traffic jam in Piccadilly. Horns blare and there is much gesticulating as sweat-drenched drivers get out of their cars and add their voices to the din. Turning right, Alex waits patiently for a swarm of Japanese tourists to stop photographing each other and continues his short journey to the hotel. His shirt is sticking to him and he is worried that the discharge from his back will show through his jacket. The traffic has started moving again, but raising his cane skywards he steps out on to the road in front of a taxi and, ignoring the torrent of abuse, makes his way to the front entrance of the Ritz.

The noise and heat of a chaotic London is eliminated as soon as he enters the hotel. All is peace and expensive opulence. There is a sense of theatre with the winter garden designed to fill the view of everyone entering. Framed by impressive columns and steps that give it the impression of a stage set. Recently mirrors had been added creating an extra sense of space, whilst daylight came from a central roof light.

As arranged a waiter was on hand with a double measure of his favourite Irish whiskey. Adding water, Alex positioned himself opposite the entrance. It was ridiculous but he was as nervous as a young man going on a first date.

As she was always late he reckoned he would have time for a quick top-up. Not so. He sensed her arrival before seeing her. She had come in from the side entrance in Arlington

Street. She never ceased to surprise. Latterly she had taken to wearing all manner of ethnic dress, African robes, Indian saris and even Scottish tartan. He struggled to his feet. She was wearing a variation on a Mao suit, but not one the chairman would have approved of. Tight fitting and made of silk, it was set off to great effect by her hair shorn close to her scalp. Shorter even than the gamine style she had favoured back in the 1920s. Bizarrely she wore no shoes.

She reached up and gently kissed him on the cheek. Her perfume lingered as she linked arms with him and without speaking they made their way to the restaurant. There was a pause in the babble of conversation as they were escorted to their table overlooking Green Park. One couple rose and for a horrible moment Alex was sure they were going to applaud. Champagne was uncorked. 'You look wonderful' he told her. 'Of course!' she replied with a theatrical turn of her head until her face was transformed into the cheeky grin that she reserved for him, an expression that few of her fans ever saw. They raised their glasses to each other. Reaching across, she gently stroked his cheek. Those wonderful hands that had aroused and comforted him over all those years. Without understanding why he started to cry.

Later that evening Alex Brett took a cab to the London Palladium. A huge illuminated sign proclaimed the show titled *Glorious Gloria*. In less sensitive times she had been known as *The Glorious Blackbird*. He was met at the entrance by a uniformed attendant and escorted upstairs to a box overlooking the stage. He felt rather exposed, left to watch the performance all on his own. It was rather sad that he could think of no-one to accompany him. Having been a fairly gregarious man all his life, he realised whilst having many acquaintances, he was left with few true friends.

Gloria did not appear in the first half of the show. It featured dancers, a comedian whose singing was better than his jokes and a very good impressionist who was making a name for himself in a popular television series. Alex was nervous about Gloria's performance. The reviews had been mixed. *The Mirror* and the Express, lavish in their praise for this ageless icon. Others emphasised the enthusiastic response of the audience. She obviously retained a hard core of devoted fans. It was left to the theatre critic of *The Times* to suggest that it was perhaps time for Gloria to gracefully leave the stage.

During the interval he was brought a glass of champagne and some light refreshment. Looking down on the audience returning from the bars, he reflected on how much he loved the theatre and the many hours he had spent painting from the wings or from a box similar to the one he currently occupied. From opera to music hall, his work from that period of his life remained some of his best.

Gloria was on stage from the moment the curtain went up. For decades she had appeared initially on the extreme right of the chorus, always purposely being out of step, before taking centre stage and thrilling the audience with her astonishing dance routines. The trouble now was that despite her legendary long legs still looking as good as ever, Alex found her routine embarrassing. Exotic dancing should be left to the young. Her performance recovered when she took to the piano. She ranged from honky-tonk to a classical selection. The British love a little uplifting culture provided they do not have to endure it for too long. By now she had the audience under her spell. Her singing voice had gained added depth over the years and her rendering of 'Love is the greatest thing' drew enthusiastic applause. Then in a departure from her normal programme, she invited the audience to join her in a selection of Beatles' songs. People were standing belting out the lyrics, the whole theatre was rocking.

It needed something quite different for her finale. God, she is a true pro, Alex thought as the whole mood changed. This song, she said, was in memory of her son who had been killed in the Korean war, but also for a dear friend who is here tonight who also lost a son in a previous conflict. Alex was embarrassed as a spotlight lit up his box and the audience broke into applause, although most of them would have had no idea who he was. Gloria started singing 'Where have all the flowers gone' in German before switching to French. Finally, she started singing in English. Losing control, her shoulders shook and, obviously in distress, she staggered from the stage. Last time she had done this was at a disastrous performance at The Talk Of The Town, when she was booed and given the slow hand clap. This night the audience went wild. The chorus and supporting cast took their bows then, seemingly recovered, Gloria appeared to a thunderous reception. Bouquets were presented, curtain calls taken. The evening surely a triumph.

The uniformed driver ushered him into the Bentley parked outside the stage door. A knot of fans and some photographers awaited Gloria's appearance. Alex was fascinated but suspicious about Gloria's performance. How was it that the spotlight was turned on him so quickly? It was surely pre-arranged. He was fairly sure that she had manipulated the audience with talk of her son's death. True, Steffan had been killed in Korea, but she had scarcely seen him since he was a child. She had been an absentee mother, leaving the boy to be brought up by his father's family. Her daughter had also been largely abandoned and left in the hands of a succession of nannies and housekeepers. All through her life she had sacrificed personal relationships in favour of furthering her career. She had always been a diva, now he concluded she was a devious diva. It was strange that her relationship with him had endured. She had proved to be a passionate, yet considerate, lover and a loyal friend. Yet within her profession she was not liked. She made impossible demands on those closest to her. She was dismissive of artistes appearing with her, including the chorus girls who she normally totally ignored outside their rehearsals and actual performances. Theatre managers wilted under her constant demands and yet her public continued to adore her. Alex felt he was in no position to criticize her and certainly not now. In black moments that had increased with age he decided that he was a fraud, both personally and artistically.

Suddenly there was movement in the crowd. Gloria had appeared wearing a stylish cocktail dress and crowned by an eye-catching blue turban. She signed autographs, whilst a couple of press photographers snapped away, pictures which would probably appear in the later editions of the daily papers. Inside the car she told him that she had a surprise for him. They moved off into the familiar streets of Soho. Minutes later they pulled up in Dean Street outside Quo Vadis. Alex reckoned he had eaten in pretty well all of the

Soho restaurants and currently Quo Vadis was not one of his favourites, although he had not been there for some time.

As they entered the restaurant it suddenly dawned on him the significance of the venue. They had eaten here many years ago just days after it opened. It was only half the size then and quite humble, with red gingham tablecloths and bentwood chairs. They had been served by Pepino Leoni, the owner. Gloria was animated, 'Do you know how long ago it was when we first came here?'. He confessed he had no idea. 'Fifty years ago', she said, '1926 and we are still together.'

Beneath her generally hard exterior Gloria had this sentimental nostalgic side and Alex did his best to join in her enthusiasm. They even ordered the food they thought they had eaten all those years ago. Mussels and a simple spaghetti dish. They recollected that the wine they drank that night did not even have a label to indicate its origin. Gloria was in full flow, obviously thoroughly enjoying herself after what she maintained had been a great final performance.

Alex decided that now was not the time to query her breakdown on stage. Unlike her he was feeling troubled and sad. Remembering that night half a century ago prompted mixed emotions. He had been beguiled and besotted by her, but guilt almost ruined that evening. Whilst they had made love later that evening his wife Helen was asleep at home with their son in Bushey. It was not the first time he had been unfaithful. Two years previously Gloria had reappeared in his life whilst making a huge impression in the Green Room at the Cafe Royal.

He had booked a table for Helen and himself, but she said she felt unwell and insisted he went alone. How was it possible to feel guilt after fifty years, but the emotional conflict that consumed him then still niggled away. He had wanted to tell Gloria that, despite loving Helen, he was prepared to give up everything just to be with her. In a bedroom at the Piccadilly Hotel he had gone on his knees to tell her just that when she raised a single finger to her mouth to stop him in his tracks. It was an image that stayed with him and any thought of them being together permanently was never discussed again. Love was not on the agenda at that stage of Gloria's career.

Her mood swings were well known. Now her eyes blazed in anger. He had ruined the evening by being miserable. He had not even congratulated her on her show-stopping performance. He was becoming old and boring. He did not disagree. She flounced out of the restaurant, leaving him to pay the bill. By the time they reached her hotel her mood had changed, again insisting he stayed the night. She strode across the foyer at the Grosvenor House Hotel aware that, as usual, all eyes were on her. They took a side lift that whisked them up to the top floor. Her suite had a huge living room complete with a grand piano. Beyond was a dining room with a table large enough to seat a dozen people. Below, London was spread out with the noiseless traffic looking like illuminated toys.

'Pour yourself a nightcap', she called from the bathroom, but he was too tired. Utterly exhausted, he peeled his clothes off, hanging up his suit and tidily folding his shirt before getting into bed. He was asleep by the time she slipped in beside him. Her naked body familiar and seemingly unaltered over the years. Her hand slid up his back and gently stroked the wound that never healed.

It was past eight o'clock when he woke. She had gone and he assumed she was jogging in Hyde Park, which she normally did when staying in London. Keeping her body in trim by exercise, but gradually killing herself by her addiction to sleeping pills and a cocktail of drugs. A fine spread had been laid out for his breakfast. He was on his second coffee before he noticed an envelope propped up on a side table. Inside written on hotel notepaper was scrawled:

'Until the next time.
All my love, G.'

There was no next time. They never met again.

Chapter 2

October 1918

He hobbled past the protesting ticket collector. The platform was engulfed in smoke and soot as ahead the engine wheezed and groaned into life. A whistle sounded and a porter waved his green flag. The platform was wet underfoot making his progress more difficult. The carriages shuddered as the train started to move. He had just reached the rear door of the last carriage when a soldier opened it. Using all the strength he could summon, he heaved his heavy suitcase into a sea of boots followed by his walking stick. Hands reached out for him and he was dragged aboard head first onto the floor. Every muscle and sinew in his body shrieked in protest. He felt sure he was going to faint. A flask was thrust into his hand. 'Have a swig of that laddie, then after a slight pause 'sir' was added. It was like no whisky he had ever tasted. Quite possibly it was not whisky at all. Whatever the liquid was it exploded in his stomach like a bomb, bringing tears to his eyes. Some Highlanders gently pulled him to his feet and he was reunited with his hat. 'Bloody hell, sir, you should be in hospital.' 'I am fine' he assured them, although he did not feel it. He was told that first class was right at the front of the train, so thanking them he started to make his way through the crowded corridors. Civilians appeared to have taken most of the seats and Alex had to pick his way through a tangle of kitbags, tin helmets and rifles.

He was making slow progress when he became aware of a disturbance ahead. Shouting and swearing mixed with wolf whistles. Forcing his way through the crowd, he could make out a young woman being mauled and kissed by a group of soldiers drinking from beer bottles. 'Stop that now!' he shouted. 'You should be ashamed of yourselves.' Their expressions were sullen, but they let the girl through. Taking her by the arm he said gently, 'Come with me.' 'Fancy a bit of chocolate, do you sir?' Alex felt a rush of rage. Using the crook of his walking stick he pulled the loudmouth towards him. 'You were saying, corporal?' 'Nothing sir.' Having noticed the impressive row of decorations on this officer's uniform, none of them was going to argue the point. They stood aside as he gently guided the young woman forward.

Ignoring other remarks and whistles, they eventually reached the front carriage. The compartment nearest to the engine was occupied by a junior staff officer and a Royal Artillery Major. He sensed the pasty faced Lieutenant was about to object to Alex's companion, but thought better of it, vacating his seat to move opposite the Major who opened one eye and resumed his gentle snoring. Unable to summon the strength to hoist his case onto the luggage rack, he managed to heave it onto an empty seat. Holding out his hand to the young woman he mumbled, 'Alex.' 'Gloria', she replied. Her hand was cool, her accent American, her looks exquisite, but in spite of himself tiredness overwhelmed him and he fell into a deep sleep.

The compartment was empty by the time a porter woke him on arrival at Victoria station. He had slept all the way from Dover. Grappling with his heavy suitcase, he noticed a card on the floor. It listed a theatrical agent called Harry Goodman with an address in central London. Rather grandly it boasted of offices also in Paris and New York. He presumed it had been dropped by the pretty young lady he had rescued from the rowdy gang of squaddies. He slipped it into his pocket and made his way to the taxi rank for a trip across town to St. Pancras for his journey north. He was met at Kettering station by a uniformed driver and his father's gleaming new motor.

Prior to the war his father had run an increasingly successful company manufacturing corsets for the domestic market and exports worldwide. Switching most production to meet military requirements had obviously transformed the business. The call for webbing used in the production of belts, gaiters, haversacks, kitbags and camouflage was endless. Whilst previously the family had lived in some comfort employing several servants, their move into Stratton House astonished Alex. It was a house he had previously only glimpsed whilst out riding as a youngster. He had often wondered what lay behind those impressive gates, with the drive gradually rising to the highest point where the impressive pile had been built. It had been designed by Sir John Soane in 1824 and had been in the De Voyle family until six months previously. The De Voyles had been bankers, steadily increasing their wealth over generations until Robert De Voyle took over. A hunting and racing man with a love of gambling. Unmarried, he managed to decimate what his family had accumulated in a lifetime of excess. Alex understood it was his mother's passion for hunting that led to the purchase. Although his father did not hunt, the kudos of hosting a meet appealed to his desire for social recognition. Many old established families were now selling up country estates and migrating to their London mansions because of high taxation imposed by the government.

Approaching the house by the main drive, Alex was astonished by the size of the place. Far too large surely for a small family. There were formal gardens with a lake to the west which could be crossed by an ancient stone bridge. Pulling up in front of the main entrance, he was embarrassed to see a coat-tailed butler waiting to welcome him. Why was it that having made money, so many Britons could not wait to emulate the aristocracy? The butler introduced himself as Greaves and escorted Alex into the house. The first impression was the smell of fresh paint. Numerous doors ran off a grand central hall. He could tell his mother had been at work organising the decor. All very tasteful, a sea of gentle yellow and grey. The overall impression rather reduced by dull paintings of horses pictured in stables and hunting prints, presumably bought as part of the overall purchase. Greaves informed him his mother was in the music room. He walked down a long corridor towards the sound of a piano. She looked up as he entered, but continued playing. Having completed the piece, she rose and made her way towards him. She was still dressed in the Edwardian manner that suited her slender figure. Her black skirt extended to her ankles, and the crisp white blouse she wore was patterned in lace and rose high to just below her jaw line. Her hair was piled high and secured by combs. She remained quite beautiful and, to Alex, an enigma.

When he was a child she had been kind but distant. She did sometimes tell him bedside stories. Not from a book, but strange tales of knights, damsels and misty castles. The only time he ever saw her animated was when hunting. Fearless and riding side saddle, she was pursued over the years by a range of red-faced, red-coated grandees. She never turned down their advances, rather she deflected them, leaving them dangling and confused, but never quite giving up. Surprisingly, they noticed that George, her husband, almost appeared to welcome the attention lavished on his wife. They viewed him with suspicion. He was undoubtedly rich, but with no real breeding. Actually, a bit of a rough diamond. Snobbery was alive and well in rural England. They were not alone in wondering how and why his parents had ever got married. Seemingly they had nothing in common. George was relentless in his pursuit of financial success, whereas his mother came from an impoverished, aristocratic Irish family. Possibly a marriage of convenience. For her there was the prospect of financial security, whilst his father was able to boast of an injection of aristocratic blood into his family line. George wanted control in his life. In business he was ruthless, whilst in his family relationships he was more benign, although Alex sensed that his parents' marriage was not a happy one. He was able to understand his mother's need to lose herself in a love for horses, music and surrounding herself in an aura of mystery.

She kissed him briefly. 'God you look terrible.' 'Thanks, mother.' He was not surprised by her coolness. He had received regular letters from his father and younger brother Marcus whilst in France, but nothing from his mother. She studied him carefully. 'I knew you would come through it alright. You will always be lucky in life.' She rang a hand bell and told a young maid to show Mr. Alex to his room and to run him a bath. As he turned to leave she gently caught him by the arm and whispered, 'I did worry about you.' He realised beneath her distant, almost frigid, attitude did lurk some emotion. As he followed the maid up the grand staircase he was confused by his mother's strange welcome. Should he be annoyed that she did not react like a normal mother, or feel sorry for her being trapped in a world that perhaps only she understood.

That evening at dinner both his father and brother were warm in their welcome. Marcus had avoided military service, apparently due to poor eyesight. Alex sensed his father had pulled strings. He was master of the local Masonic Lodge and Alex had never noticed any problems with his brother's eyesight. In fact Marcus was a crack shot. After what he had witnessed in France, Alex felt incensed that money and influence continued to buy favours. It was a look from his mother that cut short his intended tirade at the injustice. She had always had this disconcerting ability to read his mind ever since he was a child. She continued to communicate more through knowing looks than words. Alex had already disappointed his father by refusing to join the Masons, and so for tonight he decided not to inform him that he had no intention of joining the family firm.

Hr was informed that Marcus was apparently training to be an accountant. Financial control was central to all successful enterprises, and to have young Marcus fully qualified would be of great benefit in the future, his father assured them. Now it was time to consider what Alex could offer the company. Maybe sales, his father suggested. He was worried about losing government contracts after the war and fashion trends suggested that corsets may fall out of favour. He was thinking of entering the leisure market with the manufacture of women's swimwear. Alex had always spent hours drawing and sketching. Perhaps, his father suggested, designing swimwear may see Alex make a useful contribution. Alex let his father drone on about the potential market for leisure wear. People would go on holiday again. There would be a pent up demand, whilst the wealthy would holiday in the south of France. He noticed that daily flights were scheduled from early next year. Alex stopped listening, his father's voice was just a background noise. He was watching his mother. Whilst the men drank wine with their meal, his mother stuck to her Paddy whiskey. Whilst he never saw her refill her glass, the carafe in front of her was by now half empty. She noticed his attention and half turned away. Switching back to his father's lecture, Alex informed him he needed time to think about his future. 'Of course, old boy, we can discuss it after your medical board.' Actually, Alex had no idea what he wanted to do with his life other than not joining his father's burgeoning organisation.

The decoration of the house had not yet extended to the upper floors. Alex's bedroom was gloomy, with rotten window frames and wallpaper beginning to peel off damp walls. Exploring other bedrooms along a long corridor, he found one full of light overlooking the vegetable garden which would suit his purpose.

Next morning he rode a bicycle into Kettering and ordered an easel, canvasses as well as a full set of oil paints to be delivered. At school his popularity was helped by his ability to draw wicked cartoons of the masters. He disappointed his mother by his lack of enthusiasm for hunting, preferring to stay at home sketching. It was this skill that helped him remain sane during almost three years at the front, capturing the carnage and devastation. Although he had rarely painted in oils, he needed to record an image which remained, haunting him. Whilst he could remember little of when he suffered his own severe injuries, the moment Corporal Grant witnessed the death of his brother was so awful he felt that trying to recreate the moment might act as some form of catharsis. Setting up his easel, he tentatively started sketching the life size face that was going to dominate the canvas.

The following week Alex went down to London to attend his medical board. He was asked to explain how he had sustained his injuries. In truth he could remember very little. He had been inspecting a forward trench when it received a direct hit. He had vague memories of a field hospital and then a complete blank until waking in a ward containing men with the most terrible injuries. Limbs missing, faces half torn away. It was like waking in some kind of hell. As he gradually improved he was transferred to a ward where at least the occupants were expected to survive. His right leg had been severely damaged, but more worrying were the wounds to his back. A jolly doctor told Alex that his back reminded him of a piece of Gruyere cheese. After an operation to remove the shrapnel, it was decided that one shard was too close to his spine to be removed. He was told it would be better to live with the discomfort than risk being paralysed for the rest of his life. It was obvious that he would be given a discharge, although it was not confirmed on the day.

Feeling rather nervous he took a cab to Bond Street. Carrying his portfolio, he entered the premises of the Fine Art Society. He explained to a very attractive receptionist that he had some drawings he had made in France that he wanted to show. She disappeared into an inner office whilst he looked at some of the paintings on view, the quality of which made him doubt the wisdom of him offering his humble sketches. He was ushered into an office and introduced to a director of the gallery. Tea was poured and he was asked about his experiences in France. He had made over a dozen studies including Ypres, St. Quentin and the Lens-Arras Road. Each work was studied closely before finally, much to Alex's relief, he was told that his work was admirable. Furthermore, the gallery was holding an exhibition of war related material early in 1919 and the gallery would be happy to include them. It was pointed out that he would have to pay for the framing. He did not care, he was just thrilled that his work would be shown at such an influential gallery. He was asked if he had anything else that may have been of interest and he mentioned the oil he had just started. It was suggested that he send a photograph of the work when it was completed.

Feeling quite elated, he treated himself to a lunch at an upmarket French restaurant in Conduit Street. Reaching for his wallet to pay the bill, he accidentally pulled out the card he had discovered on the train he had taken from Dover. Remembering the beautiful American girl, he wondered what had become of her. He had inherited a sense of superstition and premonition from his mother. Premonitions which had served him well in France and led to his men referring to him as 'mad Alex'. He took crazy risks with a confidence that defied logic and yet he survived, until finally his luck ran out. Now it amused him to think that this random meeting with the American young woman was somehow meant to be. In his heart he knew this was nonsense, but it felt like his lucky day. So it was with a spring in his step that he set off for the short walk to Harry Goodman's Theatrical Agency in Soho Square.

A theatrical agency in Soho conjured up dingy premises in some darkened alley, but Harry Goodman occupied a smart, double-fronted building with fine views over the Square. A receptionist informed him that Mr. Goodman was in the States. He explained that he was trying to track down an American girl called Gloria, whom he assumed was on the agency's books. He was told that she was forbidden to hand out any details about their clients. On the point of giving up, Alex noticed an attractive girl who had been listening to his attempts to get information about Gloria. She introduced herself as Mr. Goodman's secretary and she told the receptionist that she would deal with this gentleman. It must have been his uniform that influenced her. She informed him that her fiancé was still serving in France. As he talked about his experiences, he sensed she was going to help him. Flicking through a card system she found the details of Gloria Bird. She told him Gloria had come to London with a recommendation from their New York office. She was booked for a few shows in a London night club before travelling on to Paris, where she was due to appear in the chorus of a new revue. Telling Alex she would be sacked if Mr. Goodman ever found out, she informed him that Gloria had digs in Church Street, just off the Edgware Road. Thanking her he limped off into a wet, chilly London afternoon. She felt pleased to have helped this man who reminded her of her fiancé. Everyone needed a little kindness in this terrible, never ending war.

It was market day in Church Street. Asking the cab to wait, Alex entered a mayhem of activity. Stall holders shouted their wares, an ex-serviceman stood in the gutter playing an accordion, medals proudly pinned to his coat. There was a smell of freshly baked bread and a grey haired Indian was offering to tell fortunes by feeling the bumps on your head. A butcher with a bloody apron carved a joint of beef, whilst below his stall two cats fought for some scraps. There were stalls groaning with vegetables next to a man selling caged birds. Have a tooth removed for sixpence, a placard declared, or have a painless extraction for a shilling, the only difference being the extra payment involved the banging of a drum to mask the screams of pain.

Peering through a sea of activity, Alex spotted the wool shop where Gloria was apparently lodging. The shop was lit by a single gas lamp. A tiny woman, hardly tall enough to look over the counter, was marooned by packets of wool, some half opened. Knitting wool bulged from fixtures and covered all the surfaces, including the floor. Pattern books were propped up on the window sill. Informing the owner that he had come to see Gloria, he was told that she had not been seen since the day before and besides she was allowed no male visitors, adding that she kept a respectable house. A ten shilling note quickly overcame that obstacle. 'Last door on the right at the top of the stairs' he was told.

Picking his way gingerly across a small parlour also festooned with wool covering chairs and a dining table, he climbed the rickety stairs and inched his way along an unlit corridor. Alex tapped on the door a couple of times before he heard a muffled reply. She was sitting crumpled in an armchair. The air in the room was stale and the bed unmade. He knew at once she was unwell. He felt her brow which was hot and clammy. He knelt in front of her trying to gain her attention. Her eyes were dull and unseeing. He poured her a glass of water. She swallowed it with difficulty and then said quite clearly, 'Come to rescue me again?' She seemingly lost consciousness, although she did vaguely remember him telling her he was taking her home. Later she recalled she imagined home was somewhere close by and not eighty miles away. She had no memory of being carried to the taxi or the train journey. Alex had acted on impulse, a characteristic that remained with him all his life. Finally, with the help of a porter at Kettering station, they managed to carry her to the taxi rank.

It was dark by the time they arrived at Stratton House. He instructed Greaves to make the guest room ready and got a sturdy man servant to carry Gloria into the house. His father had already gone to bed, but his mother appeared in the hall to see what the commotion was about. Peering at the figure swathed in a blanket, she arched an eyebrow. She gave Alex a knowing smile and, without saying a word, made her way unsteadily up the sweeping staircase to bed.

Chapter 3

Gloria

Whilst my grandfather's initial homecoming to Stratton House was muted, the same could not be said when he arrived with Gloria. He was awoken the following morning to his father shouting. Amongst a tirade of swearing he heard her referred to as a native girl. Whilst his father raged he could just make out his mother's murmured response. Her tone was conciliatory, but George was having none of it, storming out of the house and slamming the door. His mother told Alex later that his father was worried about their neighbours' reaction as he tried to get the family socially established in the county.

The reaction of Doctor Armitage, who was summoned to attend to Gloria, was even worse, but on medical rather than racial grounds. He informed Alex that he had endangered the young woman's life by dragging her all the way from London. It would have been far better leaving her where she was and getting her medical help. As it was, he told Alex that the next two days would be vital. Duly reprimanded, Alex awaited the return of his father to state his case. During that day he had been pleasantly surprised to witness his mother spending hours at Gloria's bedside applying cold towels. His father's attitude had softened somewhat by the evening, but was still insisting that Gloria should be shipped back to London once she was in a fit condition. For two days she appeared to hover close to death, never gaining consciousness.

There remains some doubts about the origins of the Spanish 'flu, but subsequent consensus was that the pandemic was misnamed. It is likely that the initial outbreak was in China or at a military facility in the American mid-west. Starting with chickens, the virus apparently mutated to pigs before transferring to humans. The rat infested western front trenches proved a perfect breeding ground for the virus, and crowded trains bringing troops home accelerated the spread further. Newspapers were encouraged not to give too much coverage to the illness to avoid causing panic. Symptoms were varied and often initially mild. A slight headache followed by aching limbs and a high temperature could spiral alarmingly. It was possible to feel fine at breakfast and be dead by tea-time. The barman at the Savoy Hotel obviously had a rather macabre sense of humour by serving a cocktail known as a 'corpse reviver'.

On the third day after her arrival, Gloria opened her eyes and panicked slightly, having no idea where she was. Alex was called to her bedside and, although very weak, she recognised my grandfather and was assured she was safe. Despite his initial reaction, George was persuaded to allow Gloria to dine with the family. Although now desperately thin, she looked remarkably elegant dressed in clothes donated by Alex's mother. Within days Gloria had won George's heart as much as his son's. He even took Gloria on a tour of his Desborough factory.

By now Alex was hopelessly smitten. His experience of women had mostly been confined to French brothels, although his parents had arranged for him to walk out with a couple of local girls before he left for the front. The fact was he overwhelmed Gloria with his devotion. He proudly took her to the neighbouring town of Market Harborough where they lunched at the Three Swans. Wherever they went people stopped in their tracks and stared at this exotic creature. Most of them had never seen a black woman before, although her colour was more that of milk chocolate. A retired Colonel eating at the Three Swans had served in Africa, but he spluttered over his soup when the young couple entered the dining room. He thought it was almost as bad as natives invading the officers' mess. Gloria smiled sweetly at him and by the time he left he had recovered enough to wish them a curt good afternoon.

Matters came to a head about a week after Gloria's arrival. Alex's attention was beginning to annoy her. She told him repeatedly that their lives were on totally different paths. He would surely feel uncomfortable inhabiting her world as she did his. Although really grateful for his help, she needed to break away. It was only later that Alex learnt that it was with the help of his mother that Gloria was magicked away from him. She denied him any emotional farewell. 'One must learn to stand back and let a girl come to her own conclusions. You were like a young puppy and annoying.' He was surprised by his mother's wisdom in matters of the heart. 'Don't go looking for love, let it find you' she said. He knew she was right, but he felt squashed and humiliated. Gloria had spent much of their time together actively trying to put him off.

Although there have been several biographies written

about Gloria, they concentrated exclusively on her career and dramas in her adult life. No-one had been able to divine much about her childhood or why she arrived in Europe when a war was still raging. The fact was that Gloria was a serial liar, so her biographers stuck to the known facts. Alex probably had the greatest insight regarding her childhood and early teenage years, although the story changed with each telling.

It is not surprising details of Gloria's early life are so sketchy as there are few records to back her version of events. What is certain is that she was born in either 1900 or 1901. The first five or six years of her life were spent in a place called Robertville, about five miles outside Charleston in Southern Carolina. Robertville no longer exists and was at best just a few shacks and one small clapboard house. Gloria always claimed that her father was either German or Swedish. It is more likely that he was French, accounting for her light colouring. A Robert Gordon ran what we today would call a scrap metal yard, requiring it to be located out of town because of the noise created by the breakdown of old cars and obsolete household equipment. Merle, Gloria's mother, was ostensibly Robert's housekeeper, whilst his small workforce lived in ramshackle tin shacks.

Robert was a great influence on Gloria's very early years. Seemingly a quite refined and educated man, it is strange that he took to a trade that required more brawn than brain. It is quite possible that he was trying to escape a dubious past. He taught Gloria to play the piano, to read music and play poker by the time she was five. All skills that she used to great effect. He also spoke to her occasionally in French, which gave her a basic grounding in the language. Apart from the constant noise of screeching metal, these formative years were happy enough for a young girl who knew no other life. This all seems to have come to an end in a terrible accident reported in the local press. Robert Gordon was apparently killed in some horrific accident involving crushing machinery. Her mother shielded her from actually seeing the results of the accident, but they moved later that day into the black quarter of Charleston.

Living in a run-down shack, Merle scraped a living taking in washing and ironing. Gloria, as well as being able to play the piano, was also showing an aptitude for tap dancing, so she was shipped off into town to perform for a few cents dancing on street corners before being moved on by the police. Merle found that taking in a lodger paid better than ironing and so started a series of 'uncles' featuring in Gloria's life. From the age of eight Gloria was sexually abused on a regular basis. She assumed that this was just part of life and her mother never acknowledged what was going on. Her mother was earning enough to clothe and feed themselves. Not all the influences in Gloria's life were bad. Walter Martin was a man probably in his seventies. He originated from New Orleans and lived a few houses away from the young girl. She was drawn to his door by his piano playing. Shyly she inched her way into his life lingering on the stoop outside his front door. Walter was very black, his colour emphasised by his grey hair. Seemingly he could play anything by ear. Gloria had only ever played classical pieces that she had learnt from Robert Gordon, but now Walter opened up an entirely new world to her. He was delighted to have such an enthusiastic pupil. Soon she was playing show songs, ragtime and even stride. Stride is a jazz piano style where the right hand plays the melody whilst the left hand alternates between single notes played an octave or two higher. Gloria spent hours with the old man and he marvelled as she increased her repertoire to include gospel and church music.

Music was a great escape for the young girl, but according to her, at the age of fourteen she decided to escape the procession of uncles by getting married. Again there is no record of the marriage to Mathew Head, which according to Gloria only lasted a year due to his drunkenness. Back living with her mother, it was not the abuse that she was still being subjected to that caused her to seek a new life in New York. The Ku Klux Klan, which had been formed in the 1860s, now had several million members in the southern States. These white supremacists proclaimed that blacks, Jews and Roman Catholics were not true Americans. Gloria became increasingly frightened by the fiery crosses announcing their presence in the area. Wearing their weird pointed dunces' hats with slits for the eyes was disconcerting, particularly when they paraded through the black parts of town. One night their door was kicked in by an angry mob seeking a boy who had made lewd suggestions to a white woman. Gloria was terrified by their aggression and hatred. She understood that life for black folks was much easier up north, so she started making her plans.

Her chance came when she managed to get a lift with a shirt salesman, who was travelling into North Carolina. Typically, she never even said goodbye to her mother, who had admittedly done very little to protect her daughter.

Selfishness certainly ran through that branch of Gloria's family. It was going to take well over a year to cover the 800 miles between Charleston and New York. A time of sharing grubby hotel rooms with a succession of salesmen and truck drivers. Whilst waiting for transport, she worked as a waitress and increasingly was employed as an entertainer. She sang, played the piano and danced. Many of these bars and dingy clubs encouraged her to stay, but she was set on reaching New York where, she was convinced with an almost fanatical belief, that her fortune lay.

Her introduction into big city life was harsh. Work was not easy to find. Sure, she could play the piano, but so could hundreds of black kids. Despondent and fast running out of money, she took a one-bedroomed apartment in Harlem. Her next door neighbour was Patrice Delage, an ageing show dancer. Being a homosexual at that time was not easy and within weeks the couple had moved in together as a form of mutual protection. Patrice was fundamental in changing Gloria's life.

A solid person, seemingly the one person who actually existed amidst a web of lies and deceit, Patrice saw Gloria's potential as a dancer, but a bad diet had left her lacking the fitness required for a professional. He spent hours putting her through exhausting routines. This proved invaluable over the years to come, as Gloria became fanatical about her fitness and diet. He introduced her to French cooking, preparing delicious meals for them over a period of months. Importantly, he also encouraged her to speak French and by the time she left for Europe she was almost fluent.

Gloria liked to pretend her time in New York drew her to

the attention of leading producers and agents. She boasted of success in clubs on West 29th Street and at the Hollywood Club at 23 West 49th Street. This was impossible as the club was not in existence during her time in New York. What is true was the fact that her colour still counted against her. Even amongst the black community there was prejudice. Her light mulatto skin set her apart from the mainstream, whilst whites treated all coloured folk with a lofty disdain. Patrice would tell her that Europe was a place of opportunity for a girl like her, particularly France where a more liberal attitude existed. Seemingly stymied in her search for fame in America, she started on a calculated plan to get to Europe. Rather than rave reviews on her performances in run down clubs, her access to a new life came via the bedroom. Joe Strauss was a modestly successful agent representing some well known names. A happily married man in his early fifties, Gloria set out to seduce him. She had learnt from Patrice that Strauss had good connections with a leading London agency. She was not the first or the last pretty girl to set her sights on a vulnerable middle aged man. Others had tried to influence Joe with sexual favours over the years and he had steadfastly remained professional in all his dealings, but this girl was different. The usual background – his wife was more interested in their children and despite all his hard work he felt unattractive and unappreciated. Gloria played him like a fish on the end of a line. He felt she had bewitched him. Afternoons were spent in a rented apartment. He started neglecting his work and eventually guilt took over.

Gradually, rather than wanting this minx, he needed her out of his life. Over the weeks they were together she had turned down offers of local jobs. She was insistent that she wanted to go to Europe. Sensing a chance to rid himself of this strange beautiful, but persistent girl, he contacted Harry Goodman in London. He lied about her ability, that he actually thought she was no better than hundreds of hoofers on his books. He paid for a steerage birth on the S.S Midlothian to Liverpool. She kept her departure date from Patrice, although it was he who had suggested that she should go to Europe. Did Gloria genuinely hate farewells? More likely it was cowardice that led to her leaving her mentor and friend just a brief note of farewell.

It is certain that Gloria arrived in Britain in October 1918. Why she was on that train from Dover was never really explained. She told my grandfather initially that she was returning from a huge success in a revue in Paris, which was untrue. More likely she had travelled to Dover hoping to wangle a trip over the Channel, but the volume of military movements had frustrated her plan.

Rejection is always hard to take. Alex was obviously vulnerable at the time of his meeting Gloria. Although he never talked about his wartime service until late in life, it had obviously affected him. Like many returning, he was subject to huge mood swings, surging from elation at what life now promised to deep depression. In the days following Gloria's departure he was overcome by self doubt. Was he unattractive to women? Wallowing in self pity, he thought of himself as a cripple. No woman would ever want him. His experience with women at home was confined to a few awkward dates with local girls with trips to the pictures and local dances. The odd kiss and furtive grope. All that changed. Along with friends whilst on leave in France, he visited local brothels. Now he worried that unlike his mates who opted for the youngest and the prettiest, he chose older women, not as old as his mother but probably in their late thirties or early forties. Maybe it was their lifestyle that made them look older than they really were. They were kind and understanding, but he was aware of his friends laughing at him for what they thought was his bizarre taste.

His rejection by Gloria gnawed away at him. With confidence at rock bottom he threw himself into painting. Here too there was frustration. The image in his mind refused to show itself with a number of false starts. What had seemed easy in pencil and wash drawings deserted him as after days of struggles and canvasses hurled across his makeshift studio, he decided on a change of tack. His father was delighted as Alex rushed off a succession of swimwear designs. This diversion unlocked his painter's block. Two preparatory sketches allowed him to start the work with renewed confidence. It took him three weeks, often working well into the night, for him to bring the image alive. The danger now was to constantly change it, whilst seeking perfection that no artist ever achieves in their own mind. Alex was content. It was shocking, but then it was meant to be. Like all artists, writers or composers, he had created a form of alchemy. From a blank canvas he had produced an image created exclusively by him. The following day he arranged for a photographer to take a number of shots that he could send down to the Fine Art Society. As the photographer was packing up, Alex's mother came in, 'Good God, that is disgusting.' 'War is disgusting mother"', he said.

Within two days of sending the photographs Alex received a telegram telling him that the gallery was impressed with his work and that their shippers would pick it up for transportation to London. Later that week another telegram arrived informing him they had some very exciting news and inviting him down to the gallery the following week. My grandfather's life was about to dramatically change.

Chapter 4

Despair

I t was strange looking at his own painting in a different setting. Now beautifully framed and taking centre stage in the gallery, it was as if he had no connection to the frightening image that now demanded his attention. The life size face seemingly wanting to burst from the canvas to envelop you in his abject misery. Bloodshot eyes caught in that second before that same face crumpled into tears. Behind the central figure lay the prone, bleeding body of his dead brother.

My grandfather told me he was amazed at the impact seeing his work again had on him. Back in his makeshift studio at Stratton House the picture appeared crude and amateurish. Here in these rather grand surroundings it was somehow transformed. Still unaware why he had been invited to the gallery that day, a photographer was on hand to picture Alex standing in front of his painting. I still have that photograph. Alex, who had still not received his discharge papers, stands rather self consciously, walking stick in hand. He looks rather grand in his uniform. Good looking rather than handsome, possibly due to a moustache that really did not suit him.

The photography was taken under a cloak of secrecy that was intriguing. Blinds had been drawn and the door onto the street shut. As the photographer cleared away his tripod and cameras, the painting was taken down and taken into the back office where Alex had first met Arthur Swanton, the director of the gallery. It was there that Alex was informed that, subject to final confirmation, his picture would be purchased by the Imperial War Museum. This would be kept secret until the eve of the exhibition of war related works, to be held the following February to maximise publicity. 'You, young man, will become famous overnight', Swanton assured him. 'But I am just an amateur' Alex replied, concerned what his early success would have on his future career in the art world. Whilst they enjoyed a cup of tea, Alex explained that he really needed to learn so much more about all aspects of painting whilst Swanton felt that a formal training might negate the immediacy of his work, but Alex was adamant that pitching in against professional artists was like asking a village cricketer to open the batting for England. Various art schools were discussed, but Alex said he would prefer to study under an acknowledged master if that could be arranged. Swanton mentioned that Stanhope Forbes had formed an artists' colony in Newlyn before the war. This had produced any number of well-regarded artists, including Dod Procter, Alfred Munnings and Laura Knight. Alex knew of Knight's work, which he particularly admired. Forbes was known as 'the professor' and was generous in sharing his expertise. Time in Cornwall really appealed to Alex and Swanton said he would write to the great man recommending Alex, giving my grandfather the Newlyn address so that he could contact him too.

There were still a couple of details that needed attention.

First a title was required for Alex's painting and then he needed to sign it. 'Despair' said Alex, without hesitation. 'Despair is what that poor man was experiencing at that very moment. The image that remains seared into my mind.' When it came to the signature he wrote simply in neat capitals 'Alex'. Well, a single Christian name was good enough for Van Gogh. 'Let us hope this is a good precedence.' 'Alex' was the signature that he continued to use for the rest of his life.

Suddenly the calm of the gallery was shattered by a uncontrollable scream. Rushing out of the office in alarm, they saw members of staff hugging and dancing round the gallery. 'It's over' a receptionist shouted, 'Dear God, it's over.' Outside they could see office workers and shop owners pouring onto the street. People were hugging, kissing, jumping and dancing. The war was over. A bottle of champagne was produced. My grandfather felt guilty, for whilst all around him was joy, he could not help thinking of all the friends and comrades he had lost. Pushing these thoughts aside he downed another glass of champagne and, thanking Arthur Swanton, he went outside to join the crowd of revellers.

Flags and bunting had appeared as if by magic. Through the melee he spotted a cab. 'Where to, sir?' Not caring and feeling slightly tipsy, he said, 'Just drive, I want to take all this in. What a day. What a bloody fantastic day.' By the time they reached Trafalgar Square it was impossible to drive any further. Walking under Admiralty Arch, Alex joined a throng lurching down the Mall towards Buckingham Palace. People were singing, alternating between patriotic songs and popular ballads like *Keep the homes fires burning*. The crowd was swaying with the pressure from behind. Someone shoved a bottle of brown ale into his hand and he took a deep swig. Unsteady on his feet, he was in danger of falling. Strangers shook his hand and embraced him, whilst a middle aged woman covered his face in lipstick. Now close to the Palace, the crowd was calling for the King. Drink was produced from coats and handbags. Alex lost count of the mixture of wine, beer and spirits which were offered. He was befuddled, which was good because his mixture of emotions were too complicated for him to unravel. For the moment he was just happy to be part of this mad mob celebrating after years of pain and loss. To a great cheer, the doors to the balcony of Buckingham Palace were opened. Moments later the small figure of the King dressed in uniform appeared. Beside him was the dominating presence of Queen Mary. The King waved in a rather jerky movement, as if his arm was being controlled by an unseen puppeteer. Despite the monarch's seeming unease at appearing in front of his subjects, the crowd broke into an enthusiastic, rather drunken version, of the national anthem.

Later that afternoon Alex found himself propped up at the bar of Brown's Hotel in Albermarle Street. He had no recollection of how he got there or of much of the rest of that evening. Although he had been told there was not a spare hotel room to be had in London that night, he managed to secure a room normally reserved for chauffeurs. His account next morning informed him that he had eaten in the restaurant and his bar bill was eye watering. Perhaps the most extraordinary memory of that crazy night was reserved for the following morning. Waking with the worst hangover he could ever remember, he was aware of a blonde figure tottering to the door. In a beautifully modulated voice she said, 'Bye, lovely to have met you' and then she was gone.

The persistent rain that failed to dampen Armistice Day celebrations was followed by two days of glorious sunshine, as if belatedly welcoming the onset of peace. On his return home Alex fired off a letter to Stanhope Forbes in Newlyn. Within days he received a warm reply. Whilst welcoming my grandfather, Forbes warned that life in Cornwall was very, very quiet and the living conditions pretty basic. He asked Alex for the day and time of his arrival and that he would arrange suitable lodgings. Excited rather than daunted by the prospect of a quiet life, Alex prepared for his departure. His father was still horrified by his son's decision to turn his back on a golden opportunity to further himself, but remained convinced that Alex's resolve to scrape a living as an artist would soon cool. The family enjoyed a final dinner together the night before Alex's departure, his parting made easier by a group of swimwear designs that Alex had prepared for his father. Worryingly, he had enjoyed creating the designs whilst his attempts at a second oil painting had ended in the canvas being destroyed. His feeling of shattered confidence was soon overcome by the expectation of what was to come.

By the morning of his departure his mood had changed again. Despite loving a challenge, he would go with no set goals other than to watch and learn, whilst trying to develop whatever talent he possessed. With his suitcase already packed and waiting in the hall, he paused outside his mother's bedroom. The door was ajar. Knocking, he entered.

The stunning dress she had worn the night before was lying on the floor along with scattered underwear. He pitied her maid who had to cope with his mother's notorious untidiness. About to leave, he noticed a book jutting out from under the pillows on her bed. Curious, he pulled it out. Leather bound, it contained an old collection of Irish love poems. The front inside page had a message written in a flamboyant hand. 'All my life, my lover, G.' Another 'G', obviously this had no connection to Gloria but neither was it his father's writing. The inscription was faded and had obviously been written years ago, but fascinating none the less. Feeling guilty at his intrusion, Alex returned the book to the safety of the pillow and made his way downstairs.

Passing the morning room and the library, he was again drawn to the sounds from the music room. He stood at the entrance listening to his mother. Seated at the piano, she was singing one of those sad Irish ballads that he remembered her singing to him as a child. He stepped back into the shadows, not wanting to break the spell. He felt a surge of love for her, but she had always kept him at a distance, either frightened or unable to express her own emotions. He felt sad as he was sure she was unhappy, except that the previous week he had witnessed a totally different side to her personality. She had hosted the local hunt. Alex had joined a team of servants offering glasses of port and whisky from silver trays to those on horseback and hunt followers. His mother, animated and mounted side-saddle on her grey hunter, elegant and vivacious, pursued by red-coated groups of men seeking just a moment of her undivided attention. She was in her element, only for this happiness to dissolve once she entered the house.

Suddenly she noticed him and immediately stopped singing and closed the piano. It was as if he had intruded and exposed her in some way. She came and stood very close to him. Too close, almost touching, more like lovers just about to embrace. Instead she raised her hands to his face and traced his features as a blind person may have done, trying to memorise every feature. He stood feeling uncomfortable, but unable to move. Gently she kissed him on the lips. It was not a kiss of a lover, but not of a mother either. There were tears in her eyes. She ran her fingers through his hair before turning abruptly and walking hurriedly towards the staircase, leaving Alex feeling sad and confused.

Chapter 5

Newlyn

It was already dark by the time the train from Paddington arrived at Penzance station. His luggage was heaved into the back of a cart pulled by an old grey horse who appeared in many of Stanhope Forbes' paintings. His lodgings were in a terraced house a few doors down from the Tolcarne Inn. His landlady, Mrs. Perkins, had a hot meal waiting for him, even before taking him up to his room. He was obviously going to be well fed and looked after in a motherly way. There was no sign of a husband, but she had a young son who was in his early teens. His room was small and dominated by a huge wardrobe that just about left room for an iron bed and a small side table. The floor was covered in linoleum. Alex opened the window and thought he could just about hear the sound of the sea before turning in for the night.

The following morning, carrying a portfolio of a number of sketches he had made since returning from France, he made his way to Higher Faugan, the house that Forbes had built in 1902. It was a handsome, white faced building with bay windows either side of the front door. It was set on high ground and had spectacular views over Mounts Bay and St. Michael's Mount. Alex was met by Forbes' wife Maudie, who was much younger than he had expected. Leaving him in a comfortable sitting room, she went upstairs to fetch her husband. Stanhope Forbes was a tall, sparsely built man with greying hair. It seems he was something of a philosopher as well as a great artist. He informed my grandfather that whilst all those joining him in Newlyn over the years had come to paint, they were also either coming to discover themselves or, more likely, to try and forget something in their past. Alex found the older man so easy to talk to. Not exactly a father figure, perhaps more like a favourite uncle. Forbes was particularly interested in Alex's military experiences, which my grandfather found difficult. Apparently Forbes had lost his own son Alec, killed in 1915. This followed the tragic death of his first wife Elizabeth, who was also an acclaimed artist. Maudie had been a student and eventually a help in guiding him through such a terrible time in his life, which led to their marriage in 1916.

Arthur Swanton had sent Forbes the photograph of Alex's painting 'Despair'. Like the gallery owner, he was concerned that a formal tuition would take away the raw talent that Alex obviously possessed. Upstairs the studio was a long, narrow gallery. Fanlights along its length gave maximum light. A line of perhaps eight or nine easels were set up, but there was only one young man working. He was introduced as Frank King, who was starting on an extensive beach scene. Forbes explained that there was no set routine. Artists came and went as they pleased and that he was always happy to help if required. Forbes had studied in France and been influenced by the Barbizon School, who favoured 'en plein' air approach of painting outdoors, although currently he had turned his attention to the difficulties posed by artificial light. Rather than start straight away, Alex spent much of the first day watching how Forbes applied paint and was able to create memorable images seemingly with just a few brush strokes. He was also fascinated to see that Forbes worked on more than one canvas at a time. Whilst he was putting the finishing touches to an almost completed painting, he was already working on studies for a new composition.

Over the following few days Alex set up his easel on the quay. The fishermen were used to seeing their day recorded, but Alex was struggling. Abandoning the busy harbour quay, he persuaded his landlady's young son to pose for him. Again he was thoroughly demoralised by his inability to transfer onto the canvas what he saw in front of him. He knew he needed help. He was embarrassed to show his attempts to 'the professor'. Whilst being kind, it was obvious that Forbes was not impressed by my grandfather's daubs. However, he did make a really interesting suggestion. Based on his 'Despair' work, perhaps Alex should try painting something from his past that remained lodged in his memory. He had spent hours in a dug-out with comrades, and an abiding memory was watching two of them playing endless games of chess to a background of mortar fire. 'Then try that' Forbes suggested. Alex lay awake that night thinking through the composition.

Rising early he left for the studio without even waiting for breakfast. Because of the claustrophobic effect of the dug-out he selected a relatively small canvas. He had hardly started work when the door opened. A hooded figure paused by his easel. 'Hello' she said, before going to the far end of the studio. Glancing surreptitiously, he felt a flutter, a churning in his stomach. This young woman was staggeringly beautiful. He realised that he was in a vulnerable, emotional state, but that old feeling of premonition again grabbed him. He remembered his mother's advice. He was not going to make a fool of himself this time. He tried to concentrate on his initial sketch. Forbes greeted him as he came in to work beside him. With lunchtime approaching, the young woman prepared to leave. Forbes, as if noticing her for the first time said, 'Of course, you two will not have met. Helen, this is Alex Beck who has just joined us. Alex, this is Helen Moon.' They shook hands and she was gone. That night he gave no thought to his painting, but the image of Helen Moon engulfed him. She had hair that fell to her shoulders like corkscrews, the colour of autumn leaves. By contrast, her skin was so white as if it had never been exposed to the sun and, startlingly her eyes were of the clearest blue. She also appeared sad and preoccupied. He was determined to show no interest in her when they met again, but he would have to find out more about her from Forbes.

In fact it was Maudie who was more forthcoming. Possessing a woman's insight, she said, 'She is very beautiful, isn't she?' and added, 'Be very careful, Alex, she has been through a terrible time lately.' Alex protested rather too readily that he was only showing a polite interest. The knowing look Maudie gave him suggested she knew this was not true. Maudie told him that Helen's fiancé had been killed in the same year that Alec Forbes had also fallen. Despite himself, Alex felt a lurch of jealousy that she had already had a sweetheart, and yet it would have been inconceivable that anyone so gorgeous would not have had a string of admirers. Apparently there had been other disasters in the young woman's life that Maudie said it would be unfair to tell him.

'Perhaps she will tell her yourself if you get to know her well enough' Maudie suggested, again adopting a knowing stare. Over the following week he only saw Helen a couple of times. On both occasions he just offered a gruff hello. His work on the dug-out painting was beginning to take shape and Forbes was encouraging, offering a couple of welcome suggestions.

An opportunity arose the first week in December. Both Alex and Helen had been working on their respective paintings, rather forgetting the time. It was already dark outside. As she was clearing her brushes away he offered to escort her home, as her digs were only a short walk from his own. They walked mostly in silence. Alex was increasingly annoyed with himself at not being able to break the ice with a joke. Instead, their limited conversation was awkward and stilted. He wanted to shout how he was entranced by her, but instead they formally shook hands before she disappeared into the warmth of a cosy parlour.

He continued to work on his painting, which was now beginning to look really promising. The two men were hunched over the table, one with his hand poised over a white rook. A whisky bottle and two half empty glasses are caught in the light, but not to Alex's satisfaction. In the background is a blanket drawn across the entrance in a vain attempt to keep out the damp and cold. Forbes was also not happy with the way Alex had attempted to paint the reflected light, informing him that he was currently working on a painting that fascinated him because of the challenges of reproducing gas light. The following day Alex accompanied Forbes as he began work on a painting entitled 'The Saffron Cake' which was eventually exhibited at the 1920 Royal Academy exhibition. Meantime Alex ensured that he was on hand to take Helen home each night when it got dark. She obviously did not object and gradually they were becoming more comfortable in each other's company. The annual Christmas dance was being held the following week and Alex suggested they should go together. She agreed without showing any great enthusiasm. As Forbes had warned Alex, their pleasures in Newlyn were simple, but he looked forward to the evening with huge anticipation. Nights spent alone in his room reading left him feeling bored and restless.

On the afternoon of the village dance Alex and Helen took a bus into Penzance. Standing at the top of Market Jew Street, the town tumbled down before them. With the afternoons already drawing in, the lights in the shops glittered into the distance. The odd motor car was parked alongside tethered horses, pony traps and farmers' carts. The pavements were crowded with Christmas shoppers. Walking down towards the market, they stopped at a tea shop. It was whilst they hungrily ate a traditional Cornish cream tea that Alex learnt more about Helen's background. It was prompted by his reaction to her illustrations that she had produced at Higher Faugan. She worked incredibly slowly in fine detail, but it was the subject matter that intrigued Alex. Currently she was working on a wistful looking young woman staring out of a window so small that it gave the impression of a type of prison cell or some remote castle, rather like those his mother had mentioned to him as a child. Behind the ghostlike figure was an un-made four poster bed, but this had been depicted out of proportion. It was too high and narrow, adding to a feeling of claustrophobia. All the tones were in shades of darkish blues and only the elongated figure was picked out in off-white. The previous work she had completed was even more depressing, again done in pen and ink with a blue wash, it depicted an imminent execution. In the foreground a young woman kneels, begging forgiveness from two impassive male figures. In the background a priest and an executioner with axe in hand waits. Behind them it is just possible to make out the turrets of a castle. Perhaps the two illustrations were connected and the girl in the bedroom is awaiting the verdict as to her fate. The quality of the works were exceptional, but the subject matter strange.

'Are you really that unhappy?' Alex asked. 'I am' she replied, then after a pause added, 'At least I was.' Alex felt a surge of delight, but he was learning and did not react. Instead he listened to how first she had lost her fiancé to be followed this year by the death of her father. She had been engaged to a young teacher called Toby. He taught in a very deprived area of Holloway. Something of an idealist, he was set on trying to encourage his pupils to aim high and not accept that their futures lay in humdrum jobs. Helen described him as being not particularly physically attractive, but a great outward going personality with a wide circle of friends. Something of a man's man, keen on sport and a visit to the pub later. Alex could imagine he probably would have liked him if they had met. Tragically, Toby was killed within two days of arriving at the front. Much to Helen's distress, his body was never identified meaning that she would never be able to visit his grave. Alex murmured his sympathy, but there was more and he began to understand now the depth of her despair translated to her work. In January Helen's mother had discovered her husband hanging from a beam in the garden shed of their Crouch End home. What was even more upsetting was the fact that he left no note as to why he had taken such drastic action. On the surface his was a happy marriage. Not knowing what caused his obvious despair led to Helen's mother having a nervous breakdown. Currently she was in Shenley mental hospital. Helen had been working as a graphic designer at an advertising agency, but with a legacy left to her by her father she had also been attracted to a complete break in Cornwall. She had arrived in the autumn with a view of trying to reset her life.

With a legacy left to her by her father she had opted for a complete change in direction. Contacting Stanhope Forbes she had arrived in Newlyn in the autumn. Despite a warm welcome she still felt vulnerable and sad. Alex had also given her some idea of his own upbringing, rather playing down the wealth of his family, although he did tell her about his father's wish for him to join the family business. However, it was his intention to become a professional artist. He did not mention the astonishing success of his very first serious painting.

They arranged to meet again in an hour so that they could go off on their separate shopping expeditions. Alex was unsure what to buy Helen. Nothing too generous which may feel he was putting her under pressure, but nothing too trivial either. He wandered into a jewellers. Certainly not a ring, he decided, but what about a necklace or brooch. Eventually he spotted a silver locket in a cabinet and decided that it was very attractive, but not too extravagant. Nestled in a smart box and gift wrapped, he was feeling rather pleased with himself. He bought Stanhope Forbes a book of 20th century poems and Maudie a silk scarf. For Mrs. Perkins a bottle of gin that was her favourite tipple. Laden with their purchases, they waited for the bus to take them back to Newlyn to prepare for the dance later that night.

The parish hall was packed by the time they arrived at seven o'clock. Trestle tables were set out along the walls allowing plenty of room for dancing. The band, consisting of an accordion, banjo and piano performed from a raised stage. The proprietor of the Tolcarne Inn had set up a bar which already had a queue waiting to be served. There was an inevitable vague smell of fish mingled with smoke from pipes and cigarettes and increasingly, as the night wore on, of sweat mingled with perfume. A heady mix. Couples started to dance as the drink broke down inhibitions. He spotted Helen surrounded by a group of admiring, fit looking young fishermen. Normally Alex only saw Helen dressed in her artist's smock or her hooded coat. Tonight she wore a dress of green satin, which billowed out as she was energetically whirled round the dance floor by Stanhope Forbes, dressed smartly in his best suit. Alex asked Maudie to dance. He had come to really like and trust her. 'Go and rescue your girl' Maudie suggested, 'My old man is a terrible dancer.'

It was the first time Alex had ever held Helen in his arms. She was shorter than he had anticipated, her face only coming to just above his shoulder, but he had noticed she was wearing flat shoes. Looking up at him and smiling, he was again struck by her beauty. She was, in his view, simply flawless. The night slipped away on a tide of dancing, laughter and cider. As always at these type of events, a couple of young girls got crying drunk, and there was a scuffle at the bar that developed into a fight outside between two brothers who had been vying for the same girl. None of this affected Alex's enjoyment. He walked arm in arm with Helen to her front door. Emboldened by the drink he drew her towards him and kissed her. She reacted violently, pulling roughly away from him. Noticing the look of disappointment on his face she said, 'Sorry, I hate moustaches, they tickle', before opening the front door to her lodgings. As soon as he arrived home Alex reached for his cut throat razor and with a few expert strokes he was clean shaven. He had grown a moustache on his mother's advice to give him a look of at least some authority, which she reckoned would be needed to command the men under his control. Looking now at his new image in the mirror, he decided he still had no understanding at all about women. But for now there was only one he needed to understand and hard though it was he would bide his time.

Christmas that year was the happiest Alex could remember. Everyone from Higher Faugan attended the midnight service at St. Peter's on Christmas Eve, their voices lubricated by an earlier visit to the Tolcarne Inn. A surprise in that morning's post was a card forwarded on from Stratton House. Post marked Paris, it read simply 'Missing you. Until the next time. Love, G.' He had hardly given Gloria a thought since meeting Helen, but he kept the card and I still have it. My grandfather was a great hoarder, a fact that made my task recording his life so much easier. I also have the locket that he gave Helen that Christmas. Inside is a photograph of a young, smiling Alex.

Christmas Day saw a gathering of all the resident artists, including Charles Napier and Frank Heath. They were joined by Harold and Laura Knight who were visiting. With a dozen people crowded round the dining table, they tucked into roast goose and a large cockerel. The wine that Forbes imported direct from France flowed. Presents were exchanged and toasts proposed. It was the type of Christmas that we all seek, but so few achieve. No rows or disagreements. After the meal Alex sat with Laura Knight, who was rather embarrassed by his obvious championing of her work. The celebrations went on long into the night, and it was almost midnight by the time Alex walked Helen to her front door. Now at least they did kiss on parting, but Helen remained shy and hesitant, quickly pushing him away. This did concern him, but he stuck to his strategy of taking things slowly.

Early in the new year Forbes was preparing to send four submissions for the summer exhibition at the Royal Academy. Two were a breakaway from his usual rural interior or beach scenes. 'The Munitions Girls' captured dozens of young women toiling in a crowded factory setting, involved in the manufacture of weapons for the front. Another 'Shell Workers' maintained the war theme. More traditionally, he also included a painting of the moor pond and a view of the new mount. Alex had completed his 'Chess Mates' picture and Forbes included the work with his submissions. Whilst many artists shunned the R.A. Forbes reasoned that the work would help cement Alex's reputation, rather than selling the painting through a gallery. So, fully framed, the works were despatched to be considered for inclusion by the selection committee.

At Alex's prompting, Helen began creating a number of illustrations suitable for the children's book market. Photographs of children playing and a couple of nursery rhyme themes were sent off to publishers, without her receiving any immediate response. Winter began to merge into Spring and they started to take long walks along the beach looking out to St. Michael's Mount. Several times Alex was on the verge of asking Helen to marry him, but he was still not convinced of her love. Despite being genuinely affectionate towards each other, she had never said that she loved him, and somehow in his mind it was better to let things drift rather than being faced with rejection. It was early in April when he finally felt impelled to act. Helen had still not had a single response from publishers and she informed Alex that she could no longer afford to stay in Newlyn. She needed to go back to London and get a job. Returning from a blustery stroll, they walked up to the quay where boats were off-loading their catch. In view of cheering fishermen, Alex took her in his arms and asked somewhat plaintively, 'Helen, will you marry me?' Her reply shocked him. 'What took you so long?' she asked.

In Paris Gloria looked down with some distaste at the figure lying naked in her bed. His gentle snoring caused a ripple of flesh to wobble its way over his vast, hairy stomach. He was truly disgusting, but it was a small price to pay as he had promised to give her a solo part in a new revue.

Chapter 6

With this ring

Gloria was a spasmodic letter writer. Letters to my grandfather would sometimes arrive in clusters, with others sent months apart. She was often funny and frequently crude. Some were boastful, but when things in her life were going off the rails they were sad or, on occasions, maudlin. None of Alex's letters to Gloria survive, so it is a rather one sided conversation. Alex was a complex character. Often impulsive and sometimes reckless, he was above all someone who liked order. The letters covering over half a century were all filed in date order, squeezed into shoe boxes and housed in their original envelopes. Clearing his apartment in Albermarle Street after his death took days. It appeared he rarely threw anything away. His clothes were spread over the seven bedrooms, all clean and pressed. I contacted the Victoria and Albert Museum and they gratefully accepted suits dating back to the twenties and thirties, together with a selection of two-tone 'cads shoes'. There were dozens of photograph albums all neatly annotated and dated. Photos dating back to his childhood, but also signed prints of many of the famous actors, film stars, writers and artists of the first half of the 20th century. Rather more bizarrely there was a blizzard of restaurant receipts, their only interest showing the rise in prices over the years. He also kept a comprehensive scrap book of Gloria's reviews, but very few press cuttings covering his own long career.

It is an eerie task emptying a home of a loved one. Alex and I had become very close during his final years. My own life was in something of a turmoil at the time of his death, so I dumped all his memorabilia into a spare bedroom. I did try to look through it periodically, but it was only in recent years that I had enough time to thoroughly go through the rather intimidating mountain of material. It was then that I began to realise that here was a story that had to be told.

Gloria's initial letters were only headed 'Paris'. I assume that this was because she was living in reduced circumstances. She was nothing if not proud. As her career blossomed subsequent letters were posted from impressive locations and some of the world's swankiest hotels. Her first letter to Alex early in 1919 set the tone:

Dear Alex,

I miss you. Life here is tough. I have just junked a blubberball of a theatre owner who promised me the earth. The only thing he gave me you would not want to hear about. Fame is proving to be more elusive than I had imagined. There must be some regular guys in our business – I just can't find them.

Until the next time.

Love G

I can imagine this letter would have driven Alex mad if he had not met Helen. I can imagine him heading off to Paris in search of her. Instead he had other matters on his mind.

Having dithered for so long in asking Helen to marry him, Alex now was set on a speedy wedding, although they both agreed that they wanted to get married in Newlyn among the friends that had become their new family. He knew this was likely to upset his parents, but he could not stand the thought of a provincial society wedding attended by scores of people he scarcely knew. A date was set for the first Saturday in May. He sent an invitation to his parents, enclosing a photograph of Helen. Three days later he received a long letter from his father. In it he said how sad he was that Alex was not only turning down a wonderful career, but had also chosen to snub his parents, he was dreadfully hurt after all he had done for his son. He regretted that he would be unable to attend as he would be abroad on business. He did concede that Helen was a very pretty girl and also enclosed a very generous cheque that made Alex feel doubly guilty. There was no word from his mother.

So it was with mixed feelings that they started to make plans for the big day. One sense that remained with my grandfather all his life was that he had never had to struggle financially. He had grown up in some comfort surrounded by servants. His father had always been generous towards him, allocating him a ten percent share in the business on his eighteenth birthday. The dividends he had received whilst in the army were going to be enough for them to buy a substantial house, unlike most youngsters in their position. Making a living as an artist may be difficult, but finally Helen had received a commission to illustrate a children's book featuring fairies and hob goblins.

Whilst there were regular weddings in Newlyn, this was the first to stem directly from Higher Faugan. Maudie was in her element. A great organiser, she planned the hiring of the parish hall and the catering arrangements for the day. Helen was recommended to a dressmaker in Penzance and on the day of her first visit Alex also bought her engagement ring. It was a single emerald set in a white gold band. Frank King, the young artist Alex had first met on his arrival, was asked to be best man.

Like all young engaged couples, Alex and Helen spent hours discussing where they would live. Despite their love of Newlyn, both agreed that it was time to move away and make a fresh start. Certainly Northamptonshire was out of the question. They would obviously visit his parents, but they needed their own space. Alex favoured London whilst Helen wanted somewhere more peaceful. Suburbia sounded unattractive, but they would start hunting straight after a short honeymoon. There were several visits to the vicar of St. Peter's who lectured them on the importance of the sanctity of marriage and arranged a practice run for the actual service. Helen's dress fittings were attended by crowds of women and girls keen to be part of this great event. It is important to emphasise the difference in attitudes a hundred years ago. Today we have become blasé, but for the inhabitants of Newlyn the wedding was of huge interest and importance. Even those not attending the service dressed up. Hoary old fishermen struggled into their Sunday best suits, whilst their women folk donned bonnets of straw and little girls wore flowers in their hair.

The night before the wedding Alex was despatched to the Tolcarne Inn to spend the night honouring the tradition of not spending the night before the wedding under the same roof as his bride. Despite a valiant effort to stay sober, Alex was plied with drinks from well-wishers and woke the morning of the great day feeling queasy and hung over.

May is the month of singing birds and it was the dawn chorus that woke Alex that morning. He noticed that swallows had arrived that very day after their monumental trip from Africa. Their arrival heralded a new start for him and a happy omen. The morning dragged on slowly, but by midday he was in his place in the front pew at St. Peter's. Behind him a hum of anticipation. People whispered how handsome he looked dressed in a smart suit, a tall elegant figure nervously fidgeting and continually glancing over his shoulder to witness the arrival of his bride who was already late. Suddenly there was a commotion as the doors were noisily flung open. Down the aisle came a figure the like of which nobody in Newlyn had ever witnessed. Her long black skirt swished over the floor. She wore a tight fitting cream blouse with a ruffle secured by a stunning cameo brooch. The dramatic effect was heightened by her wide brimmed hat fashioned with black lace, and her face emphasised by a screech of vivid red lipstick. Looking to neither left nor right, she approached the groom and kissed him tenderly on the cheek. Leaning forward she whispered, 'Is she pregnant?' Before he could answer she turned round and addressing the congregation announced, 'Hello everyone, my name is Orla, I am Alex's mother.' There was a buzz of excited conversation cut short by the organist playing the wedding march.

There were obviously formal photographs taken outside the church but only two survive. One is of the happy couple, my grandfather looking rather smug and proud as Helen stares up at him with the faintest of smiles. More interesting is the image of the bride. Perhaps it is the fading of the photograph that adds to a feeling of a much earlier age. Almost medieval, maybe pre-Raphaelite would be more accurate, helped no doubt by her tumbling hair garlanded by spring flowers. Yes, pre-Raphaelite, but representing Burne-Jones rather than Rossetti. Helen's dress is simple but stunning. A fitted bodice is complimented by the dress which extends in a gentle sweep to the floor. Her figure is so slender as to be almost childlike, but she has a beauty that still translates to modern life.

The evening included a full sit down meal before the floor was cleared for dancing. My grandfather told me that his most vivid memory of that evening was of the transformation of his mother. No longer the vague, enigmatic figure. Here was someone hell bent on enjoying themself. She sang, she played the piano and she caroused. She danced with abandon, whirling round the floor, often whooping and dragging young men from their seats to dance with her. Her sense of fun was contagious and although exuberant, was not embarrassing. For days after the wedding the talk in Newlyn was of Alex's fantastic mother. By eleven o'clock it was time to leave for the hotel Alex had booked in Penzance. This was to be no quiet taxi ride. A cart festooned with flowers and greenery had been prepared, to be pulled by the same grey horse who had first brought Alex to Newlyn. On board as well as the married couple was his mother, Frank their best man, and about half a dozen revellers determined to continue the evening's celebrations. So it was a rowdy group that staggered into the reception area of the Queen's Hotel. My grandfather maintained that well meaning friends had spiked his drinks that night. Whatever, he was obviously seriously drunk by the time they reached their bedroom. He had vague memories of making a grab for his bride. Sober herself, she easily avoided him and he fell in a drunken heap across the bed. He awoke the following morning still fully clothed and feeling dreadful. Helen lay asleep in an armchair.

They were joined at breakfast by Alex's mother. Orla appeared none the worse for her riotous night. Smart in a fashionable grey suit topped by a dramatic cloak, she dominated the conversation whilst Alex's head continued to pound. Having eaten a full English breakfast, his mother produced a small leather box which she gave to Helen. Inside was a stunning large sapphire of the deepest blue and mounted on a white-gold band. She informed Helen that it had belonged to her mother and that her father had bought it in a leading Dublin jewellers. The box contained an address in Colombo. Aware that the finest sapphires came from Ceylon, Alex was astonished at his mother's generosity. He felt that good manners would have dictated that Helen, at least initially, would have refused such an expensive and personal present. Her only response was to assure Orla that she would treasure the jewel and never part with it. Leaving Alex to his hangover, he watched the two women walk arm in arm along the promenade as the high tide crashed onto the sea wall. Helen never told him what they talked about that morning, but their walk extended to almost an hour. The sapphire, which appears on photos of Helen's dresses over the years, is certainly not amongst the mountain of possessions I inherited. Although never conclusively confirmed by Alex in our many long conversations, it seems quite likely that he honoured Helen's pledge never to part with the jewel. It is quite likely that it was buried with her.

My grandparents' honeymoon was spent at Tregenna Castle, a turreted hotel set in over 50 acres of ground with panoramic views out to sea. Honeymoons, particularly in those far off days, were often difficult and so theirs proved. Being thrown together for the first time with no supporting cast could be a strain, as a young couple began to get used to each other. It was often commented that the person you thought you knew prior to marriage changed once they were confronted with a whole life ahead of them. This did not apply to my grandparents, they were at ease together. Alex found Helen affectionate, thoughtful and loving. The problems were confined to the bedroom. Alex put most of the problem down to his own inexperience. Perhaps he was too eager, clumsy and awkward in his approach. Whatever, it was three nights before the marriage was consummated. It was a problem that existed through most of their married life. He understood her shyness, but her attitude was more one of acceptance or duty, rather than even a hint of enjoyment. At this early stage of their marriage it did not really worry Alex as Helen was so loving and fun to be with. He was also visibly proud, as over the years she continued to get flattering glances from men and yet, unusually, her good looks did not appear to pose any threats to the women she met.

The weather was kind to them on this, their first holiday

together. They enjoyed long walks and trips into St. Ives for shopping and lunches overlooking the sea. It was whilst sitting on the terrace at the hotel that Alex spotted the advertisement for the house they were to buy. Amongst the properties listed on the front page of The Times was a gentleman's residence in Bushey Heath, Hertfordshire. They had decided to spend the following week house hunting, and again Alex's sense of premonition set in. He had ringed several properties listed in the paper, but this one stood out for him. It described a charming country property, yet within easy reach of London.

The house, built in the early nineteenth century, afforded four beautifully proportioned living rooms, kitchen and a scullery. Upstairs there were five bedrooms with two attic rooms suitable, it suggested, for servants. The well stocked gardens extended to over an acre with fine rural views to three sides. Three days later they stood on the front drive to the property. The advertisement had failed to mention that paint was peeling off throughout the house and several window frames were rotten. Outside the beautifully laid out garden had been allowed to be overwhelmed with weeds, and the lawn was really just a field. Despite all this they both loved it. They were impressed by the rather grand portico. A morning room and dining room led off a central hall. Behind was a good sized square kitchen. At the back was a small study and a lovely living room overlooking the garden wilderness. They decided it was perfect even before venturing upstairs.

The price being asked represented the fact that it had been left un-lived in for a couple of years. Even so it was going to stretch them financially, particularly as neither of them had a guaranteed income. Alex was left with two choices. Buy the house outright leaving nothing for furniture and fittings, or take a small mortgage which would allow them to have money to make the house a comfortable home. Days were spent whilst Alex haggled to get a lower price. Luckily the house market was still very deflated by the impact of the war. The deal was done, allowing a very modest amount to spend on necessities. Alex was and remained a gambler. He was convinced that the sale of the paintings to be exhibited in London would provide them with a buffer until they could sell more works. His optimism was justified for within days Helen also received a positive response to her work by Frederick Warne, a leading publisher.

It was early in June that my grandparents moved into Hollybanks, their Bushey home. Now just part of the endless spread of London's suburbia, a hundred years ago Bushey was little more than a village. Although Alex did not know it at the time, Bushey had once been home to the influential Herkomer's Art School and the village still attracted artists like *Lucy Kemp-Welch*. Strangely, all of the three properties that Alex bought during his lifetime attracted an artistic community. Through the summer of 1919 Alex and Helen were surrounded by groups of workmen. Fresh paint was applied and windows replaced, and despite all the chaos surrounding them it was a time of intense happiness. Helen continued to surprise. He had not realised that she was a superb cook, but her real passion was gardening. Once they had furnished the house, following visits to Heal's in Tottenham Court Road and to local sale rooms, the house began to reflect Helen's skill at mixing antique and contemporary furniture, and running riot in her choice of curtains and furnishing fabrics. In between this hectic nest building, she started to devote her energies to the wilderness that was their garden.

Weirdly, Helen maintained that there were really only two seasons, summer and winter, with two static times bound together by the changing months of spring and autumn. The tide of the year is quicker in the spring than its ebbing in autumn, when the whole country year had to be embraced and celebrated. After a busy day they sat in their emerging garden and she would excitedly point out the different birds, identifying many solely by their song. This was all new to Alex who had never really taken notice, although even he was fascinated that larks continued to sing in the wastelands of war-torn France. Through her enthusiastic instruction he began to identify even rare birds like the grasshopper warbler and butterflies like the large meadow brown.

Although much of the upstairs remained in need of urgent attention, they decided on the bedrooms that would act as their separate studios. They made a pact that each was a no-go area, a private space for them to work without any interruption or outside influence. This was an agreement they both honoured.

Whilst the newlyweds were settling happily into their new home, Gloria had secured herself a job at a down-at-heel club, just off the Rue de Sebastopol. Whilst it paid very poorly it had the advantage of being close to Les Halles, the fresh food market for Paris. Named as the 'belly of Paris' by *Émile* Zola, it allowed Gloria to get food very cheaply, or even without charge when she flirted with the stallholders.

Looking back, she still found it astonishing that the squalid Club Antoine was to be her launching pad to international fame.

Chapter 7

A strange peace

Amongst the blizzard of restaurant and shop receipts, one took my particular interest. It was from Liberty's, the department store. Although undated it listed an evening gown of green silk velvet, hand embroidered in pure silk. It was priced at a hefty 25 guineas. This was the dress that she wore for the preview of the exhibition at the Fine Art Society. In the photograph that I still have, Helen looks up proudly at Alex, who cuts a dash in a dinner jacket popularised recently by the Prince of Wales. They had worried about what was a suitable dress code and solved it by booking a table at the Embassy night club, just up the street from the gallery. The gathering was generally of the great and good. My grandparents were probably at least thirty years younger than the rest attending. Alex certainly did not receive universal approval of his major painting, particularly from the men. They were all genial enough towards him, but typically said "very good, old chap, but a bit modern for my taste." It was left to women to understand and appreciate the work. It upset one lady so much that she had to be escorted to the cloakroom. Press photographers and critics were circulating. One confided in Alex that it would be hard to produce other works of such impact. Alex saw hardly anything of his wife as she was surrounded by a group of admiring men old enough to be her father. Four or five of Alex's sketches had been reserved by the time my grandparents slipped away, having stayed long enough not to cause offence.

They walked the short distance to the Embassy, but Alex's leg was playing up and he walked with a pronounced limp. As they approached the club's entrance, the smartly uniformed doorman snapped to attention. Alex's bearing still reflected his time in the army. 'Evening sir.' 'Thank you, I bet you were a Sergeant?' Alex said with a smile. 'Sergeant Major, sir.' Alex shook the man's hand, noticing for the first time the eye patch he was wearing. Alex had been told that the club employed a good number of ex-servicemen. It was just so sad seeing them having to accept such menial jobs. There was huge discontent in the country as returning servicemen were consigned to homelessness and unemployment. There was genuine concern that resentment would spill over from strikes to violence and, conceivably, revolution.

Inside, the club was crowded to capacity. The air was thick with cigarette and cigar smoke. They were escorted to their table right next to the dance floor. Having ordered champagne, Alex turned to the two couples who occupied the table next to him. He greeted them, 'Good evening.' Both men were immaculate in white tie. One wearing spectacles, with protruding teeth and slicked down hair, replied with a sneer, 'Do I know you?' and without waiting for a reply turned away. Alex's champagne had been uncorked by a waiter, but poured by an assistant who had an empty sleeve tucked into his jacket pocket. 'Can you believe it' one of the women at the next table brayed, 'A one-armed waiter, quite ridiculous.' 'I don't know' 'Snaggle touch' lisped, 'He is obviously perfectly 'armless.' This reduced them all to hysterical laughter. Alex grabbed Helen quite roughly and propelled her onto the dance floor to avoid their obnoxious neighbours.

Alex was a clumsy dancer. Without his stick his balance was very poor. He apologised as he knocked into couples on the crowded dance floor. None took offence until he veered into 'Snaggle tooth' and his be-jewelled partner. As they waltzed away he heard the man lisp in stage whisper, 'This place is full of bloody cwipples.' Alex pursued him, 'What did you just say?' He loathed people with an inbuilt sense of entitlement and superiority and who are not used to apologising. Despite the look of anger on Alex's face, he replied, 'If you are cwippled you really should not....' He never completed the sentence. Alex hit him with a pent up fury and the slightly built figure was catapulted into a line of tables, sending glasses and bottles smashing to the floor. The wretched figure's glasses had been smashed, his teeth re-arranged and blood gushed from his nose. His companion screamed and a voice demanded that the police should be sent for.

As people gathered round trying to assess what had happened, a single figure strode across the floor. He had been sitting with his wife on the other adjoining table to the prostrate figure. Without saying a word, he shook Alex's hand and then embraced him. Everything had gone quiet until a voice cried out, 'Well done sir!' It was the waiter who had served Alex his champagne. Taking Helen's arm they made their way towards the entrance, people parting to let them past. Suddenly a ripple of applause started. Chefs and kitchen staff had appeared. There was a real tension in the air. Here in this moment was the dilemma the whole nation faced. Privilege being challenged as never before. The moment passed and the staff returned to their work stations. Outside the doorman hailed them a cab. In an unusual spark of genuine humour, Helen asked, 'Why don't you pick on a chap of your own size?' This broke the tension Alex had been feeling and they were still laughing when they reached their hotel.

That night they made love as they never had or ever did again. It was an act of deep love between them. Abandoned, tender and memorable. Later that night Helen was woken by the whole bed moving. Beside her Alex was shaking as if consumed by a terrible fever. Suddenly all the pent up emotion of his time in France came crashing to the surface. They did not speak or ever refer to this moment again during their marriage. She simply held him to her, stroking his head and running her fingers through his hair as a mother would do to a child. Gradually his convulsions lessened and he fell into a deep sleep. Helen lay quite still at his side, as if any movement would waken the demons that still lay within his soul.

The following day had been designated 'Peace Day.' The government had brought the Victory Parade forward from its intended date because of the general unrest in the country. Strikes and discontent were shown in sharp focus when the King was booed whilst reviewing recently discharged troops. What had been the use of the extraordinary sacrifice made by the British people if life was not going to change for the better? It was hoped a day of flag waving celebration would lighten the public mood.

Crowds were already lining the pavements as my grandparents made their way to the offices of Smedley and Co., one of George Beck's most important customers. Their offices on the corner of Whitehall and Trafalgar Square gave them an unrivalled viewing point for them to witness what was a fantastic example of superb and meticulous planning. Close on twenty thousand troops had been billeted in London overnight to enable them to take their place in a unique pageant. Despite the drizzle in the air the crowd was not going to let it dampen their enjoyment. They had gathered from all over the country. Special trains and buses had been laid on, and it was not only London accents that could be heard rising to where Alex and Helen waited in anticipation. Bunting hung from public buildings, and Buckingham Palace had been decked in decorations of red, white and blue. The pageant was extended to the Thames where warships lined the banks.

On Whitehall a temporary cenotaph had been erected. This 'empty tomb' had been built by Edwin Lutyens within ten days. This was a day to honour all who had contributed to the war, a fact underlined by the seven mile procession that took hours to pass the cheering crowds. The parade of some twenty thousand men and women began at 10 o'clock. The route started at Albert Gate and ran to Hyde Park before turning south and crossing the Thames, taking in less fashionable areas of London before returning north by Westminster bridge. Onwards past Parliament and Big Ben, onwards then to Whitehall where all paused to salute the hastily erected cenotaph. The route now took in Trafalgar Square and into the Mall past the Victoria memorial where the King was to take the salute, then along Constitutional Hill before finally returning to Hyde Park.

During his lifetime Alex attended most of the great state events open to the public. Weddings, coronations, funerals and the WW2 Victory Parade, but for him and many of his generation, Peace Day was the most poignant. A bitter-sweet day of elation that at last the war was finally over, tempered by memories that refused to fade. From their key vantage point Alex and Helen watched as endless lines of soldiers marched past the predominate khaki, relieved by the brightly turbaned Indian troops. African soldiers were also represented, as were Belgian and French troops. Sailors got an extra cheer from the crowd, as did the Scots, kilted and accompanied by bagpipes. No sooner had one military band passed before it was possible to hear another approaching. Every organisation that contributed to the war effort was represented. Cheers swelled again to welcome nurses proudly swinging by in their pristine uniforms. They also saw General Foch mounted on a black stallion and General Haig, but this was a day not for Generals or the top brass, but for the ordinary tommy. When the last troops were gone many in the crowd seemed reluctant to leave, whilst others headed for the Mall hoping to see the Royal Family appear on the balcony of Buckingham Palace.

Against the tide of humanity, my grandparents went to pick up their car for the drive home. Helen had picked up a couple of newspapers. Although souvenir editions both contained photographs from the previous night of Alex and Helen taken in front of his painting, Alex's response was to blurt out, 'Oh shit, obviously I am going to be identified.'

Laughing, he asked Helen if she would be prepared to visit him whilst in jail. The following morning two policemen arrived to interview my grandfather. They explained that Earl Henty had suffered a vicious attack and that he had identified Alex from a photograph in yesterday's papers. Alex did not respond, allowing the senior man to continue. It appeared that other people present, including staff, gave a very different description of the assailant. Variously described as short with ginger hair, or alternatively as thug-like and dressed in a cheap ill-fitting suit. 'Are you able to confirm that you were not at the Embassy Club last night, sir?' Alex replied that he was at the Fine Art Society, which could be confirmed and that was all he was prepared to say. Actually it was pretty obvious that the police were not about to take any further action, there had been a closing of ranks to protect him. The policemen were obviously sympathetic, shaking hands warmly with my grandfather. As they were leaving he asked them to confirm that Henty was not some war hero. 'Not exactly sir, he spent the entire war in Portugal. Neutral country sir. Have you ever drunk Henty port sir?' 'I have' Alex replied, laughing, 'But never again.' 'Me neither sir, but you may have to use his coal, it appears his family own half of Derbyshire.'

Reckless behaviour erupted periodically throughout Alex's life. Shortly before his death I probed into why he became known as 'Mad Alex'. He insisted his bravery was either down to being drunk, or a desire during his final year at the front to be shot. He did his best as his row of medals for bravery prove. He was so disillusioned that he wanted to die to get away from what he considered to be pointless carnage. He shocked by saying that at one stage he had seriously considered deserting. Was he joking? We shall never know. Alex was hard to read and as I continued to delve into his life the more complex a character he turned out to be.

'Despair' was acclaimed on both sides of the Channel, with a photograph of my grandparents appearing in some French newspapers. The following week a letter arrived from Gloria, again with no address.

My dear Alex,

I am so jealous. I want fame and recognition and you get both. It's just not fair. Then to cap it all you go and get married. She is very stunning. I hate her.

Until the next time.

Love, G.

By the end of the year Gloria had sunk into a deep depression. Her career was going nowhere and a succession of short lived affairs left her disillusioned by men generally, and particularly those promising to re-launch her career. She resolved to leave Bar Antoine once the new year festivities were over. New year, new hope. Antoine had pointed out a man who had come in for the previous two nights. He ordered a bottle of Chablis, drank scarcely a glass and left as soon as Gloria finished her act. He appeared again on the third night, ordered the wine, watched her perform, but this night asked Antoine to invite Gloria to his table. He was tall with grey hair and a rather distinguished bearing. Not the type the bar usually attracted. Tired and grumpy, Gloria sat down, poured herself a full glass of wine and said, 'I suppose you are going to tell me that you are going to make me a star, but only after I have warmed your bed.' The man's face remained impassive. He informed her in answer to her first question that he thought she was talented and it was possible that he could help her to become a star, although it was doubtful. In answer to her second question he informed her he had two daughters older than her, and his wife had warmed his bed for the last thirty eight years and he hoped she would continue to do so. He spoke fluent French, but with an accent she could not quite place. Changing to impeccable English he said, 'Allow me to introduce myself. My name is Harry Goodman.'

Chapter 8

New beginnings

Harry Goodman had been in Paris negotiating a deal for Maurice Chevalier to tour Britain. It was his secretary who reminded him about the young American woman whom she had met whilst he was abroad in the United States. Gloria was in Paris working in a succession of unfashionable clubs. With no engagements on his last night before returning home, he decided to take a trip to Bar Antoine. He saw a raw talent and, playing a hunch, opted to extend his visit. By the third night of watching Gloria he decided to make her a very unusual offer. Initially it was based on her piano playing. A huge interest in jazz and ragtime had migrated from the States to Europe and, as ever, Harry was not about to miss out. Whilst he realised her keyboard skills were instantly saleable, her singing had nothing to set her apart and her dancing was frankly embarrassing. Overtly sexy, but crude. He arranged for Gloria to meet him at his hotel the following morning.

The receptionist rather dismissively informed him that there was a person wishing to see him. Having established it was Gloria, he gave instructions for the young lady to be brought up. Gloria had been prevented from entering Hotel Athenee by a uniformed commissionaire. Still denied access through the main reception area, Gloria was escorted to a side entrance and brought to Goodman's suite via a service lift. This was not a humiliation that Gloria ever forgot. Goodman was horrified to see the young girl still shivering in cheap summer clothes. Gloria appeared quite overcome by the grandeur of the suite with its views over the Eiffel Tower. Aware that she had not been listening to him, Goodman gave her time to relax a little as he poured them both a coffee. What he proposed stunned her. In the new year she was to be flown to London. Once there hotel accommodation with food would be provided, together with a nominal wage. In return she would be put through the most rigorous training programme. This was likely to last months rather than weeks. It would include voice training, a fitness programme and intensive dance coaching. There would be more, but that would be explained to her later. If she did not meet the required standards work would again be found for her in clubs. If, however, she applied herself and met the standards required by her tutors, he had plans that could catapult her into national acclaim.

Harry Goodman was a unique presence in British show business. A graduate of Oxford university, he had planned an academic career until the death of his father. Since then he had transformed what was a small business into becoming one of the most influential and successful theatrical organisations in London. Harry was renowned for his negotiating skills and also for spotting trends in the market. He also had a knack of uncovering new talent. As Gloria prepared to leave and with her head still in a spin, Goodman peeled off a couple of large denomination notes, telling her to go and buy herself a warm coat, adding as his parting shot, 'I don't want you turning up in London with pneumonia.'

Alex had never tried to hide the circumstances of how he had met Gloria from Helen. In fact he had gone out of his way to let her read Gloria's letters, not that she had ever seemed that interested. This latest one really intrigued him.

My dear Alex,

I will be arriving in London soon. Really exciting developments. I cannot say more, but things are looking up.

Until the next time.

Love, G.

The letter had been posted in Paris and there was still no address for him to contact her with his own exciting news. Helen was pregnant with the baby expected in June. They were both thrilled at the news. Helen was blooming with no morning sickness and looking lovelier than ever. Her career as an illustrator was also taking off, with a commission from the Medici Society to illustrate the Pied Piper of Hamlin. It was proving a more difficult time for Alex. Although he was loving life in Bushey, his work was not going well. Flower studies and garden scenes were wooden and not good enough to be offered for sale. He needed something to spark him, but for the time being he basked in happy domesticity. Helen concentrated on her art work in the mornings, turning her attention to gardening in the afternoons, provided the weather was kind. Each evening she prepared a beautifully cooked meal, before they settled down to reading or playing a board game. Despite his good fortune worries niggled away. He needed to earn some money. His only immediate prospect was the hopeful sale of the 'Chess Mates' at the summer exhibition, but that was not until June. Did artists really have to rely on inspiration? Maybe it was more perspiration and hard work that was needed. Despite still feeling rather glum, he entered his studio with a renewed sense of determination.

In a sense the smell of vegetables and ripening fruit pursued Gloria from Les Halles in Paris to London. The rehearsal room Goodman had arranged was situated in a room off the main hall in Covent Garden. Unsold goods were stacked in crates whilst Gloria was put through her paces. It was a smell she never tired of and one that continued to prompt memories throughout her life. Gloria was astounded at how much her life was to be regulated. Her hotel, the Strand Palace, was only a short walk from the market. It was a hotel that gave the veneer of luxury, but was designed for the mass market. Glitz, but at a very reasonable price. Harry Goodman had warned Gloria that during her time in training she was to keep a low profile and do nothing to draw attention to herself. To further this intention she was surprised to find three dowdy outfits laid out in her room which she was to wear until told otherwise. Women of colour were still something of a rarity in London, hence the dresses in grey, navy and brown, together with two pairs of sensible shoes. She was also banned from making contact with any friends she might have in town, thus stopping Gloria making contact with Alex. Any thoughts she may have had regarding the severity of her trial period were reinforced on her first day in the rehearsal rooms. This was going to be like a military boot camp.

She was welcomed that morning by the four people charged by Goodman to transform her from a small time performer into a potential star. They were frightening. Changed in to a leotard, they viewed her much as a farmer would a beast at market. She was asked about her diet. 'No wonder you look so unhealthy', they told her. Her skin and shape were, they said, testimony to her unhealthy life style. Already feeling aggrieved, her posture and hairstyle were savaged. What did they expect living on subsistence wages whilst in France. She was on the edge of tears, but they did not give up. This was the plan to knock her confidence before gradually building it up again, but this to be based on her progress to their promptings and cajoling.

In those early days Gloria felt quite desperate and alone. Her singing coach, a former opera performer in her fifties, told her she sounded like a screeching parrot. She needed to re-pitch her voice to a lower key. When this was gradually transformed, huge attention had to be paid to her breathing and diction. Despite her piano playing being her strongest suit, a mentor was employed to help widen her repertoire. Of all her coaches it was the dance master who worked her the hardest. Effeminate he may have been, but he was remorseless and seemingly never impressed no matter how hard Gloria worked in an attempt to please him. It was about a month into her training that Harry Goodman finally put in an appearance. Taking her to one side he told her the reports he had received on her progress were encouraging. As if in acknowledgement, he invited Gloria to his house for Sunday lunch. Working six days a week left Gloria exhausted by the time she returned to her hotel, so a change of scenery was something to look forward to.

A car was sent to pick Gloria up for the trip to Hampstead. The house was large, but comfortable rather than flashy, bulging bookshelves predominating. Gloria was introduced to Judith, Harry's wife, and his eldest daughter Rachel. Over the following weeks many Sundays were spent with the warmth of their welcome, in stark contrast to her hectoring tutors. Walks were taken with Harry across Hampstead Heath and his plans for her gradually being revealed, but there was still plenty of work to be done.

Deportment and etiquette councillors were added to her team of tormentors. Hours were spent simply walking up and down the room, to the background noise of crates being loaded and porters swearing. She was advised to slow her natural movements. Even picking up a glass had to be done at three-quarter speed. All of this helped to create a dramatic effect. Even her use of cutlery had to be overhauled. Goodman had noted her table manners would not pass muster in the world's swankiest restaurants. Table settings were laid in the rehearsal room as if for a banquet. Knives and forks had to be held in the European style. Soup spoons and fish knives all had to be identified for Gloria and, importantly, how to use them. The different type of glasses required for hock, claret or burgundy. Whisky, brandy and sherry glasses also, there was so much to memorise. It did occur to Gloria that they were trying to turn her into a lady as well as a performer, which they never achieved, but then she had no wish to be or behave like a lady. After three months of exhaustive training even her tutors reckoned she was ready for what was going to be the most outrageous gamble of Harry Goodman's career.

The influenza epidemic was beginning to decline in 1920 to be replaced by another, less destructive and more exciting. The young longed to forget about the war, the effects of which had infiltrated almost every home in Britain. Now they wanted to have fun. Most of all they wanted to dance. This was a way of throwing off the feeling of national gloom. For them there was no appetite for stately waltzes or foxtrots. Even the twizzle or the shimmy were now considered old hat. What they wanted was jazz, even ragtime was being pushed aside. Couples were invited to rock 'n' roll. Jazz was exciting, even its meaning had young ladies colouring in embarrassment when explained to them. Dance halls were opening up all across the country. A watered down version of jazz had even been played at Buckingham Palace by the Original Dixieland Band, whose members were all white. But if you wanted to dance there was really only one venue that counted. A dance hall that could accommodate five thousand people offering non-stop dancing, as one leading band took over from another.

The site of a former bus depot was seemingly a strange venue in which to launch Gloria's career. Although opened only the previous year, the Hammersmith Palais had become the mecca for those embracing the new craze for dancing sweeping across the country. Although aimed at the mass market, even the privileged 'bright young things' were prepared to venture into a part of London they scarcely knew existed. Entering the Palais was to leave London behind and embrace the illusion of a mock Chinese palace. Brightly coloured lacquered wall panels and giant columns soared to a vast black lacquered ceiling that extended to a lavish pagoda. There was a welcome to a grotto of 'peerless delight' and Chinese lettering signifying good luck. No expense had been spared on this make believe wonderland. The huge dance floor was constructed of the finest Canadian maple. This was conducive for the dance experts to perform to the highest professional standards, although often the floor was so crowded it was difficult to move.

Despite no alcohol being served, it was still difficult for the Master of Ceremonies to be heard above the buzz of conversation. Gradually the floor was cleared and a grand piano placed centre stage. Shouting to make himself heard, the MC gave Gloria a big build up. They were, he informed them, lucky to witness the first British appearance by Gloria Bird, fresh from rave reviews in Paris and New York. A spotlight picked out Gloria seated at the piano, dressed in a man's tailed suit and wearing a silk top hat worn at a rakish angle. Within moments crowds were returning from bars scattered through the building. They were drawn by a type of piano playing they had never heard before. The crowd pushed forward surrounding Gloria as she vamped and played honky-tonk and stride. She sang jazz numbers and show songs, before inviting everyone to join her in a rowdy version of 'Alexander's Ragtime Band'. She finished her performance with 'Ca C'est Paris', her French perfect, her voice husky and intimate. She left to thunderous applause, the audience being told that she would be conducting a sensational dance routine at the next interval.

Now the dancers were happy to clear the floor and make way for Gloria and her dance partner. The Tango had originated in Spain, been developed in Argentina and further sexualised in the brothels of New York. Gloria and her tutor James had spent long hours perfecting their routine. Interpreting their moves to the music of the Palais's resident band, they thrust and pouted in unison. As the music reached a crescendo Gloria arched her back in an act of submission. The young ladies looking on were shocked, whilst their boyfriends whooped and cheered. British audiences were just not used to such overtly sexy performances. What followed was truly shocking.

In a routine that predated the Paso Doble by a decade, the couple now performed a mock bull fight accompanied by three Spanish guitarists. At one end of the vast dance floor James stood theatrically pawing the ground in mock anger. Still impeccably dressed in white tie and tails, he also wore a pair of frightening bulls' horns. Facing him was Gloria the matador, dressed in a skimpy leotard. She was holding a black cape which she used to encourage the bull. Charging straight at her, she avoided his frantic thrusts with a furl of the cape. The strumming of three Spanish guitarists reached a crescendo. The cape was now reversed to show a vivid red. As the bull made his last desperate charge, he fell exhausted at Gloria's feet. To the cheers of the onlookers, she thrust the Malacca cane in to his body.

Maybe that would have been acceptable, but standing astride him was not. Her six inch heels pierced his shirt. The Malacca cane was held aloft. James pleaded in supplication whilst, as pre-arranged, press photographers recorded the scene for the national newspapers. It is quite possible that many gathered there that night did not fully understand the implications of what they had witnessed. A black woman humiliating a white gentleman in evening dress was going to prove incendiary. Harry Goodman expected an outraged response and he was not disappointed.

Two days before appearing at Hammersmith, Gloria broke her promise to Goodman by contacting Alex. Her letter both confused and fascinated him. Written on headed notepaper from the Strand Palace Hotel, it read:

My dear Alex,

It is only a few hundred yards from this hotel to the Savoy, but miles apart in the clientele they attract. Would you believe I am just about to make that short journey. I want you to meet me at the Savoy at midday this Friday. By then I think my life will have changed. I told you I was going to be famous too. Don't be late. If you fail to appear I will never forgive you.

Until Friday. Love, G.

Although puzzled, Alex showed the letter to Helen. 'You must go' she told him. 'Only if you come too' he said. Obviously this was the last thing Helen wanted to do. Being pregnant and traipsing round London would be no fun. So it was that on that Friday Alex took the train to London. It was mad, he thought, that even Gloria could achieve fame overnight. Not for the last time she was just about to prove him wrong. Of course the Times he was reading on the train made no mention of Gloria, but he thought he caught a glimpse of what may have been her on an inside page of the Daily Mail that a man sitting opposite him had been reading. Suppressing his curiosity, he purchased a couple of daily papers at Euston. There on the front page of the Daily Express was a photograph of Gloria astride a stricken white man. He was not sure of his reaction. Shock certainly, but was this really the way she wanted to achieve notoriety? It all seemed rather tacky and he was sure she was going to lay herself open to abuse rather than praise. Arriving at the Savoy he had to negotiate his way past a group of photographers.

There was no sign of Gloria in reception and he wondered if her suggestion to meet was a hoax. Enquiring at the desk he was informed that Miss Bird was expecting him and arranged for a bell boy to take him up to her suite. The door was ajar. 'Come in, Alex.' The voice was familiar and yet somehow different from what he remembered. She looked different too, slimmer, healthier and stunning. The last trip Harry Goodman had arranged in her transformation was a visit to the hairdressers. Her hair had first been cropped and then her head shaved. The effect was extraordinary. It emphasised her high cheekbones and flawless complexion. Dressed in a silk dressing gown, she embraced him chattering like an excited schoolgirl. Had he heard about her performance at the Palais? Did he know her picture was all over the papers and that she had been booked to appear all the next week at the Apollo Theatre on Shaftesbury Avenue? He tried to respond, but she was not listening, talking now about starring in a show in Paris in June. In an abrupt change of mood she accused him of not showing enthusiasm for her triumph.

'Kiss me!' she demanded. He pecked her on the cheek. 'Not like that, properly!' He tried to wriggle away from her. She undid her dressing gown and let it slip to the floor. He was stunned, excited and alarmed. She engulfed him, her body thrust against him. Again he tried to pull away. 'Gloria, for God's sake!' 'What is the matter with you?' she demanded. Rather weakly he replied, 'I'm married.' 'So what?' 'But Helen is pregnant.' She sidled up to him again, 'Then you must be desperate.' Still, in spite of himself, he protested. Again her mood changed. 'Are you queer?' she said, raising her voice. 'No Gloria, don't be silly.' 'That's it!' she was shouting now, 'You are queer, a Nancy boy.' Bursting into tears, she hurled an empty glass onto the floor shattering it before throwing herself onto the bed and curling up in the foetal position, sobbing uncontrollably. Looking up from gathering the broken glass, Alex was amazed to see Gloria now sitting up and giggling. 'Well' she said, 'If you do not want to roger me, we may as well go and get some lunch.'

She was not going to make things easy for Alex. She was a minx. She dressed very slowly, almost like a striptease in reverse. Sighing, she ran her hands provocatively over her body, smiling, inviting him to respond. He turned away and her mood went into reverse. Now she was hectoring. A table had been booked at Rules, just five minutes' walk from the hotel. She would join him there as she was under oath not to be seen in the company of any man other than Harry Goodman during her stay in London. He wanted her to create an aura of mystique. Rules in Maiden Lane is London's oldest restaurant. Alex had been taken there for a family treat before the war. As he pushed by the photographers outside the hotel, he began to curse his middle class morality. Maybe, but having sex would ruin their friendship. Anyway the moment had passed and he could go home with a clear conscience.

Alex was shown to a table under the dramatic domed glass roof. He ordered champagne and waited for what he imagined would be a dramatic entrance. Actually she slipped in beside him with the minimum of fuss. She wore a modest, but expensive looking, black dress. Her moods could change like the wind, but she was in good form by the time she had enjoyed a couple of glasses of bubbly. Whilst Alex tucked into a generous helping of steak and kidney pie, she picked absentmindedly at a rabbit salad. Outside a gaggle of photographers had gathered, presumably to snap Gloria leaving. Her life was about to be constantly scrutinised. The initial press coverage had been curious rather than hostile, but that had changed. Whilst the British attitude to black people was less prejudiced than in the States, there was a scarcely concealed contempt, but also an irrational fear. Perhaps it was hatched in childhood. A fear of the dark. Black was frightening and dangerous. Black looks, black holes, the grim reaper swathed in black. Blacks were commonly referred to as natives, negroes or, most insultingly, as niggers. There were wild rumours about black people's sexual appetites and of black men's sexual prowess.It sent a collective shiver through the thoughts of young ladies. For some it was in anticipation, rather than fear.

Scanning the three London evening papers on his journey

to Bushey, it was obvious that Gloria's appearance in Hammersmith was causing real controversy. The Archbishop of York was worried that the country was in moral decline, exemplified by the obscene photograph of a native woman humiliating a white man. The writer, Aldous Huxley, was horrified that negroid music and morals were infecting our young. It was becoming an age of excess and selfishness after all the sacrifices made during the war. Turmoil was the order of the day. Strikes and lack of respect was rampant. The young were irresponsible, cocking a snook at the established order.

Back home in time for supper as he had promised, Alex and Helen sat in the garden enjoying the warmth of an early summer's evening. Alex could not help musing on the extremes between Helen and Gloria. His wife had spent much of the day tending her vegetable garden, whilst Gloria had attempted to seduce him. Helen provided him with a happy and contented home life. Despite her growing girth, pregnancy suited her. She was serene and beautiful, all any man could want, except in the bedroom. From the day that she had learnt that she was pregnant Helen had slept in the guest room. Her excuse was she would become restless in the night and sleeping apart ensured that Alex would get a good night's sleep. It always struck Alex as strange that Gloria, who had suffered abuse as a child, had a healthy, if not an excessive, sexual appetite, whilst Helen, who had experienced no such traumas, avoided intimate physical contact whenever possible.

Whilst Gloria's show at the Apollo was a triumph with the audiences attending, it drew a barrage of criticism from the press and the establishment. The Daily Mail complained of jungle music corrupting the young. The Bishop of Winchester, who admitted he had not seen the show, said that Gloria's dancing was derived from primitive rituals of negro orgies. The louder the complaints, the more the young were drawn to jazz and the throwing off of inhibitions that had ruled their parents' lives. For the less privileged youth, this related to their passion for dancing. For their richer cousins, sex, drugs and booze were added to the equation.

For Harry Goodman the whole exercise had been a huge success. All the time, money and planning he had invested in launching Gloria had paid off. For him all publicity was good publicity. With London audiences demanding and begging for more of Gloria, he arranged for her to appear next in Paris. Always leave the public crying for more, was his maxim. He rationed the appearances of his super-stars and he was confident that Gloria was about to enter that elite stable.

As the summer evenings grew longer and the birth of their baby came closer, Alex was still tormented by the memory of a naked Gloria oozing sexual allure. Would he have the resolve to resist her next time? Would there be a next time? As sleep eluded him, down the corridor Helen was also awake, but only because of the movements of a baby anxious to make its appearance.

Chapter 9

Separate paths

No publicity stunt, no matter how controversial, is sufficient to launch an enduring show business career. Harry Goodman's hunch was vindicated. A combination of factors played in Gloria's favour. She had a natural talent that had been honed by hard work. The arrival of jazz and her colour set her apart from any rivals. Her fluency in French was also appreciated by the Parisian audiences. Her show alongside the Southern Syncopated Orchestra received rave reviews from the critics, who embraced Gloria without the hurtful criticism she endured in London. It was probably this more liberal approach that encouraged Gloria to spend much of the following decade in France. She did make visits to Britain, including a season in Blackpool where her erotic dancing had to be tempered to pass muster with the Lord Chancellor. The censor was always on hand to make sure British passions were held in check.

Although Gloria continued to write to my grandfather, there appears to have been a cooling in their relationship since their meeting at the Savoy. They did not even get together when she was up in Blackpool. It was a period of over three years before they met again, the longest period during their almost sixty years relationship. Her letters were mostly concerned with her latest triumph and often included press cuttings. Her greatest success during this period was starring in a lavish production of the *Folies Bergère*, where her abandoned dancing caused a sensation. This followed her starring in the *Revue Nouveau* at the Theatre des Champs-Elysees.

Whilst Gloria was embracing her new found fame, my grandfather was still seeking a spark that would re-ignite his career. The month of June did bring good news. First his painting 'Check Mates' was well received and sold to an American collector for an unexpectedly high price. More importantly, two days later Helen gave birth to a baby boy. After much discussion he was christened Patrick, a name thoroughly approved of by Alex's mother. Life at Bushey resumed its relaxing rhythm. Helen was a natural mother, although for a time Alex felt he was being excluded. Months after the birth Helen was still insisting on sleeping separately, the excuse now being her need to attend to Patrick without disturbing Alex. He also noticed other changes. Helen had always had a healthy appetite and being such a good cook the temptations were obvious, but her weight was soaring. He understood that many young mothers suffered from post-natal depression after giving birth, however Helen was obviously incredibly happy, but frankly fat. In his darker moments Alex even imagined she was trying to make herself unattractive to stop him pestering her for sexual favours. Despite her weight gain she remained a very attractive woman. On Orla's promptings Patrick became known as Paddy, a name that stayed with him all his life. He was a bonny, endearing child and gradually my grandparents came to an accommodation regarding their life together, but Alex remained frustrated, both physically and artistically.

It was a visit to Bertram Mills circus that propelled Alex out of a period of sloth and introspection. The circus was now an annual event, having first been launched in 1919. Helen agreed to accompany Alex to Olympia and a babysitter was organised, but at the last moment Helen changed her mind. This was going to be a recurring theme over the years. She was far happier at home and only ever ventured out to the shops, or to take Paddy to the local park. Alex was disappointed as he had just changed his Bullnose Morris for a sparkling new Humber. His mood was soon improved. He loved the atmosphere and excitement generated by the audience.

This was to be a springboard for the next phase in his artistic journey. Horses, lions and elephants were very much the stars of the show, but he was drawn to the high-wire acrobats and particularly the clowns. He was so anxious to get home and record what he had seen, that he left well before the show finished. Performers and audiences were now to become the focus of his interest, which would see his reputation as a major artist revive and grow.

It took some time for me to realise that Alex and Gloria were bound together over the years by a weird sort of synergy. Their successes and dramatic failures mirroring each other, as if influenced by an external force. The image that Alex retained from his visit to the circus was of a white clown. It was an image that even today is associated with him. Produced as a print, it sold in its thousands across the world. What was it that resonated so strongly? The long sad face covered in thick white make-up and the single tear poised before it falls from view. Whatever the reason, Gloria acknowledged in a letter sent from the Grand Hotel in Menton that Alex too was now a star again, in his own right.

Strangely the positive response to the white clown brought a succession of requests from leading personalities and politicians, including Ivor Novello, to be recorded by Alex for posterity. Alex politely declined; he had no interest in boosting already inflated egos. Whilst not drawn to low life, he wanted to record the life of ordinary people. His visit to the circus led him towards an interest in the theatre. Music hall particularly appealed to him. He had been taken by Orla as a child and he loved the raucous excitement of an audience just as likely to boo a performer as applaud them.

On a cold October evening in 1923 he drove to Islington Green in north London, home to Collins' Music Hall. Earlier the building had been a pub offering entertainment, but was now one of London's premier music hall venues. Stupidly Alex had imagined he could get a ticket on the night, but the house was fully booked. Disappointed, he was drawn to the excitement as a crowd gathered outside. People were spilling out of the Fox pub next door to the theatre. Raised voices, ladies in their best clothes and a father carrying his young daughter on his shoulders. A group gathered round a glowing brazier where a cloth capped figure was selling roasted chestnuts, whilst another stall was selling whelks. People gathered round and Alex attempted to catch the moment on a sketching pad that he always carried with him. They were boisterous and friendly. One lady suggested that he could come and see her etchings any day, before being pulled away by her husband. Alex knew instinctively that night that he had discovered what he had been searching for, and his series of theatre and crowd scenes formed the most significant body of work he recorded during the following decade.

Back in his studio he created 'Roasted Chestnuts', a large canvas that was to be one of the major attractions at the Royal Academy 1924 exhibition. The work also led to a change in the way he interpreted his subject. Rather than search for accurate detail, his paintings were viewed as if seen through a rainy window. Slightly distorted and yet conveying the atmosphere of the moment. Having completed 'Roasted Chestnuts' he switched his choice of venue to the Metropolitan Music Hall on the Edgware Road. It was an easier journey, from Canons Corner it was a straight road, although often clogged with traffic. With many more cars coming onto the roads it was a constant battle, as open topped buses, cars, lorries and horse drawn carts jostled for position.

The Metropolitan Theatre was built in the 1860s on a site that had been a pub since the 16th century. It had a seating capacity of two thousand and Alex was fascinated as he watched the noisy audience gather. He had booked a box for three consecutive nights, anxious not to miss anything. The artistes appearing would have been appalled if they had known that he took absolutely no interest in any of their acts. His focus was solely on the audience that spilled out in front of him before being lost in the darkness of the upper circle. Music halls had previously been the scene of many a drunken disturbance, but legislation before the war had banned alcohol being taken into the auditorium. The atmosphere was still electric, veering from abusive shouting and booing to ecstatic applause. Having a night out at a music hall was to witness the British losing all their supposed reserve. People were on their feet singing one moment and trying to break up a fight the next. Bouncers were employed by the theatre to eject the culprits, to a chorus of cheers and boos. His three nights at the theatre drew two relatively appreciative audiences and one of increasing and finally total bedlam, where the performance had to be halted until order was restored.

Back in his studio in Bushey he felt exhilarated that at last he had found a subject that allowed him to express himself. His obvious happiness also improved his relationship with Helen. Far from molly-coddling their son, Helen was bringing him up to be tough and adventurous. Young Paddy, although quite small, was growing up to be confident and outward going. Although Helen spent far more time with the child, Alex was building up an easy rapport with him. He regretted that his gammy leg prevented him playing football with the child, but they did enjoy games of tennis and cricket together on the lawn.

Each year Stanhope Forbes and Maudie came to stay with them during the first days of the Royal Academy exhibition. Helen was a wonderful hostess and Alex sometimes worried that the problems they continued to have in their physical relationship were actually his fault. He talked to her about it too much when perhaps what was needed was some gentle wooing.

It was months since Alex had heard from Gloria when suddenly, in the early summer of 1924, she wrote to say that she was appearing in the Green Room at the Cafe Royal and she expected to see him there on the opening night. She enclosed two tickets. She had informed him previously that she was now splitting her performances between lavishly produced shows to smaller intimate cabaret appearances. Alex tried very hard to persuade Helen to go to the Cafe Royal that night, but he knew it would be a forlorn hope. She would not leave Paddy for the night. He said that in that case he would not go either, but she insisted. It was with a high sense of anticipation that my grandfather set off for the West End that night.

Alex parked his car in a street behind the Langham Hotel. Regent Street was in the final months of having a face lift. Much of the road was still dug up and he passed the emerging mock Tudor building that was going to house the exotic goods offered by Liberty's department store. Many other buildings were being refurbished. Walking into the Cafe Royal you entered a world of excess. All was ornate gilt, contrasted by black lacquered columns. Here was a meeting place for famous writers, composers, artists and, latterly, film stars. He was directed up a grand staircase to the first floor where many people were already eating. Feeling rather self conscious he was escorted to a table nearest the small raised stage. Ordering a double whisky, he was surrounded by tables containing up to eight people. Others were for set up for two or four guests He was the only singleton.

Not for long. He was joined by a tall, rather distinguished looking man who introduced himself as Harry Goodman. They had just enough time before Gloria came on stage to agree that the three of them would meet up later at a restaurant that Harry had already booked. Declining the menu offered by a waiter, Alex ordered himself another whisky and a soft drink for Goodman. Alex had not really known what to expect from Gloria's performance, but he was genuinely impressed. She had obviously learnt the art of responding to her audience. For this sophisticated intimate gathering she was, if anything, understated. For her lavish shows in Paris her dancing could be outrageous and erotic, before effortlessly changing mood by switching to playing ragtime and jazz numbers teased from her piano.

In Blackpool any pretence of sophistication was sacrificed as she reacted to the holiday audiences. This night all was control as she coaxed the audience to embrace her talent. Still not as well known in Britain as in France, she started by playing Gershwin's new masterpiece 'Rhapsody In Blue', which drew polite applause. The atmosphere lightened as she switched to ragtime and blues. By the time she sang 'What'll I do?' she had the audience under her spell. Moving amongst the diners she picked out an elderly gentleman and sitting on his lap sang 'It had to be you'. Several couples rose to applaud, whilst the old man wiped his brow and feigned a heart attack. No wonder, dressed in a tight azure blue dress she exuded sex, but in an unthreatening way that women could appreciate and enjoy. She finished her act with a memorable version of 'Limehouse Blues'. Then as an encore with the resident band on stage, she performed probably for the first time in Britain the dance that was sweeping America. The Charleston was crazy and quite unlike any other dance. Fiendishly difficult for many to learn, Gloria performed it seemingly effortlessly, but with verve and panache. Many years later Gloria was acknowledged as one of the greatest cabaret performers of the twentieth century.

Goodman had chosen one of London's best French restaurants, the Moulin d'Or in Romilly Street. He had obviously wanted a chance to chat to Alex before Gloria joined them. It appeared that whilst he was thrilled with her professional progress, he was worried about her private life. He told Alex that Gloria often spoke about him and how she valued his friendship. Goodman was worried because Gloria was very vulnerable and generally tended towards people of doubtful character. She was now earning a great deal of money and he was unable to keep a close watch on her to protect her from the sharks. This was particularly difficult as she spent so much time in France. Because of this and the fact that Goodman's own health was causing concern, he was thinking of appointing someone who would act as her assistant and gatekeeper. He had someone in mind. Alex, listening carefully, wondered why he was being told all this, but realised that Harry was genuinely fond of Gloria and in some sense was responsible for her well-being. Perhaps Alex was just a sounding board for Goodman's concerns, but he felt rather touched by the older man's trust in him. He promised he would always remain friends with Gloria and do whatever he could to help her. A promise he kept for over half a century.

Gloria was quiet and restrained during the meal, despite both men congratulating her on her performance that night. She deferred to Goodman, listening carefully to all he said. He had obviously become something of a father figure to her. The conversation turned to Alex's painting that Goodman obviously admired and was knowledgeable about. Throughout the meal Gloria remained pensive and sad. She brightened briefly when Goodman rose to leave them. Clasping Alex's hand he said quietly, 'Remember, Alex, real friendship is the most precious gift anyone can give.'

Gloria remained subdued during their taxi drive to the Langham Hotel. 'I must be psychic' Alex told her, because that was where he had parked his car. 'Are you driving home tonight?' she asked. Taking the plunge, Alex blurted out that he was hoping to stay with her. In the darkness he could not gauge her reaction, but her response was not encouraging. He was not about to be put off. He had imagined his seduction of Gloria for months, his conscience cleared by Helen's continued rejection of his advances. Her suite at the hotel was not as grand as the one at the Savoy, but certainly a romantic setting for a night of romance and love. Unfortunately Alex completely fluffed his lines. With the door hardly shut he made a grab for her. Later he reflected it was not that different from his disastrous wedding night. Gloria did not resist him, but his pent up passion for her was spent almost immediately. The gentle, passionate love making that he had imagined was over almost before it began. The look Gloria gave him was one he needed to forget. Sadness tinged with distaste. She had obviously felt exhausted after her performance and he had acted like a schoolboy.

She was asleep the moment her head hit the pillow, whilst Alex lay awake feeling furious with himself and guilty at the thought of Helen and Paddy asleep in Bushey. Gloria was already dressed when he finally woke up. The previous night was not mentioned. Gloria was friendly and affectionate. She was off to see Harry, who was planning a European tour for her. Suddenly she started crying. Taking her into his arms, her whole body shook. She was inconsolable. Was she really that upset about his behaviour? Had it ruined their friendship? It took some minutes for her to calm down. Gradually it emerged that her mood was nothing to do with Alex. 'Did you not see how ill he looked?' she asked, accusingly. Alex had noticed that Goodman did have a rather sallow, unhealthy complexion. 'He's dying' Gloria wailed, 'What will I do?' Alex did his best to comfort her, but selfishly he just welcomed the opportunity to hold her in his arms. Life was very complicated.

Chapter 10

Monica

Gloria was notoriously fickle. Fickle towards friends, lovers and husbands, each embraced in an initial wave of enthusiasm only to be discarded and forgotten just as quickly. As her fame and wealth grew she became dismissive and often cruel to those serving her. Only two people remained constant pillars in her life from the second half of the 1920s. For over fifty turbulent years they survived and tried to influence the chaotic nature of her life. One was my grandfather, their relationship probably strengthened by their never meeting on a regular basis. No time for Gloria to get bored or feel constrained. The other long lasting relationship was Monica Wiseman.

Gloria was introduced to Monica by Harry Goodman. She was the daughter of an old family friend and someone he could trust. As his health declined he realised that Gloria was attracting some very dubious company. Already wealthy and left alone to tour unaccompanied, she was vulnerable and needed help. Monica's father was a second generation of Jewish/Polish immigrants. He had run a small jewellers in Dalston until his death earlier in the year. Being fluent in four languages and having always expressed an interest in travel, Goodman reasoned that Monica could provide a stabilising influence on his volatile star. He was only partially right. For their long association the two women bickered and argued, but eventually settled into a grudging understanding.

Gloria and Monica were polar opposites. Where Gloria was unpredictable and volcanic, Monica was calm and considered. Starting as little more than a companion and bag carrier, she became central to Gloria's life, assuming the role of gatekeeper and ultimately her manager. Highly intelligent, she trained herself to represent Gloria at every level relating to business and financial matters. During long hours spent in hotel rooms whilst Gloria was out socialising or sleeping off the excesses of the previous night, she even studied contract law. Successive highly paid lawyers were astonished at her detailed knowledge. She quickly built a reputation for being a ruthless negotiator on Gloria's behalf. Long before Harry Goodman's death in 1926, the two women had agreed a method of working together. Monica was responsible for organising Gloria's life from booking hotel rooms and travel arrangements to increasingly negotiating deals for Gloria's appearances at leading venues.

Monica was four years older than Gloria, but even as a young woman she was ageless and anonymous. Monica's sphere of influence did not extend to Gloria's personal life. As agreed she never interfered with any of Gloria's many relationships, no matter how distasteful she found them, unless she felt that they endangered Gloria's financial well being. Gloria was hopeless with money and although Monica was extremely well paid, her honesty was never in doubt. It was a strange relationship for two women who had so little in common, but who saw each other almost every day for over forty years.

Neither even really liked each other. Monica continued to be appalled, if resigned, to Gloria's morals. Not just sexual, but also at the way she treated people, becoming incensed when Gloria refused to attend Harry Goodman's funeral even though she was in Britain at the time. She was quite unable to deal with grief. For her part Gloria could just not begin to understand that someone's idea of having a good time was mooching round junk shops and auctions looking for jewellery she could sell on her return to Britain. Having learnt a great deal from her father, this hobby proved incredibly lucrative over the years. When Monica did finally retire she had already built up a small portfolio of houses on the south coast. She died a wealthier woman than Gloria. It appears she had no romantic relationships during her entire time with Gloria and few friendships either. I have a number of photographs where she appears in the background as an almost ghostly figure. Certainly no beauty, but not unattractive either, it was only greying hair that aged her in any way.

What I had never appreciated was that although Gloria wrote to my grandfather from numerous private addresses and swanky hotels, she never owned her own house or apartment. It was part of her nomadic instinct, a wanting to constantly be on the move, a need to meet new people as if imprisoned by any form of permanence.

With Monica already conducting Gloria's schedule, she did visit London again a few months after Alex's fumbled seduction. She appeared at Quaglino's, a leading night spot in Bury Street off Jermyn Street. Strangely there is no letter from this time and it is possible that another romantic interlude was underway as she was photographed in the company of Reg Gibson, a saxophonist with the Bert Ambrose Orchestra. Her proposed European tour was also put on hold, but she did star in *Creole Goddess*, a revue staged at the wildly lavish setting of Luxor Balkanska in Belgrade. Arriving in style on the Orient Express, the readers of the leading local paper voted her 'the loveliest woman in the world'.

Whilst life in Bushey seemed low key by comparison, Alex was also enjoying critical acclaim for his music hall paintings. Life at home had improved also. Helen had returned to their bedroom at a time that she was beginning to shed some of the weight she had piled on. His feeling of guilt increased during this period as Helen was being particularly attentive. The wound on his back had flared up and he was in continual pain and discomfort. For days Helen bathed the affected area and gently applied cream prescribed by their doctor. It was in a part of his back that Alex could not reach and although generally very proud about not giving in to the pain, her care led to them being closer than at any time since their marriage. They also both revelled in seeing their young son growing up.

Paddy had started attending a local school. It was on a visit up to Stratton House that Alex's father suggested the young boy should be sent to Oundle, the school Alex had attended. Oundle was a private school much favoured by Northamptonshire farmers and local businessmen for their sons. It had a good academic record and was very sports orientated. Whilst Alex had enjoyed his time there he was not in favour of boarding, despite the school not taking boys until they were eleven. There was still a long time before they had to make the decision, but Helen surprised him by being in favour. Orla was very animated by the prospect. She had a wonderful rapport with the young boy and she looked forward to having him stay during exeats. It was strange that his mother had formed such a bond with the young boy, far stronger than she had achieved with her own children. Their regular visits to Stratton Hall were always enjoyable and without tension.

Over supper there was much discussion about Gloria's continuing rise to stardom. George declared that on first meeting he was convinced that she would become a household name. Orla rolled her eyes whilst Helen started giggling. It was Orla who asked Alex if he still saw Gloria on her trips to London. 'Only if I get permission from Helen!' he joked. His mother's gaze did not waver. He knew she suspected him. He was convinced she was psychic, or perhaps it was just a mother's natural intuition. The conversation moved on.

Among a pile of letters on their return was one from Gloria. In spite of himself Alex felt a flutter of excitement. Written from Hotel Normandy in Deauville, it read like a royal command:

My dear Alex,

Meet me at the Kit-Cat Club in The Haymarket next Tuesday, the 23rd. I have arranged an early slot as my act does not normally end until about two in the morning. I have to make a short appearance in the Piccadilly Hotel as I start a week's run there the first week in July. I have booked a new Italian restaurant in Soho.

I have missed you.

Love, G.

Alex's first reaction was to refuse. Her letter was annoying and she had only enclosed a single ticket. The trouble was that she continued to enthral him. A conflict between love and desire is seldom simple. True love may triumph in films and popular fiction, but desire usually wins in the short term. In any event after his previous attempt it was unlikely that Gloria thought of him in any way other than as a good friend. Having settled that in his own mind Alex told Helen about the invitation. As he had expected she insisted that he went to London without her. Either she did not suspect or possibly did not care if Alex was romantically involved with Gloria. Rather, she seemed genuinely pleased that he was very friendly with someone so famous.

He already had a feeling of guilt as he set off that morning. Helen packed his suitcase, carefully wrapping his dinner jacket in tissue paper to avoid it creasing. She stood at the gate holding a squirming Paddy as he drove off. The Kit-Cat Club was the place for the 'bright young things' to be seen. It had only reopened a couple of weeks previously, having been shut down for contravening the licensing laws. It was a unique venue able to accommodate over fifteen hundred guests. Unusually the club was below street level. A balcony had tables set out where those dining could look down on the ballroom and the main restaurant. There was a charged atmosphere as people spilled out of the American bar clasping cocktails in order to get a good view of the cabaret. The setting was breathtaking. A gold ornate ceiling was complimented by ivory columns rising to the balcony and walls throughout in contrasting turquoise. A bank of lights above the dance floor had the effect of changing the colours to dark blue and orange. Waiters wearing tailed suits swayed amongst the guests carrying trays of drinks. Normally the club did not get busy until after midnight, but Gloria's appearance had ensured a full house. Her act was very similar to the one Alex had seen at the Cafe Royal, but her reception was far more boisterous with the younger clientele.

After a couple of encores Alex went outside and was directed into a waiting car. Despite only a short wait, Gloria had already changed into a less flamboyant cocktail dress for her short appearance at the Piccadilly Hotel. She greeted him warmly, but there was something different about her. It was only as he watched her captivate her new audience that it occurred to him. It was her voice, her speaking voice. The American, French and perceived English had merged together to create an accent that was unique and one that she kept for the rest of her life. It combined the informality of America, the sexiness of France, tempered by the formality of the English. The result was a voice that was instantly recognisable. She successfully transferred the same effect to her singing. To be instantly recognised is the holy grail for any entertainer. As she explained to Alex later that night, it was an attribute seized upon by the burgeoning record industry, with her first recording contract being concluded with HMV.

As they were leaving the hotel Alex was introduced to Monica Wiseman. He was rather embarrassed when she asked him to sign her autograph book. No-one had ever asked him for his autograph before and it obviously irritated Gloria who tried to hurry him out to the waiting car. Monica was not about to be hurried, fixing Gloria with a ferocious stare. Monica was obviously knowledgeable and interested in art. She informed Alex that she had seen his work at the summer exhibition and was an admirer. Gloria hated not being the centre of attention and stomped off leaving the two chatting away. Alex instantly took to Monica, realising that she would be prepared to stand up to Gloria, something that was certainly needed to control her growing ego.

It was almost midnight by the time they arrived at Quo Vadis in Dean Street. Alex was surprised that Gloria had chosen such a modest restaurant. The owner, Pepino Leoni, served at table himself. He realised that news of Gloria visiting his restaurant was enough to ensure full bookings for months to come. She signed a couple of menus for him and promised a signed photograph would follow. That photograph can still be seen in the restaurant today. After their modest but enjoyable meal they walked arm in arm to the hotel. The adrenalin that Gloria experienced after every show had declined and her mood now was calm and affectionate. Alex had booked a single room at the hotel. Collecting his key from reception he joined Gloria in the lift. The cheeky grin that he was convinced she saved for him alone spread over her face. Never failing to catch him off guard she said, 'Come on big boy, this time show me what you are made of.'

My grandfather's reputation had been built on his ability to record the lives of ordinary people in a way that photographs generally failed to convey. Despite numerous requests he avoided painting the rich and famous. A choice on his part that extended to his family and close friends, none of whom became subjects. The one exception was a very intimate painting of Gloria, which was one of Monica's most treasured possessions. It was created years after a sketch he made of her after that night at the Piccadilly Hotel. For him it was a record of a memorable night of unrestrained passion. The sketch he made was of Gloria sitting on the edge of an un-made bed. She faces head on with a smile that is beguiling and open to interpretation. Gloria's attitude to sex always shocked and confused Alex. She felt that he and most British men were repressed and confused. For her, sex was to be enjoyed and spontaneous. She described it like having an itch that needed to be scratched, enjoy the encounter and move on, talk of love just complicated things. Alex never really knew whether to believe her. He explained that in England any young woman behaving like that would be considered a slut. Gloria just laughed, but then her life was based on selfishness and compulsion.

Back in Bushey Alex hid the sketch of Gloria away in his studio, forgetting about it for several years. Whilst Gloria resumed her lucrative career, appearing in a series of revues in Paris, life for Alex was serene but lacking excitement. The garden now showed the time and attention Helen had devoted to it. There was a rose garden with borders bursting with colour and a lawn with a surface like a billiard table. As the seasons changed one vague worry niggled away at Alex.

Helen had now lost all the weight she had gained after Paddy's arrival. Actually she looked as beautiful as when he first became captivated by her, but she seemed rather frail and lacking in her normal energy. She laughed off his concerns, telling him that she felt fine.

His attention was diverted by a constant stream of letters from Gloria. Her first recordings were selling well and there was talk of a film contract. In the meantime she had discovered skiing. She sent photographs from the slopes of Austria and Italy, usually standing alongside a young male companion. Again he felt a pang of jealousy when she declared that it was not just skiing that the instructors had to offer. Throughout their relationship Alex always felt that she was purposely trying to keep him at arm's length emotionally. As more of her time was devoted to leisure and holidays, it seemed inevitable that she would discover Monte Carlo and the lure of the gambling tables. As with booze and later in her life drugs, Gloria threw herself into the thrill of the spin of the roulette wheel. This led to an ongoing battle with Monica as she tried to restrain Gloria's impulsiveness. A truce was reached when reluctantly Gloria agreed to a daily rationing of money she was allowed to invest. Retreating from the high roller tables, people still crowded round her as she placed her chips. Like most gamblers Gloria only ever mentioned her winning streaks. What she had not realised at the time was that Monica also became interested in the game. Spending nights quietly watching the players, she also bought all the books she could find on systems and mathematical formulae for success. None of course were foolproof, but it did lead years later for the two women to join forces in an attempt to find a winning formula.

By the beginning of 1928 Alex's concern about Helen's health had deepened. She was now painfully thin and she was so listless that she was even ignoring the garden and cooking appeared a chore. A new interest was listening to the wireless. Alex invested in one of the earliest mains-operated sets known as a baby grand. Housed in an impressive mahogany case, it provided them with many hours of entertainment despite regular breakdowns in service. It was another modern investment that finally led Alex insisting that Helen should go to the doctor. Making telephone calls through the local exchange could often be a long and frustrating exercise, but it was following a call to his mother that finally convinced him that Helen needed help.

Their local GP was fairly sure that Helen had become diabetic. Her loss of weight and constant thirst were good clues. A simple test confirmed his suspicions. A few years previously being diagnosed with diabetes was a death sentence, with few patients surviving for more than a couple of years. With no cure the only remedy was to adopt a starvation diet, but this only delayed the inevitable.

Luckily a lifeline had been thrown to sufferers with the discovery of insulin in 1922. Their doctor referred them to a leading specialist. Doctor James Matheson had been involved in the early stages of the development of insulin and lectured across Europe. A short ginger-headed Scot, he had a practice in fashionable Highgate. As Matheson talked Helen through the problems of injecting herself, Alex was fascinated by the specialist's huge hands that appeared to be out of all proportion to the rest of his body. Helen opted to inject herself rather than have a nurse call on a daily basis. She attended a clinic for several weeks as she became used to what was to become a daily ritual. The need for sharp and spotlessly clean needles and accurate dosages was constantly underlined until Helen felt confident enough to inject herself at home. Hypos were explained and the need to carry lumps of sugar at all times in case her blood sugar levels fell. Despite a few scares during those early weeks Helen soon got in to a daily routine. Gradually her health improved, although it was Alex who discovered her on the kitchen floor after suffering her first hypo. Quickly revived, they both felt more comfortable with dealing with what continued to be a scary illness.

A letter from Gloria informed him that it was she, not Harry Goodman, who had negotiated her first European tour. It was whilst she was in London tying up the loose ends regarding the tour, that news of Goodman's death was announced. Unforgivably, Gloria returned to Paris, leaving Monica to attend the funeral.

Chapter 11

A slippery slope

Drugs had been part of the London scene long before a Chinese man known as 'Brilliant Chang' arrived to dispense his oriental delicacies. Laudanum and opium were freely available in the nineteenth century. Chang, a good looking and charismatic man, ran his empire from his expensive and prestigious restaurant situated in Regent Street. This provided him with a ready-made clientele of 'bright young things'. He became the darling of an aristocratic and wealthy elite looking for additional kicks to their already frenzied lives. Despite being reputedly associated with a number of tragic deaths and the resulting bad publicity, Chang remained free to carry on his trade. Many clients, including Lady Diana Cooper, were drawn from the pages of Debrett's. He was finally deported in 1924 when he transferred his operation to Paris. Attracting unwanted attention from the police, he moved to Nice where Gloria was introduced to him. As usual Gloria embraced this new influence in her life with reckless enthusiasm. It started a dependence that remained with her for much of her life. Strangely it was her exposure to the effects of war during the 1940s that led her to being totally free of any drugs influence at the time.

Her initial plunge into heroin taking led to some very

shambolic performances on the French Riviera and withering reviews in the press. Showing a lack of respect for paying audiences was a problem that returned to haunt her later in her career. Once an icon in France, she needed a new stage and she found it in Berlin. So started a mutual love affair. Monica now stepped in to save Gloria on two fronts. She had taken control of Gloria's finances in 1925. This was the year that Winston Churchill as Chancellor of the Exchequer restored Britain to the gold standard. This had the effect of making Britain's exports too expensive. By 1929 the trade position had weakened further leading in part to the crash of the stock market and the subsequent slump. The major part of Gloria's considerable wealth had been invested in stocks and shares. Losing faith in Gloria's stockbroker, Monica started to convert Gloria's holdings to cash. With so much time on her hands Monica had spotted the trends and saved Gloria from financial ruin, a fact that Gloria never acknowledged. Soon it would be time for Monica to intervene regarding Gloria's growing drug habit. For now it was time to slink away from critical France and into the warm embrace of the Weimar Republic.

Gloria spent much of her life seeking excitement and new experiences. Arriving in Berlin in June 1929 provided a perfect backdrop for even her to experience events beyond both her wildest dreams, but also fears. A month earlier, about forty communists had been shot by police after a May Day rally. She witnessed street fights between left and right wing armed gangs. She was also verbally abused by a group of brown-shirted fascists. Despite this Gloria loved Berlin and the tension that under scored everyday life. The punitive conditions demanded by the Allies at the end of the Great War created a general feeling of resentment in Germany and it was now being left to the opposing political factions to fight for supremacy. This humiliation was to have far reaching consequences that still had to be played out.

Whilst in Britain the 'bright young things' imagined they were living dangerously, it was tame stuff compared to their German cousins. Whilst politicians, rabble rousers and street fighters fought for control of Germany's future, another section of society parried and spiralled into a period of unprecedented moral decline. Life was being lived at such a pace as if somehow those involved knew of the dangers that lay ahead lurking in the wings. There was tension both politically and sexually. Gloria had found her ideal habitat. Decadence was dangerous, but so alluring.

Gloria spent much of her life in luxurious hotels and none more so than in Berlin. The wide sweep of Unter den Linden provided the backdrop for her stay. The Adlon was a vast Germanic pile whose bleak exterior camouflaged the luxury within. The first impression on entering was of lavish floral arrangements in the public spaces, which were replaced daily. Giant palms were set alongside vast columns that rose to gilded balconies. There was a spectacular orangery and it was possible to take breakfast overlooking the historic Brandenburg Gate. It was a place of live theatre, almost like a giant film set. Gloria loved the hotel and initially the management were happy to welcome such an international star, but her erratic behaviour did test their patience. 1960s' rock stars were not the first to trash hotel bedrooms. Monica managed to smooth things over, but she was furious at being put in such an embarrassing position. A threat to leave Gloria for good did see a temporary improvement in her behaviour. Massive rows culminated in Monica rationing Gloria's drug intake. In truth she did not need any further stimulant, she realised that here was the life she craved presented on a plate.

Gloria had been booked to appear for a season at the famous El Dorado night spot situated on the corner of Kalckreuthstrasse and Motzstrasse. Revitalised and excited by the atmosphere, her first night's performance was met by an ecstatic reception and endless encores. El Dorado had been the haunt of homosexuals for years and now added transvestites, transsexuals and lesbians to the menu. There were men dressed as women and women dressed as men, together with some tourists wanting to be shocked before retreating to the safety of their hotels. There was a man wearing a military styled hat, leather shorts and a studded dog collar being led round by a huge fat man in a tight fitting leotard. There were women with breasts flattened and dressed in dinner jackets, their hair cropped and smarmed with brilliantine. Here was decadence and debauchery, but Gloria had won over a new set of fans. It started a love affair between the gay community and Gloria that remained throughout her career.

Each night Gloria was mobbed by her new fans before she ventured out in search of new adventures. She found herself drawn to even more bizarre venues. Fascinated, she watched live sex taking place on a small raised stage, conducted by every conceivable combination. Shocked but fascinated, for several nights she had been pursued by a very attractive blonde dinner-jacketed individual. The story Gloria told my grandfather was that she had no idea this figure was a woman, only finding out when they were in bed together. Alex did not believe her. Gloria continued to be attracted by women into her latter years. The truth probably was that Gloria was attracted by both sexes and never saw any reason to temper that attraction. Whether or not Gloria did know this statuesque blonde was a man or not hardly matters, but her experience that night was apparently true.

Ursula Steinman was the wife of a wealthy financier. As the two women cavorted in bed, the door to their hotel room opened and a man, probably in his sixties, came in. Freezing in fright, Gloria was sure that she was being caught in some elaborate sting and possibly blackmail. But no, Rudolph Steinmann politely introduced himself before pouring himself a cognac and sitting on a chair next to the bed. Pulling the blanket up to conceal herself Ursula told her to take no notice. 'He just likes watching,' she said and Gloria, befuddled by drink and mixed emotions, did not resist as they resumed their writhings. So started an astonishing 'menage et trois'. For the length of her stay in Berlin the girls were joined by Rudolph, who watched on happily sipping his brandy. When their energies were finally spent the three of them would venture out for a late supper. Gloria was never sure if she was genuinely bi-sexual. Over the years she tended to sleep with people whom she found attractive, usually avoiding any romantic involvement. My grandfather did tell me that she reckoned women made better lovers. Men, she insisted, were clumsy and selfish, whereas women were sensitive and considerate. Whatever the truth it made him realise that his life at that time was really rather dull.

Alex always felt a sense of guilt that unlike most artists he had never really struggled financially. Maybe it was this privileged background that led to his lack of interest in money. Despite his paintings fetching increasingly eye-watering sums, his style of living remained modest. He liked well cut clothes and enjoyed eating in good restaurants, but he never sought the trappings of a wealthy man which he certainly became. It was this lack of interest that led to a significant loss of money during the stock market crash. Like Gloria he had invested in shares through a broker used by his father. He was too slow to react to the impending slump and for the first time since they got married Alex and Helen had to be prudent in their spending. Dividends from the family business were also hit as his father's firm saw their export trade decline. George was also forced to seek new partners to boost the company's finances, which also saw a drop in the percentage of shares that Alex held.

Sending Paddy off to boarding school was a significant milestone in my grandfather's life. He had enjoyed watching the young boy grow and develop his own very distinctive personality. He was quite different in both looks and personality than his parents. Certainly more out-going than either of them and he made friends easily. Whilst only average academically, he had a natural aptitude for a whole range of sports. He was captain of both the cricket and football teams at his prep school, which undoubtedly helped in getting him accepted at Oundle, the school his father had attended. Public schools had been in existence for centuries and had initially been formed to help the less privileged get a first class education. By the eighteenth century these seats of learning had become the preserve of the ruling classes. Although Alex was not really in favour of boarding at such a young age, it had always been taken for granted that Paddy would be packed off aged eleven. Unlike his father some twenty years earlier, Paddy was excited at the prospect and viewed living away from home as a great adventure. Obviously Helen had spent far more time with their son as he grew up, but she also appeared more than happy for him to fly the nest.

It was a strange feeling for Alex to return to the school where he had spent seven years of his life. Nothing seemed to have changed, he even recognised a couple of the gowned masters who were no longer frightening or intimidating. In the main assembly hall was a list of boys who had won places at Oxbridge colleges, with another indicating those masters and boys who had been killed in the war. Alex helped Paddy carry his trunk up to the same dormitory that he had occupied. The spartan conditions the boys were subjected to was reckoned to toughen them up for life to come. There were no tearful goodbyes. Helen was relaxed and Paddy scarcely had time to say goodbye as he joined other boys in exploring their new home. Alex and Helen stopped at a tea room in the ancient old market town before their drive south. Helen was looking gorgeous and he had noted the admiring glances of other parents. She was in an ebullient mood, whereas Alex had anticipated her being tearful and upset. Not for the first or the last time did he realise that he just did not understand women. He was constantly wrong-footed, but then that was a great part of his charm. On their return home there was a letter waiting for him from Gloria.

My dear Alex,

Gosh, Berlin was unbelievable, can't wait to tell you about it. Some very exciting news. I am off to New York to appear in a new revue. Talk of a film deal. All is buzz, buzz, buzz.

Until the next time.

Love, G.

Within months came news that Gloria was married.

Chapter 12

Down and out

From the moment Gloria arrived in New York the omens were not good. In Europe she was used to being escorted to her suite by the general manager, but at the Plaza she was assigned some junior assistant manager who had not even heard of her. She complained her suite was far too small but was informed that the hotel was fully booked. At least it had a good view over Central Park, but she was irritated that advance publicity regarding her arrival back in the States had raised little interest. Despite being such a cosmopolitan city she was convinced that there remained a unspoken bias against black people, no matter how famous.

She appeared in *Glorious Birdsong*, a revue staged at the Majestic Theatre on Broadway in mid town Manhattan on West 44th Street. Despite relatively good reviews, booking such a large venue with over fifteen hundred seats proved a problem. In spite of advance publicity Gloria was unknown to American audiences. For the first three nights the theatre was packed, but by the second week she was playing to half full houses. She found for the first time that American theatre producers were far more ruthless than their European counterparts. Her situation worsened when her expected film debut was put on ice. She was determined not to return to Europe having failed to take New York by storm, or to kick her heels in the hope that the studio in Hollywood would change its mind. My grandfather was convinced that it was at this moment that Gloria showed her own ruthless ambition to rectify her setback.

It came with a chance meeting in the grand foyer of the Plaza Hotel. Drawn by a group of photographers and flashing light bulbs, she noticed that the centre of their attention was a fit looking young man with blond hair. Not knowing who he was she pushed her way through the throng and introduced herself. As a response he kissed her on the cheek, 'Hi, Martin Hansen.' 'I know' Gloria lied, sure she could quickly divine who this young man was. One photographer asked Gloria to pretend to hit Hansen on the jaw. The penny dropped, she had seen his photograph in a paper earlier in the week. She had just been introduced to 'the baby-faced assassin', the leading contender for the middleweight championship of the world. He was quickly hustled away by his manager and entourage, just waving to her over a sea of fans who had gathered. The following morning most of the papers featured the photograph of Gloria pretending to hit the boxer. If nothing else it had produced some welcome publicity, but by ten o'clock she had received a call from Hansen inviting her to dinner that night.

Hansen, who was unbeaten, was scheduled to fight Miguel Torres in a final eliminator for the title, but the Mexican had pulled out with a hand injury. The promoters were now searching for a suitable substitute. He had to be good enough to test Hansen, but not beat him. Whilst negotiations continued the boxer was released from his punishing training programme. Like many before him Hansen was bewitched by

Gloria. It was a whirlwind romance. Gloria was certainly really physically attracted to him. Going to bed with a trained athlete was a new experience and one that genuinely thrilled her. Taut muscles rather than flabby bellies took her desire to new heights. Much against his family's and management's advice, the couple were married in the evangelical covenant church in central New York. The ceremony was attended by members of Martin's family and a rather bemused Monica. Outside hundreds of well-wishers greeted the couple, many waving Swedish flags. Still upset with the Plaza's management, Gloria insisted that the wedding breakfast be held at the Algonquin Hotel further down 44th Street from the Metropole Theatre. She reckoned the setting to be more suitable in a hotel notorious for hosting giants of the arts. Gloria chose to ignore the cool reception she was given by his family, particularly his mother. A deeply religious woman, she could scarcely disguise her hostility to this exotic woman who had stolen her son. Her gloomy predictions for the marriage were all too accurate.

Because Martin needed to get back into full training, their honeymoon at the Royal Palm Hotel in Miami was restricted to three days. Three days of energetic coupling, but also of rifts already developing. Gloria had become used to a certain amount of refinement in her life. People she met and places she visited were, on the surface at least, civilised. Martin Hansen was not. Brought up in a rough area of New Jersey, he had been taught to honour God, attend church and be polite, but his crude manners jolted. His church-going had obviously not impeded his vocabulary of oaths and swear words that punctuated every sentence. Worse though was his childish sense of humour and the practical jokes that he regularly carried out to Gloria's embarrassment. He seemed totally oblivious to Gloria's annoyance and his strange behaviour intensified the longer they spent together. By the time they returned to New York Gloria was at screaming pitch. It was if she had married a child, albeit one who could only satisfy her in bed. The one positive of her ill-judged escapade was contact from Hollywood. A film contract had been prepared and Gloria could not wait to leave her husband to his training. A regime so tough that he admitted that at times it was so painful that it reduced him to tears. Despite this he assured her he loved it. He really was stupid.

Despite the early strain in their marriage Gloria was at the ringside to cheer on her husband against the French fighter Marcel Drevet. Although he was European champion, the promoters were confident he was a perfect choice for Martin Hansen to shine. A skilful boxer, but without a devastating punch, it was thought that Hansen would overpower the Frenchman. The fight was staged at Madison Square Garden, an ugly building situated between 49th and 50th Street in Manhattan. Its unimpressive exterior was compensated by the atmosphere generated within the vast auditorium. Instantly Gloria was swept away by the raucous, charged atmosphere, with the tiered banks of spectators gazing down on the small elevated ring. She was disappointed not to be among the list of stars who clambered through the ropes to take the applause of the crowd. The position was redeemed by her being spotlighted and introduced as the new wife of the baby assassin to a torrent of wolf whistles.

With tension rising Drevet clambered through the ropes to

waves of booing. Dark and dressed in blue shorts highlighted with a cockerel emblem, he looked really small under the floodlights. The crowd now rose as Martin took to the ring accompanied by a young woman holding the Swedish flag. Gloria felt totally detached from the blond figure acknowledging the cheers of his fans. He had a swagger, oozing confidence as the fighters touched gloves. To a groundswell of cheering the bell sounded for the first round. Hansen was the most aggressive, but Drevet was clever, boxing on the retreat and making him miss the target. The second round followed a similar pattern although Drevet, light on his feet, was gaining in confidence. For the next couple of rounds her husband increased his attacks, landing a number of telling blows. Gloria became aware of bets being placed by ringside spectators as to how quickly the fight would finish. In the sixth round there was a collective drawing in of breath. Suddenly there was blood everywhere, it was splattered over both men's faces and had been caused by a violent crash of heads. As the bell sounded for the end of the round it became obvious that it was Hansen who had suffered a horrendous cut above his left eye. It was his blood that had smeared Drevet's face and now it had been cleared away he was unmarked.

Martin Hansen had never been hurt in any of his fights and it was obvious he was distressed by his injury. His seconds applied an adrenalin stick to the cut and smeared his face with Vaseline which appeared to staunch the flow. Drevet's first straight left opened the wound again. Martin reacted like a wounded bull, charging forward throwing wild hooks and uppercuts which the French fighter skillfully avoided. Hansen was having trouble seeing and towards the end of the round was caught off balance, being downed by a left hook. The count had reached six when the bell sounded and Hansen waved to the crowd showing that he was unhurt. The cut had worsened and the fight should have been stopped, but there was too much money at stake. Drevet was caught early in the eighth round by a vicious right cross. Rising at the count of nine, the fight now took on the air of a bar room brawl. Forgetting the most basic defence, Hansen went in for the kill. Another crack of heads left him reeling. The crowd were on their feet and Gloria had to peer through a sea of spectators to see her husband caught by a desperate haymaker. Losing his senses, Hansen rose on the count of three to show he was unhurt, but he was. Another hook sent him tumbling. Again he did not take a long enough count to gather his senses. Another sickening blow sent the Swedish American to the canvas. This time he did not get up.

There was pandemonium. Bets had been lost, well laid plans ruined. Fights broke out and chairs were being hurled. A uniformed attendant escorted Gloria away into a corridor that led to the changing rooms. An elated but battered Drevet was led past her by his seconds, leaving the smell of his sweat heavy in the air. Then it was her bedraggled husband swearing to anyone who would listen that he had been robbed. He either did not see her or ignored her. She felt nothing for him. No pity, no sadness at the unravelling of his world title plans, all she realised was that she had made a stupid impetuous mistake. She needed to get away. Hollywood beckoned. She would deal with the Martin Hansen problem later when she had proved to the American public that she truly was a star, but the bad omens that she had chosen to ignore persisted when she finally arrived in California.

The general consensus was that Hansen had been unlucky. Drevet should have been disqualified for illegal use of the head. Whilst the cut was going to take weeks to heal, arrangements were immediately made for Hansen to fight Miguel Torres, his original intended opponent. Despite being given a chance to redeem himself, Martin remained in a dark mood after the fight. He had to find excuses and people to blame. First it was the referee, but then he turned his fire of frustration on Gloria. She had brought him bad luck, she was a malign influence. Their rows were volcanic and threatened to turn violent. With Monica, Gloria made the decision to travel to Hollywood a couple of weeks ahead of schedule, leaving Martin to go off to the Catskill mountains for an intense regime of training. Despite having already discussed divorce, Gloria agreed she would return to support him for his fight with Torres, providing her filming was over. By the time they went their separate ways they were at least being polite to each other, although Gloria was aware that Martin's family were creating problems for them in the background. Never one to deny herself pleasure, Gloria choreographed one final passionate coupling before they parted.

Passing through the impressive arch at the entrance to Paramount Studios, Gloria was expecting a welcoming committee of senior executives. What she got was blank stares from the uniformed gatekeeper. Referring to his clipboard he told her he had no trace of her and perhaps she should return later in the week. Standing her ground she insisted that further enquiries were made, flourishing the letter requesting her attendance. Eventually it was established that she was expected, but that her film had been put back by several weeks.

She had been informed by letter, but she had left New York by the time it arrived. Eventually a young Scot arrived with a docket for her hotel reservation and said that the studio would be in touch. Despite adopting her best diva protest she was steadfastly refused access. Beyond, workmen were erecting an elaborate castle set It was unlucky that Gloria should arrive at a time when Paramount were experiencing serious financial problems. Competition was fierce and cinema attendances were down as the slump took hold in America. Huge numbers of films were being shot, almost in the hope that a few would become giant hits. What Paramount needed was a huge new star and she was to appear the following year in the form of Mae West. Obviously Gloria had hoped to fill the new star role for the studio, but she was being thwarted at every turn. Her hotel was dismal and she fretted whilst she waited to be called.

Gloria was always unable to understand why she never really had a breakthrough in the States. Whilst she was a unique exotic presence in Europe, in America there were any number of black performers just as talented. It was a hard pill to swallow and as she continued to kick her heels awaiting the call from the studio, she started to feel unwell. She put this down to the heat and change in diet. After a couple of weeks her mood was improved by the arrival at her hotel of Mack Mottram who was going to direct her movie. A man in his late thirties, he exuded energy and enthusiasm which was just the tonic Gloria needed. He left her a script to study. To her alarm the film *Striking Gold* told the story of a young woman arriving in New York seeking fame. The problem was that in the script she never did strike gold. There was a bigger problem. There were no songs or dancing for her to perform. The film only required a straight acting role. Now in a total rage she rang Mottram threatening to pull out. 'No chance' he informed her, 'You are under contract.' After days of angry confrontations he agreed to include a couple of numbers for her to sing. Now she was convinced that it was all the unpleasantness that was making her feel unwell. Slowly and in absolute horror it occurred to her that she was pregnant. A trip to a doctor confirmed as much, but worse she was too far gone to have an abortion.

By now rehearsals were well under way and the rushes found Gloria giving a very wooden performance. Despite Mottram's encouragement she was unable to transfer the glitter of her stage performances to film. She was not a natural actress, but even the songs she performed in the film lacked her normal vibrancy. Her version of 'Bye Bye Blues' almost hit the spot, but she was unhappy about having to perform 'Half Caste Woman', a song written by Noel Coward. What no one realised was that during most of the shoot Gloria was trussed up like a chicken in a corset to disguise her thickening waistline. Despite numerous re-shoots Gloria's magic refused to break through. An unspoken tacit agreement was made between director and star. Both knew the film was a dud and no amount of re-takes was going to significantly improve it. Besides, the allocated budget had been spent. Gloria had at least got to meet Frederick March, Cary Grant and the Marx Brothers, but it was time to move on. To what? To a husband who irritated her, an unwanted baby and Martin's sanctimonious mother.

Martin and all his family were thrilled by the prospect of an addition to the family, whilst Gloria fumed at her stupidity. Her only relief was being able to discard the corset. As Martin Hansen completed his training for his bout against Torres, Gloria began plotting her future escape. The past year had been a nightmare, it was time for her to regain control of her life and career.

Gloria's pregnancy was too far gone for her to attend her husband's fight, which was again held at Madison Square Garden. Instead she settled back in an armchair and listened to the commentary on the wireless. The bookmakers made Torres a marginal favourite, but it was Martin who had the better of the early rounds, flooring his opponent in the fourth. By the sixth round Martin was in trouble. The gash over his eye had opened up again. As in his meeting with Drevet, this appeared to unnerve him. Despite the increasing promptings of his corner, he forgot his ability to avoid punishment and instead opted for an all out attack. It was a strategy that he was never going to win against the tough Mexican. Floored twice in the seventh round and with blood streaming down his face, his seconds threw in the towel to save him lasting damage. Hansen was furious, but despite his bravery it was the right decision.

Gloria switched off the radio when the commentator's voice was being drowned out by the baying of the crowd. What followed in those weeks after the fight was difficult for all concerned. Martin Hansen had seen his chance of becoming world champion disappear. Of course Gloria's prospects of true international fame had also taken a knock. Rather than console each other they both entered into a blame game. For Martin it was all Gloria's fault. She was a witch who had brought him nothing but bad luck. She became hysterical, blaming him for ruining her prospects and also for getting her pregnant. They did agree on one thing, they hated each other.

Martin's sister Ingrid tried to calm both of them down, frightened that all the trauma would cause Gloria to miscarry. In fact the baby arrived two weeks late, but was bonny and healthy. Gloria found the whole experience disgusting. She only held the baby on a handful of occasions before she slipped away. She did not even stay for the christening. Unknown to Martin, Gloria agreed that the baby be left with Ingrid and her husband to be brought up until Martin was in a position to take the child on. Almost as selfish as Gloria, Martin never lived with young Steffan, arranging for Ingrid and her husband Donald to adopt the child. The couple moved to Laguna Beach in California, where they ran a successful restaurant. Along with their other two children, young Steffan enjoyed a happy and contented upbringing until he joined the military.

There were long term repercussions for Gloria financially. A long drawn-out divorce, including a substantial payout to her former husband, continued to irk even years later. Like so many fighters Martin did not know when to quit. He fought on for years, gradually having to fight for just a few dollars, but always expecting to rediscover his former form. He swapped to a career in wrestling and was successful for a time before again sinking to the under-card. Never remarrying, he died in 1955 with what today we would term as dementia.

Monica had alerted the press of Gloria's return from her triumphant tour of the States. *Striking Gold* had only been distributed through small town cinemas in America, although it was shortly to go on general release in Britain.

As the flashbulbs recorded Gloria's arrival in Southampton, Alex was returning from a meeting with the Kaufman Gallery in Mayfair. It had been agreed that they would handle much of his output in future. As he drove up the drive in Bushey he was feeling optimistic about the future. The day had gone well and it was a glorious evening. Helen had taken Paddy up to stay with a school friend who lived just outside Bedford. Taking off his jacket, he poured himself a whisky noting that Helen had already set the table for supper. He could see her sitting in a deckchair staring out at the garden that she had transformed over the years. Walking across the patio to join her he stopped. Something was wrong. Throwing his glass into a flowerbed he knelt in front of her. She was staring out at the garden, the roses, azaleas and freshly mown lawn, but she saw nothing. Helen was dead.

Chapter 13
A friend in need

We all react in different ways when confronted with personal tragedy. Some panic, others dissolve into tears, whilst those unable to face the moment walk away. Alex did none of these. He had seen enough death in the war to realise immediately that Helen was beyond help. Quietly he went to the garden shed and pulled out a deckchair that he set beside Helen. Gently he took her hand which was still just warm. For over an hour he sat there looking over the gorgeous garden that Helen had created. July is known as a mute month and there was no birdsong to ease his thoughts. A bee settled for a moment on Helen's dress before darting off. He kept reciting a rhyme he remembered from childhood.

A swarm of bees in May
Is worth a load of hay
A swarm of bees in June
Is worth a silver spoon
A swarm of bees in July
Is worth a fly.

It was a terrible rhyme but reciting it helped numb his mind. When the sun finally dipped below the trees he went inside and rang the doctor. The next few days were a blur. He rang his parents to break the news. Not for the first time his mother's reaction surprised him. She insisted that it was a woman's job to tell young Paddy. She was driven down to Bedford and he was taken back to Stratton House. It was Orla who decided that Paddy, at twelve, was old enough to attend the funeral despite Alex's doubts. A post mortem confirmed that Helen had died from an overdose of insulin. It was explained that Helen had over-injected on a couple of former occasions. The coroner contacted Eileen Downs, Paddy's friend's mother who had been one of the last people to see Helen alive. Apparently Helen had been perfectly normal and had talked about picking her son up in a few days. Despite the massive over-injection a verdict of death by misadventure was recorded.

In the days before the funeral Alex was struggling. He hardly ate anything, compensating with a huge intake of Paddy whiskey. Unable to face sleeping in the marriage bed he fell into a hazy slumber on a settee. It was five days after Helen's death, with the funeral arranged for the following week, that Alex saw a chauffeur driven car draw up in the drive. Gloria was escorted to the front door by the driver carrying a large cardboard box. Staggering to his feet, Gloria swept past him with the greeting, 'You look terrible.' Still taken aback by her unexpected arrival, he was told to take a bath and make himself presentable. He did not argue. By the time he had shaved and bathed he was aware of a delicious smell of cooking wafting up from the kitchen. Feeling rather shamefaced and dressed in clean clothes he descended slowly, not knowing what to expect. He felt uncomfortable with

Gloria being in the house so soon after Helen's death. He had never expected to see Gloria wearing an apron cooking at a stove, but the food she prepared was superb. Why was he surprised, she queried, anyone living in France for any time could always produce a tasty meal. Not having realised how hungry he was, Alex ate two helpings of coq-au-vin followed by a tarte-tatin that Gloria had pilfered from the Savoy's kitchen. With the help of a good claret Alex gradually relaxed and poured out his heart. Gloria just listened, prompting him to move on when he became emotional. Here was Gloria, who generally cocooned herself in an eiderdown of selfishness, being true to a friend in need. That night Alex went up to sleep in the spare room leaving Gloria to clear up. Sometime later he became aware of a familiar naked figure snuggling up to him. This was a comforting friend, not an amorous lover. She reached below his pyjama top and gently massaged the wound on his back.

He was awoken the following morning by the noise of a car on the gravel outside. He reached the window just in time to see the car turn out of the drive. Downstairs Gloria had cooked him a full English breakfast waiting in the oven. Also was a familiar note:

My dear Alex,
I am so sorry. Be strong.
Until the next time,
All love, G.'

What was it in Alex's character that drew out this totally unexpected response from Gloria? It was one that she repeated in times of crisis and one that Alex certainly repaid over the years. Theirs was a unique relationship, sometimes lurching into passion, but always banked and confirmed in their steadfast friendship. It was with some shame that Alex realised that they had not even discussed Gloria's problems with her failed marriage. At this stage he had no idea that Gloria had left her baby for others to bring up. This illustrated the two Glorias that over the years Alex began to understand. Deeply flawed, but continually fascinating.

Alex had been dreading the funeral and his young son's reaction to his mother's death. As it transpired it was Paddy who kept asking his father if he was alright. The young boy, who had been really close to his mother, was dry-eyed and brave under the protective eye of Orla. There were only a few attending that day at St. Peter's church in Bushey. Maudie had made the long journey from Cornwall and there were representatives of the publishing companies who had championed Helen's work. There was also a sprinkling of neighbours, but it was only the family who attended the interment.

Left alone after all the formalities, Alex grappled with the decisions he needed to make regarding his changed circumstances. He did not want to desert the house with all its happy memories, but he realised he did need a change of scene if only to spark his career. Whilst there was little in Bushey of interest for him to paint, he wanted to keep the house on so that Paddy would have familiar surroundings to enjoy during the lengthy school holidays. Alex reasoned that he probably needed to employ a housekeeper, but the most immediate problem was to maintain the garden that had been such a central part of Helen's life. She had been helped for the last couple of years by Fred Yates, a man already in his seventies. A younger full-time gardener would need to be appointed, but for the meantime old Fred would have to do, although he was so slow spending more time looking than working. Alex asked a local charity to take Helen's clothes away. It was painful but he did not want the house to become a shrine. Then came a problem that he had been putting off as long as he could. True to their original agreement Alex had never set foot in Helen's studio. After her initial success she had rather ignored her illustrating, spending ever more time in the garden. It was something that had to be done and so it was with real trepidation that Alex gingerly opened the door.

Helen had not been in her studio for some weeks, but there was a strong sense of her presence which he found rather disconcerting. A vague whiff of the perfume she wore hung in the air. Alex had never believed in the supernatural or life after death, but he was unnerved by the oppressive atmosphere. He remembered a nurse telling him whilst he lay injured in a French hospital that she always opened a window after anyone died. He had thought this rather fanciful, but now he felt a strong urge to let some air into the room. Opening the windows he was struck by a waft of air causing one of Helen's illustrations to fall to the floor from her desk. Had he really released her spirit? It had been a cloudy day, but at that precise moment the sun broke through. Maybe just a coincidence, but Alex was emotionally touched and felt that Helen had finally left him. He never forgot her. Her beauty, tranquility and easy companionship that made it difficult for him to ever fall in love again.

Picking up the illustration that had fallen from the table, Alex started to browse through a considerable collection of work that she had not submitted for publication. There was a series of delightful children's nursery rhymes. All had pen and ink outlines and were highlighted in watercolour. Each was completed in minute detail. There was *Jack and the beanstalk*, *Mary had a little lamb*, and *Jack and Jill*, amongst a series of ten. She had also started a series of alphabets illustrating a collection of dogs. A for Airedale Terrier, B for Borzoi. A magical work with a young child holding onto the elegant Russian wolf hound. She had reached the letter L for a black Labrador where once again she left the series unfinished. The quality of the work was so exceptional that Alex was determined to get them published thus cementing Helen's reputation as a leading book illustrator. There were other random examples lying on her desk, including one of a child tumbling down a hill above a beautifully written caption *A rolling stone gathers no moss* and some preparatory sketches of *Alice in Wonderland.*

Under the stack of illustrations was a black leather folder. Opening it Alex felt a lurch in his stomach. Completed in minute detail was a study of a man hanging from a beam in what appeared to be a garden shed. The viewer was spared nothing. The eyes bulged, the tongue lolled. Alex remembered that Helen's father had committed suicide and his sense of dread deepened. It had occurred to him that Helen's death could have been suicide, but he had tried to put it to the back of his mind. Certainly the fact that she had systematically gone round all the local tradesmen and settled their bills had struck him as slightly odd. Paying the garage for servicing of their car was understandable as was the grocer, but settling their newsagent's account when this was normally paid monthly was strange.

There were a number of illustrations in the folder and each unnerved him further. She had painted a close up of her face surrounded by two looming devil like figures. Their features were fine but cruel, seemingly sneering at her. This was followed by three unfinished sketches of a young girl being raped by the same Satanic figures. Alex cast them aside in disgust only to take a sharp intake of breath. He felt giddy as if about to faint. Holding on to the desk for support he stared in horror at a detailed watercolour of Helen. She was captured sitting in a deckchair staring out over the garden. Every detail, the rose arbour, every flower and bush recorded, even the pattern on Helen's dress was accurate. She had recorded her own death scene. It was almost too much for Alex to bear.

He had seen terrible carnage during the war and he was usually able to keep his emotions pretty much in check, but this was different. Clutching the folder he rushed downstairs as if pursued by the devils that had invaded Helen's mind. There was a fire in the living room grate. The fire now completed the job that the hangman had started. Helen's father's illustration was consumed by the flames. They were followed by the three Satan's. Surely a fitting end. Sneering no more, their influence no longer able to infect Helen's soul, if such a thing existed. He paused now. Did he really want to consign this superb illustration of his wife to the flames? He did. Holding the cartridge paper to the fire, the flame turned blue, the paper resisting if only for a moment. Then, horribly,

Helen's image appeared to perform a dance of death. As the paper curled her image became distorted. The lawn was consumed along with the rose arbour. The flowers melted from view and stubbornly Helen refused to take her leave. Then like a martyr on the pyre, first her legs gave way to the flame followed by her body, but the face remained serene to the last. With a final curl she was gone and the flames rose to roar up the chimney.

Now she was finally gone Alex broke down. In spite of himself he sank to the ground. He wanted to kneel as if in prayer, but his injured leg thwarted him and he fell awkwardly on his side sobbing. Outside an early autumn wind blew down the chimney and a log fell from the fire landing on the carpet next to Alex. Forced by the smell of burning, he was jolted out of his self pity. Grabbing the fire tongs he placed the log back on the fire. The wind outside strengthened and the curtains gave a little shudder. Did he really believe she was trying to contact him? He had no idea but he still shouted, 'It is no good Helen. I am still bloody furious with you!' Furious of the waste of a life that could have contributed so much to their happiness, her suicide was a secret that he kept to himself except for one person. And that was not Gloria.

Chapter 14

Revival

After the funeral Alex fell into a period of lethargy and introspection. He was haunted by the thought that he was the reason that she had killed herself. Was it his relationship with Gloria or was there something in her past that had continued to haunt her? Perhaps it was genetic. Her father had killed himself whilst outwardly appearing perfectly happy. The fact was she had left no note or any indication as to why she took such drastic action. They had no money worries, a son they both doted on and a seemingly strong marriage. Endless turning over the reasons in his mind was dragging Alex down. He began neglecting himself again, only shaving a couple of times a week and living on sandwiches and breakfast cereals. Household chores bewildered him and dirty washing piled up. He even bought shirts and underwear in bulk to save him washing and ironing his clothes. He was also drinking heavily.

He was forced in to action when Paddy came home for the Christmas holidays. Alex employed a local lady to tidy the house and cook meals that could be heated up. Paddy arrived with a school friend and, unlike his father, was coping really well. His school report underlined this, informing Alex that his son had thrown himself in to his work. More importantly he was showing exceptional skills at rugby, already playing for the under sixteens' first fifteen. He was also taking part in dramatics and was a leading light in the art club. So Alex concluded that his son was busying himself to mask the pain he was obviously feeling. Alex made a resolution to take on his son's attitude in the new year, but instead fell back again into a period of indolence. For the first time in years he made no submissions to the Royal Academy. It was the arrival of spring and an improvement in the weather that finally stirred him into action. He had employed a very competent full time gardener to maintain and further improve what Helen had created. At last it was time to move on.

Alex wanted a life dominated by his ability to paint, but he needed the right environment. He mapped out a variety of locations in London which he thought would be suitable. He wanted to be in an area of creative activity. Not necessarily populated by artists but writers, musicians and actors. He started looking in Hampstead but found it rather too elitist. Chiswick and stretches along the Thames had been good enough for Turner and countless artists over the years, but he needed people, not boats and buildings. He had high hopes for Soho, but trawling the streets it appeared that almost all available property was being swallowed up by those running the sex trade. Having covered all parts of the northern Square Mile that contained Soho, he came across Archer Street. He was attracted by groups of men gathered chatting and smoking. It appeared they were all musicians waiting to be hired. Between them they played every conceivable instrument and repertoire that ranged from Mozart to Scott Joplin. The image of this group was already fixed in his mind as a possible subject for a major painting. It offered real characters, many of them in unconventional dress set against a urban background. Glancing down the street he noticed a sign for an Italian restaurant and feeling hungry after pounding the streets all morning he went in. It was a humble affair, all raffia-covered Chianti bottles and crude paintings of Portofino after which the restaurant was named. The food was simple but good. It was a poor location for a restaurant with little passing trade, particularly when there were so many superb competitors within walking distance. Alex lingered over his lunch and was joined by the proprietor who offered him a glass of wine. Ricardo Manzi was the chef and waiter, with only a kitchen hand to help him.

Alex reckoned it was going to be a tough job for the restaurant to survive. Their conversation turned to Alex's hope of finding a studio in the area. Just as Alex was about to leave Ricardo mentioned that there were a number of rooms upstairs that were not being used. There was plenty of space but it was in a terrible state. The two men went upstairs to investigate. The Italian had not been lying, the rooms were strewn with boxes of old clothes, random plumbing equipment and pigeon droppings. The restaurant owner had wanted to convert it into a flat, but did not have the finance. There were three rooms of a good size, one that been a kitchen in its former life. More importantly there was a galley room not unlike the studio in Newlyn. This room also had fanlights along its length which would be ideal as a studio. Alex did not hesitate. Cleared up it would be ideal. Surprisingly quiet for central London, this was to be his base for the next three decades and formed the background for most of his major works.

It took three months before the place was habitable. In addition to his studio he had a bedroom, living room, a dining kitchen and a lavatory and bathroom combined. Most evenings after a full day at the easel he ate downstairs at the Portofino. When endless pasta began to pall he ventured further afield for his meals. He quickly embraced Soho. It was chaotic, seamy and grubby, and yet most residents were friendly and the cosmopolitan background appealed to him. There were so many nationalities living in the area that one moment he felt he was in Rome, the next Madrid or even Moscow. As planned he started work on the group of musicians congregated each day just down the road. Rather like Stanhope Forbes he got into the habit of painting two or even three works in tandem. If he felt he was struggling with a particular subject, moving on to something totally different relieved the block he had been experiencing. Following the move he came across the intimate sketch he had made of Gloria sitting on the edge of the bed at the Piccadilly Hotel. He started a large oil he thought would make a suitable gift for Gloria after her kindness to him.

Despite the rent Alex was paying, the Portofino was having trouble attracting sufficient customers and Ricardo seemed in a constant state of anxiety. There was a pattern to his mood that increased at the end of each month. Alex had noticed that he had a regular visitor who never stayed to eat, but disappeared into the kitchen with Ricardo before leaving patting at his pocket. Alex had asked about these strange visits, but Ricardo was always evasive, as if even discussing it left him in some kind of danger. Matters came to a head about three months after Alex had moved in. Dissatisfied with his morning's work, unusually Alex was lunching in the restaurant. It was gone 2 o'clock and Alex was the last customer finishing his coffee, when he saw the sinister man he had seen previously. Alex noticed that Ricardo visibly stiffened as if suffering an electric shock. The two men went through to the kitchen where there were raised voices. Moving closer to the door so he could hear clearly, the stranger was demanding money. Not only the sum apparently normally paid, but double.

Pushing the door ajar he saw Ricardo being threatened with a razor. 'What the hell is going on?' he demanded. 'Leave it, Alex please!' Ricardo blurted out. 'You want some of this do you? If not mind your own business.' Smiling, Alex approached the swarthy character brandishing the razor with hand outstretched, as if in greeting. This seeming gesture of friendship caught the unofficial rent collector off guard. Unarmed combat comes back to those who have learnt it, much like riding a bike. The extended arm of friendship yanked the razor free and in one movement the rent collector was thrown to the floor. 'You are dead, fucking dead!' the man screamed, but it was nothing to the scream he gave as Alex kicked him in the groin. Ricardo was in tears; He's right, we are both dead. Oh my god, what have you done?; Alex was quite unconcerned. He picked up the rent collector and shoved him on to a chair where he was sobbing and clutching between his legs. Ricardo explained between sobs that the rent collector was a member of the Sabini gang and everyone in Soho paid for protection, otherwise they were subjected to extreme violence. No-one, Ricardo explained, crossed Sabini and stayed in one piece. That afternoon people watched in amazement as Alex led Nosher Grant by the collar towards old Compton Street where Darby Sabini held court.

Darby Sabini was a few years older than Alex. He was born in Clerkenwell, known as little Italy, the youngest of six brothers. His father died when he was only two and so it was his Irish mother whose influence that manifested itself in strange ways for a renowned gangster. He hated swearing and particularly blasphemy. He insisted that his gang members always treated women with respect. An extension of this revealed that he never became involved with prostitution. Another quirk in his character was that although constantly violent, he never used a razor to inflict damage. He was happy to wield a cosh, knuckle duster or the odd chair leg, but the use of razors made him shudder.

Although the youngest in the family, from the start he was in charge of the gang's reign of terror. It started on the race tracks where his ruthless use of extreme violence allowed him to take control. Every bookie had to pay for protection. He even charged for chalk for them to mark up their odds. Within years the gang had extended their interest to pubs and clubs in the West End. Even a hint of resistance led to the premises being trashed. Sabini even had the police co-operating with him. Raids would be made on clubs to be followed by a representative of the gang calling shortly afterwards to offer protection against any further trouble from the police.

As a newcomer to the area Alex was blissfully unaware of the danger he was placing himself under. Ever since his schooldays he had hated bullying and he showed no fear on entering the Admiral Duncan pub. Holding Nosher by the collar he propelled him across the bar and demanded to know where he could find Sabini. With eyes wide open in fright, the barman indicated a door at the back of the bar. The room had about half a dozen men gathered round a small figure seated in a Windsor chair. ;Yours, I believe; Alex said, pushing the unfortunate Nosher towards his boss, still gripping his crotch.

The sheer audacity of Alex's action appeared to catch even Sabini off guard. A couple of the heavies gripped Alex by the arms, causing him to drop his walking stick. Aware that they were just about to rough Alex up, Sabini raised his hand. 'Wait' he said, 'Get the gentleman a chair so he can explain himself.' Grudgingly they released him and gave him back his cane. Alex explained that he had overheard Nosher demanding money from his landlord. Not only demanding money but double what he had previously paid. It was this information that sparked Sabini into life. Poor old Nosher made a dash for the door despite his discomfort. He did not get far. Trying to obtain extra cash for himself was a mortal sin in the eyes of Darby Sabini. 'Sort him' Sabini instructed, as Nosher squealed his innocence as he was dragged away. Alex now realised what he had got embroiled in. Thinking quickly he insisted that Ricardo should not pay any money in future. This was greeted with gales of laughter. Sensing the increasing atmosphere of violence soon to be directed at him, he made his outrageous proposal.

He explained that he was an artist and would be happy to paint Sabini's portrait in exchange for a protection for the Portofino. Alex saw a flicker of interest register on Darby's face. He did not respond, seemingly deep in thought. How was it that this rather absurd little figure could generate such fear. His style of dress never changed. A smart brown suit, the effect rather ruined by him always wearing a white shirt without a collar. He also wore a high fronted waistcoat topped by a rather ridiculous flat cap. Still, the pair stared at each other trying to sum up the situation. Alex had played on Sabini's ego guessing that he would like to be preserved in paint for posterity. A discussion followed about the value of a painting created by Alex. After all anyone could claim they were a famous artist. 'Then make some enquiries' Alex suggested. 'I will' Sabini responded. They agreed to meet at the restaurant the following day at noon. If Alex was right they would have a deal. If not he knew what to expect. As Alex rose to leave, Sabini called out, 'I admire your balls', but Alex did not wait to reply.

Ricardo was beside himself with fear at the prospect of Sabini coming to his restaurant, but my grandfather told him to relax, the gangster would be mad to reject his offer and he was right. Sabini's mood was positively light hearted. Standing in Alex's studio he joked, 'I thought I was supposed to be the robber. The prices they charge for your painting is a crime.' Alex agreed, but the deal was made with a handshake. Alex had three sittings with Sabini. He was not used to painting portraits, but the result was uncanny. He managed to convey the sense of menace, whilst also rather flattering the sitter. Sabini was thrilled with the result, reacting almost like a child receiving their first train set or bicycle. Not only did Ricardo never have any trouble from the gang again, Alex achieved a unique status in Soho. Well known hoods stood aside for him in the street. Free drinks were offered in pubs and bars and discounts on anything he wished to buy in the local shops. He was probably the only man to stand up to the gang and survive unscathed. Within two or three years Darby Sabini withdrew from Soho to a respectable retirement in an apartment on the sea front in Brighton. Constant challenges and fights from rival gangs had taken its toll. He left his brother Harry to carry on with the family firm. Back in Brighton taking pride of place over his fireplace was the portrait that Alex had created. Strangely the two men were to meet again, once more at a time of mutual grief for both of them.

In the period after the Sabini incident Alex set to work on the painting of Gloria after their steamy encounter some years previously. Working from the sketch he made at the time he fashioned a work that he really loved. He thought he had caught the moment perfectly, the slight knowing smile, the crumpled sheets captured a lasting and memorable moment in their lives. Contacting Monica Wiseman to arrange shipment, he was anxious to get Gloria's response. He did not have long to wait.

'My dear Alex,

How dare you! I look horrible. Besides, my tits are bigger. You make them look like wrinkled walnuts. I have told Monica to destroy it. Never paint me again.

Until the next time.

Love, G'

Chapter 15

Defining moments

Gloria had an ingrained ability to self-destruct. These dramatic falls from grace normally occurred after a sustained period of success, as if subconsciously she embraced the dark days that followed. She never took kindly to advice, no matter how well intentioned. Maybe later she would change her mind, but in a reheated form and she would claim that it was her idea all along. She was particularly averse to suggestions made by Monica, which were normally savvy and well intentioned. It was certainly true of her advice for Gloria not to revisit Berlin. She warned Gloria about the changing political scene in Germany. Gloria confidently predicted that any problems only related to Jews. Monica was not so sure but she knew Gloria needed another injection of excitement. She also suspected Germany's relaxed approach to drugs was an added attraction.

Gloria's return to Paris from the States started with a very successful cabaret season at the Moulin Rouge. This was followed by a dramatic change of direction when she took the lead in Offenbach's opera *La Créole* at the Theatre Marigny. The critics were overwhelmed at her capacity to switch seemingly effortlessly from cabaret to opera. Her love life had also taken an upward turn when she started an affair with her singing coach, Jean Claude Trenier. An older man in his fifties, his vocal coaching added depth and range to Gloria's voice. But although he had brought a degree of stability to her life, within days of stepping down from *La Créole* she was bored and despite Monica's warning she was off for a two week engagement at El Dorado.

On arrival in Berlin it did not take long for Gloria to realise how much Germany had changed since her last visit. As porters struggled with her luggage Gloria made her way ostentatiously to reception at the Hotel Adlon. Without looking up the reception clerk told her quietly, 'Sorry Miss Bird, the hotel is full.' Before she could launch her outrage the look of fear on the man's face cut her short. His eyes darted to his right. Gloria noticed two men dressed in long raincoats whom she had seen staring at her at the airport. The clerk explained that Berlin had changed since her last visit and arrangements had been made for her to stay at a sister hotel. The clerk's sense of fear was obvious and for once Gloria meekly followed her baggage as it was loaded again into a taxi.

The sister hotel was away from the centre, rather gloomy but clean and comfortable enough. Gloria soon realised that the other guests were obviously either Jewish or dark-skinned foreigners. She was tempted to travel straight back to Paris, but the lavish reception she received at the El Dorado on her first two nights was exhilarating. The clientele for her show *Schwartzer Sante* was even more outrageous than she remembered. On the first night there was a religious, or rather a sacrilegious, theme. Pastors and nuns swarmed around her. One nun had cut off the front of her habit, exposing her breasts. These were possibly the most fervent fans that Gloria ever encountered and she loved them for their camp and over the top attention.

She had scarcely started her performance on the third night after her arrival when there was a commotion coming from the entrance hall. The doors burst open and dozens of brown-shirted thugs crashed in, scattering tables, shattering glasses and crockery. To screams of alarm the audience was rounded up and made to face the wall. The brown-shirts were part of a huge paramilitary group under the command of Ernst *Röhm* who had helped bring the Nazis to power. Gloria was hustled outside to a waiting car. For the first time in her life she was seriously scared. After a ten minute ride she was firmly but politely ushered into a small room with no furniture or outside windows. After what must have been over an hour she was led down a dimly lit corridor into another stark room. A man dressed in a dark suit with a swastika armband was seated at a desk.

Looking up from beneath hooded eyes he indicated to a seat opposite his desk. 'Sit!' he barked in English, much as he would instruct a dog. Gloria, having regained some composure, started to shout and scream her complaints at her treatment. The man, who was probably about the same age as Gloria, let her finish then chillingly told her that if she continued talking without permission she would be arrested and locked up. He spoke impeccable English, but with a pronounced accent. He continued to ignore her whilst studying a buff folder containing a file of type-written reports and some photographs. Closing the folder he studied her, removing the frameless glasses he had been wearing. What followed amounted to a lecture. Why, the inquisitor inquired, had Gloria chosen to appear at such a degenerate venue when there were so many fine theatres in Berlin? The El Dorado, he continued, was home to Jews, homosexuals and perverts. She should realise that Germany was to be the centre of European civilisation where these dregs of society would have no place.

She relaxed a little as he appeared to have completed his lecture, when he suddenly said, ;I believe you know the Jew Rudolf Steinmann?' She did not answer. Sneering, he opened the folder again. 'But I believe you also knew his wife.' He paused, 'Shall we say more intimately?' Gloria felt a spasm of alarm. 'Miss Bird, if these photographs became public I think maybe your career might be finished.' She wanted to scream her fury at his invasion of her privacy, but for once she remained silent. He looked at her as if undressing her in his mind. She was not sure that she had not seen him before on her previous visit, but his face did seem familiar. He continued studying her before rising abruptly. 'You will leave at once. You will be taken to the airport. Go and do not come back. Do you understand? We do not want your sort here.' 'What do you mean, my sort?' Gloria asked indignantly. He did not wait to reply. Within an hour she was on a flight to Paris. This encounter with Nazi Germany was to influence Gloria's life, which in a way even surprised her.

Strangely it was Alex's son Paddy who next experienced the growing threat of Fascism spreading across Europe. As a young teenager it was frightening to be engulfed by a marauding mob of Mussolini's black-shirts as he walked down the Via Roma with Maria in Padua. Maria Botti had been an assistant in a patisserie in Brewer Street, just round the corner from my grandfather's studio. Alex, having something of a sweet tooth, was a regular visitor. As they chatted daily Alex was taken by her warmth and infectious good humour. She was a good looking woman with a mane of jet black hair and a tendency to plumpness. He was worried that she might think he was propositioning her, whereas in a roundabout way he was only offering her a job. He needed a studio assistant to tidy for him, but also to order paints, canvasses and organise framing for his finished works. Realising this was not a full time job, he also proposed that she could help with Paddy back at Bushey during school holidays. She was very reticent but agreed to pop round to the studio. Alex need not have worried because from the moment she came through the door to the restaurant the attraction between Maria and Ricardo was evident. A perfect solution was found with Maria taking over front of house at the Portofino. Even better, Maria loved helping out at Bushey when Paddy was home and they too found comfort in each other. She never attempted to be a substitute mother, but she did offer the young boy genuine love and comfort at a time he needed it most.

Within months of their meeting Maria and Ricardo were married in St. Patrick's, Soho's only Catholic church. Although Alex was not religious, he had occasionally ventured into the church. Its vaulted interior offered complete peace and silence from the never ending theatre being played out just outside its doors. Since living locally Alex had also attended a Christmas midnight mass and was astonished to see the quantity of fivers and tenners spilling from the collection plates. Conscience money from a congregation of street walkers and hard faced hoods.

Maria had a brother who was a butcher living in Abano, a town some five miles south of Padua. So it was for the next four years that Paddy spent part of his summer holidays in Abano with Maria and her brother's family. He was taking Italian at school and he fell in love with the language, the architecture and increasingly the gorgeous Italian girls. The breathtaking great hall on the Palazzo della Ragione in Abano sparked his interest in architecture, but it was the squares and piazzas of the old town in Padua that convinced him that on leaving school he would study to become an architect. Like his parents he had inherited the ability to draw and paint, but the nuts and bolts of architecture fascinated him. This was a time of peace and contentment for Alex, which was further helped by his meeting Vivian van Damm.

When Alex first arrived in Archer Street, the Windmill Theatre had been a cinema. The owner of the theatre was the eccentric socialite Laura Henderson. Her idea was to offer non-stop revue for the first time in London. Her philanthropic intention was to offer out of work artistes the opportunity to appear on the West End stage under the show title of Revudeville. The problem was that most of the performances were dreadful and the critics savaged the whole concept. Enter Vivian Van Damm. Previously a dynamic cinema manager, gradually under his supervision the shows improved, but with a seating capacity of only about three hundred Van Damm realised he needed to offer a totally new brand of entertainment. It was through Mrs. Henderson's social connections that the Lord Chancellor surprisingly sanctioned the possibility for nudes to appear on stage on the understanding that they stood like statues, never moving. Overnight Van Damm had his unique brand and from 2pm each afternoon until the early hours queues formed waiting patiently to gain entrance.

Van Damm was aware of Alex's work and introduced himself one night as they both dined at the Portofino. Knowing of my grandfather's series of paintings covering the music hall and theatre, he expressed surprise that Alex had not shown any interest in a theatre on his own doorstep. They agreed to meet the following day and so started another important phase in Alex's artistic life. Entering by the stage door he was shown up to Van Damm's office, and was given licence to wander round as he pleased. The frantic pace of scantily dressed girls passing on the narrow staircase, the smell of greasepaint, perfume and the non-stop clatter of high heels was intoxicating. Why on earth, he wondered, had he taken so long to discover this incredible source of inspiration. By the mid 1930s the Windmill was a must visit tourist attraction. The shows were by now run with military precision. Two separate companies performed on alternate days. Each show ran for two hours and there were four shows a day, with audiences able to come and go as they pleased. Although it was the statuesque nudes that drew the crowds, it was the professional standards that Van Damm demanded that set it apart from numerous imitators that sprung up over the years. Apart from the very slick routines of the company, the Windmill also launched the careers of many comedians who subsequently became household names.

The girls soon became accustomed to Alex sketching away and Van Damm welcomed the publicity created when the first examples of Alex's 'Windmill Years' were exhibited at the Royal Academy summer exhibition. He recorded auditions and dress rehearsals for new shows which were held on Sundays. His most popular images were those of the girls about to go on stage and attending to their make-up in the crowded dressing room. Alex was quite shocked by how young most of the artistes were, Van Damm often refusing to engage young women in their early twenties as being too old.

Despite the amount of flesh on show the girls tended to be from respectable backgrounds and were encouraged not to get involved with any 'stage-door Johnnies', although there was regular romances between the cast and a few resulting in marriage. The girls certainly earned their money, which amounted to two pounds ten shillings a week. This equated to one shilling and eight pence per performance. Never one to miss out on publicity, Van Damm employed a statistician who estimated that each girl had five thousand changes of costume each year and went through seventy five pairs of shoes which were required to complete the seventy five thousand kicks they executed. The publicity rather backfired on him as the girls demanded a wage increase and Van Damm was forced to increase their wages to four pounds a week, although it was phased in over a period of months.

Alex certainly became immersed in the Windmill culture. Over a period of four or five years he produced over twenty major works, which are amongst some of the best he created, several of which are now in national collections. Despite this being one of his most productive periods artistically, the latter part of the 1930s was one where my grandfather became rather evasive and it was to take me some time to understand why.

Chapter 16

The apple never falls far from the tree

I t was more an ultimatum rather than a request. Alex could not remember his mother ever visiting London before. She had a dislike of big cities, rarely venturing into Northampton or Leicester, but her phone call had been specific. He was to meet her at Gunter's Tea Shop in Berkeley Square. Intriguingly she told him that she had some really important news.

My grandfather relayed the news to me of that day in great detail as it was obviously of huge importance to him. Only the date was in doubt. He was not sure if it was late in 1937 or early the following year. Gunter's was the smartest place in London, all bone china, tiny cucumber sandwiches and delicious cakes. Alex arrived early but he need not have bothered as Orla was a dreadful timekeeper. Rather like Gloria there was a sense of theatre about her. She loved making an entrance. As she swept between the fashionable cane tables, he was struck by what was a magnificent looking woman she was. She made no concession to the current vogue for shorter skirts. Her look was classic, a fitted blouse, long black skirt and topped with an outrageously wide brimmed hat. Her kiss of greeting merely brushed his cheek.

Removing her long leather gloves, she ordered for both of them without consulting her son. After the usual pleasantries she embarked on a succession of family news, that by the end of that day was to change his whole understanding of himself.

Orla had told her husband that she was visiting London to see a dressmaker that had been recommended to her. He showed little interest, being taken up with production problems being experienced in his Desborough factory. Actually she told Alex she had undergone a series of tests at University College Hospital before seeing the leading haematologist, Dr. Ian Robertson, who informed her that she was suffering from a form of leukaemia. Alex's medical knowledge was very limited and he made all the right noises, trying to reassure her. She let him finish before informing him that currently there was no cure available. Alex felt quite panicked by the news but Orla was calm. She told him she was quite at peace with herself and anyway the specialist had told her that she could still expect to live for several more years. The consultant had made her future sound almost acceptable. Certainly she would suffer a loss of energy and weight, but it would be a gentle decline. Imperceptible at first, allowing her to settle her affairs at leisure. The way Orla described the process did nothing to calm Alex. Despite their rather distant relationship, particularly when he was young, his response to the news left him feeling physically sick. Surely there was something that could be done. Perhaps she should go to America for treatment.

She told him that there was more that she had to tell him, but that could wait for later. Trying to jolly him out of his glum mood she suggested that he take her out for dinner that night. She did not want a swanky restaurant, but something more basic. She wanted to experience 'real London'. The choice was obvious, Orla could have a look round his studio before dining at the Portofino.

Orla's welcome to the Portofino that night could not have been more effusive even if she had been a member of the Royal family. Other diners stared, trying to place this striking looking older woman Her manner was rather grand, graciously accepting the compliments from Ricardo and Maria. Her tour of the studio drew the cryptic query as to whether her son ever painted young women fully clothed. Alex really wanted to move on from his Windmill series, but they had proved so popular that many had been produced as prints and well known celebrities were queuing up to purchase any new creation that was offered at the Kaufman Gallery.

Safely tucked away at the back of the restaurant was a perfect spot for mother and son to chat without being overheard. It was strange that they had never really confided in each other. Alex had always found his mother distant and yet at the same time often magical. It was as if she inhabited a separate universe, one that drifted apart from the rest. Seemingly unaffected by the chaos of the world around her, she was an ephemeral figure somehow unreachable, particularly for a young boy seeking his mother's overt love. Yet that had changed with the arrival of Paddy whom she doted on. Changed also by the news of her illness, which had the effect of opening the floodgates and a need to be frank at last with each other. Having ordered and relaxed after a couple of glasses of Brindisi, it was Alex who broke the ice by telling his mother of his doubt about Helen's death.

He had never acknowledged to anyone that he was haunted by the thought that she had committed suicide. Orla listened, not interrupting his anguish still raw and unresolved. In a moment of rare tenderness between them she reached across the table and held his hand. When he had finished she simply said, 'I think you are right, but do not blame yourself. She was such a beautiful girl'. She paused, 'But I think it was in her blood. Alex, it's time for you to move on.' As the first bottle of wine was finished Orla cross-examined Alex about his love life or lack of it. He was evasive, particularly regarding the young Windmill girls. As his mother stared at him from across the table, he was reminded of how Orla had an uncanny ability of discovering his misdeeds as a youngster. He felt relieved that he had now unburdened himself about Helen's death, but his feeling of guilt never left. He had witnessed terrible scenes in the war, but it was thoughts of Helen that continued to wake him at night.

It was when half of the second bottle of wine had been drunk and whilst sipping coffee that Orla shocked Alex with some astounding family revelations. As ever with her it was a story that was coaxed and teased from her memory, as if in a trance. Orla Forsyth was born into a poor aristocratic family who had lived just outside Kilkenny since arriving from Scotland in the eighteenth century. Slavin Castle had once been grand but had fallen into little more than a ruin. The family lived in the west wing in seedy opulence. Orla's mother died when she was very young and she had only the vaguest memory of a ghostlike figure seemingly always dressed in white. Orla's father always had grand plans and business schemes that invariably crashed. He was a great horseman but an unlucky gambler. Duncan Forsyth was a proud man and he tried desperately to keep up appearances, despite his world literally falling down around him. Young Orla had a strange and lonely upbringing. Religion has always divided Ireland. Her father said that his daughter was not going to be educated by what he described as prating nuns. So it was that half a dozen or so other Protestant children were assembled each day to be taught by a succession of private tutors. As she grew up Orla lost herself in the comfort of books and poetry. She had very little social contact with children of her own age other than where horses were involved. Duncan Forsyth was a great hunting and racing man. Orla learnt to ride as soon as she could walk. She rode every day of her life, noted locally for her skill and bravery. By her teens she often accompanied her father to race tracks, watching him lose the little money he had left. They travelled across the country from Thurles to the Curragh.

It was when Orla was about sixteen that she went with her father to the Tralee festival. It was here that the organisers tried to persuade him to enter his daughter for the Rose of Tralee beauty contest. It had never occurred to him that his daughter had suddenly blossomed into the most beautiful young woman, but he would not hear of it. Incarcerated and desperately lonely, Orla spent her time trying to bring some order to their crumbling home. She had to use her charm to deflect an increasing number of debt collectors who came calling. She despaired of what she could achieve in her life and suggested to her father that she move to Dublin in search of work. He was adamant that no daughter of his would ever go out to work. Things may be difficult, he told her, but standards must be maintained. She despaired that he was so out of touch and the prospect of spending the best years of her life looking after him appalled her. He remained unrealistically optimistic. He informed her he had just purchased an agency to sell corsets in Ireland for a leading English manufacturer. The defunct business was financed with borrowed money, but it had a small office in Dublin and his hopes were high.

Despite her beauty Orla rarely ventured out except on horseback, as the few clothes she had were dowdy and old fashioned. Perhaps it was obvious that she would lose her heart to almost the first young man to show her attention. She had first noticed Michael O'Mara on the hunting field because of his reckless bravery. She had also seen him riding at a local point to point. He was tall with a mop of unruly black hair and an easy charm. From casual chats she began to notice him hanging around the gates to the castle. Although she discovered he was a year younger than her, she was flattered by his attention and physically attracted to him. Avoiding the prying eye of her father, they managed to meet by riding off into the countryside. Both were inexperienced, but their excitement in each other was intense. Naive as she was, Orla realised the risk she was taking, but this seventeen year old boy released a passion that overwhelmed her. For perhaps the only time in her life she gave way to its temptations. It was not love or anything remotely like it, but raw desire that frightened her. Now it was she who was pursuing him. Trouble began when his parents complained to her father, who was horrified to be confronted with such scandalous allegations. Having previously been denied, she was now packed off to Dublin to help in the newly acquired office.

Orla did not spare herself in what she told Alex about following her arrival in Dublin. Her father had given her enough money to buy herself an outfit so that she did not look out of place in the big city. Although she had been lonely and bored at home, she hated Dublin. A dislike of big cities that stayed with her all her life. The office was small and cramped and she was forced to sleep on a mattress on the floor. The manager of the agency appointed by her father was Harold Meehan, who spent most of his day in the pub. His wife Maisie was to play an important part in Orla's life, for it was her who realised that the young girl was pregnant. Ignorant but horrified, Orla cold-heartedly set out to retrieve the situation.

George Brett had only planned to spend a day in Dublin. The Irish market for corsets was relatively small. He had been led to believe by Mr. Forsyth that he ran a sizeable sales organisation, rather than a dilapidated office in the back streets. He was also offended that Forsyth had not even turned up to meet him. He would have turned on his heel and left straight away if it had not been for Orla. She turned on an award-winning performance. Ten years her senior George, despite his commercial success, had very little experience of the opposite sex. Short, red-faced and already balding, he was clumsy and ill at ease in the company of young women, and yet here was a sensational beauty paying court to him. She was not just stunning, but charming and intelligent too. Because of business commitments he had to return to England that day, but a letter from Orla had him inventing a reason to re-visit Dublin again a week later.

This time he did not rush home. He took her to dinner, bought her clothes and she flirted and enticed. Did he suspect? Possibly, but he was captivated. They went for walks along the beach at Howth. They stayed at a hotel overlooking the harbour, in separate rooms obviously. They talked about a possible life together. Orla really rather fancied this unlikely suitor. Perhaps it would give her a chance to escape and to enjoy a life of comfort. For George, he could scarcely believe that he could attract such a gem. Such a young woman would be an asset for any man. It was with a trembling voice that George proposed to Orla less than a fortnight since they first met. She kept him waiting a couple of days before accepting, despite worrying that he may have changed his mind. They contacted her father who immediately saw the advantage of the arrangement. His daughter was marrying a Protestant and he was being offered a financial lifeline. They married at St. Mary's in Howth. Truly a marriage of convenience, but on many levels a successful one.

It had been a day of revelations which was difficult for Alex to absorb. To be told in quick succession that your mother is dying and that your father is not who you thought he was changes the whole perception you had of yourself. The soft lilt of Orla's voice added to a sense of unreality. George Beck had been a good father to him, although it was not just the physical differences that set them apart. Unlike his brother Marcus, Alex had never shown any interest or aptitude for business matters. He had always put this down to being more like his mother in looks and interest. Had the reckless streak that came out in his war experience been inherited from this young man he had never met? What had happened to him? There were so many questions.

Feeling guilty at keeping Ricardo up so late after the other diners had left, Alex guided his mother upstairs to his cluttered sitting room. Pouring them each a large tumbler of Paddy whiskey, Alex needed some answers. Orla had decided that her hospital appointment offered the perfect platform for her to explain the situation. She had pondered long and hard as to whether to inform him about his father, but decided that he had a right to know. She asked that he never discuss the matter with George or his brother as it would cause unnecessary pain. She told him that George did probably suspect, but as Alex arrived three weeks late it was never discussed between them. She also explained to Alex that she had always shown a slight favouritism towards Marcus to further deflect any suspicions George might have had. Did all these revelations really explain his mother's rather aloof attitude towards him as a youngster?

His thoughts were interrupted as Orla continued with her story. She had recently learnt that Michael O'Mara, her teenage passion, had died. She had managed to follow his progress by taking the local Kilkenny papers and daily copies of the Irish Independent. She had expected great things from her young lover. She felt sure he would make his mark and to an extent he did. He studied medicine at Trinity College in Dublin. For a time he became involved with student politics, flirting with the IRA. During these early days his real claim to fame was in his sporting achievements. He was a star in

Gaelic football and continued to be a leading jockey in point to points. His ability at a range of sports interested Alex as Paddy had developed into a seriously talented rugby player who had recently represented England's schools against Wales.

Apparently later in life Michael O'Mara also became a single handicap golfer. After practicing in India for a couple of years Michael went back to Ireland. He married Moray Donoghue and they lived in Waterford where he became a successful and popular GP. They had three children who are now scattered around the world. Still trying to absorb all this information about his real father, Orla still had one further bombshell to pass on. Reaching into her handbag she pulled out a bound notebook. Inside there were a series of sketches. Two were close-ups of a young woman's face, one pensive, the other face-on and smiling. The third was of the same young girl lying fully clothed but with her back against a hay bale. 'You?' he said. She nodded. The sketches were rushed but good. Very good. 'Don't tell me' Alex queried. Orla was smiling, 'Yes, Michael did them, the apple never falls far from the tree.'

Chapter 17

Stop the clock

Helen's death continued to have a profound effect on Alex and his future relationships. Not only did he feel a sense of guilt but he was also inhibited in his own mind by his physical condition. His leg continued to worsen, making it really difficult to bend. He still walked with the benefit of a cane but sitting down was a problem with his leg having to be thrust out straight in front of him, causing all manner of problems in restaurants and particularly when travelling on the tube. Worse was the wound on his back that continued to weep. This disgusted him and inhibited his confidence in entering into romantic relationships. Several months in constant pain had an ageing effect. He looked older than his age, his face drawn and flecks of grey hair appearing. His manner had also changed from the easy going young man of his youth. Now he tended to be tetchy, even brooding, but none of these faults that existed in his mind appeared to deter women of all ages who continued to be attracted to him.

It is impossible to believe he lived the life of a monk after Helen's death. Despite his reticence it is obvious that he had at least two romantic involvements with Windmill girls. His reluctance to talk openly about this period was probably partly because of the age difference, as most of the girls employed by Vivian Van Damm were teenagers. There was another reason that we will come to later. From what I have learnt about Alex at this stage of his life was that to many he cut a truly romantic figure. His gammy leg and obvious sadness acted as a challenge to a wide cast of women who sensed the need in him. A need for love that he was only too aware of but one that tended to elude him. We do know that he did enjoy a brief affair with the mother of a school friend. I have a photograph of Brenda Jenkins, a lady of rather generous proportions with the face of an angel. Standing on the touchline of a muddy rugby pitch was the unusual setting for the start of their romance. Brenda's husband had run off with his secretary and until he returned Alex enjoyed an uncomplicated affair. Brenda was outgoing and fun. In many ways quite outrageous for a respectable suburban housewife, but ultimately bound to her returning errant husband.

Of course there was one constant love in Alex's life, but Gloria was never going to offer him a stability that he really craved, despite that her arrival back in his life always caused a flutter in his heart and a rise in his spirits. She arrived at his studio unannounced, causing quite a stir as she swept through the restaurant. Alex had just received an excited telephone call from Paddy informing him that due to a late injury he had been selected to play for the East Midlands against the Barbarians in Leicester the following afternoon. Since leaving school Paddy had won a regular place in the Northampton Saints' team and was being predicted as a possible future international. 'Great' declared Gloria, 'I love going to ball games.' Alex did explain to her that watching rugby in England was crushed, cold and uncomfortable, but she was not going to be denied.

They set off the following morning, having rung and arranged for them all to stay with his parents that evening. On arrival at Welford Road Gloria was well wrapped up in a sheepskin coat, but topped with a flamboyant turban. Squashed in on wooden seats, nobody paid her much attention to start with, but a total ignorance of the rules did not inhibit her raucous support. She had never met Paddy, but shouted at the top of her voice, 'Isn't he just gorgeous!' Within minutes of kick-off she was on her feet yelling her support. Obviously rather nervous, Paddy had a shaky start dropping a couple of high balls, but as the half went on his confidence grew and he started to make breaks. A scuffle broke out right in front of where Alex and Gloria were sitting between Paddy and a huge opposition forward. 'You are a great big bully!' She shouted so loudly that Paddy looked up and wondered who this strange woman was. By the second half some of the crowd were becoming annoyed by Gloria's continual outbursts, but most voiced their support for this vociferous newcomer. With only a few minutes remaining Paddy made a break from full back. Like all gifted players he always appeared to have time feigning one way and leaving an opponent grasping at thin air. Covering half the length of the pitch he timed his pass to perfection, allowing the winger to score a try confirming a win for his team.

The warmth of the clubhouse was a welcome relief from a cold, wet March afternoon. Gloria eased her way through the crowded bar, heading straight to the room reserved for players and club officials. She handed her coat to a rather startled president of Leicester Tigers rugby club as if he were a cloakroom attendant. Alex followed in her wake. Removing her turban, people were beginning to realise that they had an unexpected star in their midst.

The journalists covering the game gathered round and someone alerted the local press photographer to come. He arrived just in time to capture Paddy being engulfed in a sea of kisses, a photo that featured on the front page of the Leicester Mercury the following day. Paddy had worked out who Gloria was before his father finally fought his way through to join them. She was in her element. It was adoration that Gloria craved and Alex knew what was going to happen. Hoisted onto the piano by the 'bully' who had scuffled with Paddy, she started to give an impromptu cabaret. Starting with her recent recording of 'South of the border' she then took over at the piano, playing honky tonk and then singing 'I get a kick out of you' to hoots of laughter and boisterous applause. Alex was constantly astonished by Gloria's ability to adapt to her audience. She was entertaining everyone whilst drinking pints of beer rather than her usual champagne. She was a real pro but with a genuine love of performing. She had a warmth to her that he felt she had lacked earlier in her career. As much at home with a mass of macho rugby players as the homosexuals of Berlin.

Alex had to literally drag Gloria away to make sure they were not too late arriving for dinner with his parents. Paddy had developed into a very pleasant looking young man. Not handsome, but certainly attractive and obviously very fit and toned. A couple of inches shorter than his father, he had a confidence that belied his age. To Gloria he was, she declared, 'The sexiest, best looking guy who ever drew breath.' As they travelled in the car and the compliments continued to flow,

Alex was pleased to see that rather than be embarrassed by Gloria, Paddy teased her. He told her she was every young man's fantasy. She always revelled in compliments and she showered him with affectionate kisses. Alex had never really explained his relationship with Gloria to his son other than the facts of their meeting and ongoing friendship. The young man probably realised that their relationship did not end in just friendship, but was too sensitive to his father's feelings to ever question him about it.

Orla and George were thrilled to welcome them all and they enjoyed a wonderfully relaxed evening. Alex was concerned that his mother looked drawn and had lost weight, but she was in ebullient form, thrilled by Paddy's success on the rugby field. Gloria informed them that she was booked in for a season at the Trocadero in London during May. She had already informed those at the rugby club, inviting all and sundry to let her know which night they would be attending so that she could arrange the best table for them. A more sombre note was made by George who worried about the prospects for war. Gloria told of her frightening experience in Berlin. She was convinced the Nazis were evil and Alex was aware that the visit had changed her perspective on life. To his surprise she announced that she had thought of taking out French citizenship, but with war looming she thought Britain was a better bet. 'What about America?' Orla asked, 'Surely you would be safer there?' 'I love Britain' Gloria replied and Alex wondered what the implications of her decision would be on their relationship. These were troubling times. A need for everyone to take stock.

Paddy had never visited his father in his studio. Neither

had he ever been to Soho and this strange square mile of London fascinated him. It was a place that offered a young man a menu of excitement and temptation like no other. He had been the source of much envy at school. Most of his friends' fathers were either land agents, farmers or in business. The popular prints of Windmill girls were banned from dormitories, but several were secreted under beds away from the prying eyes of masters.

A father/son relationship is often difficult particularly if the father has been really successful in whatever field. Alex and Paddy had spent relatively little time together with Paddy having been away at school for long periods. On the surface they got on well together, but Helen's unexpected death had created something of a barrier. Paddy had a sense that his father had never been willing to discuss it openly. He was also quite astute and, although he had loved meeting Gloria, there was something about her relationship with his dad that suggested a more complicated connection than platonic friendship. His welcome at the Portofino rivalled that given to Orla. He had spent many holidays in the care of Maria of whom he had become extremely fond. He was now speaking Italian almost fluently and their lengthy conversations often left Alex observing from the sidelines.

On his first day Alex took him for a drink at the York Minster in Dean Street. The memory remained with my grandfather. It represented the first real acknowledgement that Paddy was now a man. It was a regular watering hole for Alex and was run by a Belgian family. It tended to attract a Bohemian clientele. Importantly they kept a good stock of Irish whiskey. What had astonished Paddy on their short walk to the pub was that everyone appeared to know his father. Every few yards they stopped as shopkeepers, tough looking men with scarred faces and street girls asked to be introduced to the young man. 'It's really just a village' his father explained, 'All the locals know each other. Most are friendly, although you have to be careful.' By the second day of his visit Paddy was casting out alone. Some of the street girls had shown a particular interest in his son, but Alex decided it was no use trying to restrict the lad's movements. He knew Paddy had a girlfriend up in Kettering, but he doubted if that had developed far enough for him to lose his virginity. Alex's first real experience had been in a French brothel and he reasoned that one of the local girls plying their trade in the surrounding streets was probably not a bad place to start. It was best he turned a blind eye.

One of the main reasons for Paddy's visit was to see Gloria perform at the Trocadero. The huge complex run by the Joe Lyons' organisation was on the corner of Coventry Street and Shaftesbury Avenue, a stone's throw from Piccadilly Circus. Built in the last days of the nineteenth century, it stood on the site of what had been London's first tennis court. By the 1920s it was one of the 'must visit' venues in London. It offered glitz and glamour at reasonable prices. It was one of the first places to offer cabaret whilst dining in London. It was also reckoned to have the most extensive wine list, offering well in excess of five hundred vintages.

As Britain limped towards an inevitable war, the Trocadero had lost much of its original gloss and glamour. The chandeliers still shone, but the brightly gilded architraves and frescoes had lost their glow and the carpet lining the grand staircase entrance needed replacing. None of this inhibited Gloria who gave a bravura performance. The audience responded in kind. It was almost as if everyone realised that life as they had known it was shortly to come to an end. They waited for Gloria after the show and walked the short distance to Veeraswamy, which had been the first Indian restaurant to open in London twelve years previously. The food was a revelation to Paddy, but despite the success of an enjoyable evening the conversation was muted. Alex had been depressed but not surprised that Paddy wanted to volunteer for military service. He had been in the combined cadet force at school and fancied joining the Royal Air Force. Alex had already seen too much of war, but knew that his son's call up would come soon enough. It had just been announced that single men between 20 and 22 had to register for six months' military training. Gloria was pensive. War would change everything. Future bookings had dried up other than for minor venues. Her experience in Germany had left her wanting to contribute something to the war effort. One bright spot was that she had just signed a new record deal with Parlophone and the next few weeks were to be devoted to the recording studio. What was Alex planning, they wanted to know. He was too old and too infirmed to be any use in the armed forces and he felt that he was in a rut and becoming really depressed.

There was a strange atmosphere in the weeks and months leading up to the outbreak of war. Following Chamberlain's 'Peace in our time' speech in September 1938, most desperately wanted to believe him. Nine months later the mood was very different. Some continued to ignore the increasing threat, blithely carrying on as normal. Others, particularly those who had experienced the devastating effect of the Great War, were overwhelmed with worry but generally kept their thoughts to themselves. A small but vocal group became nationalistic and xenophobic. German shops and bakeries were attacked. Weiss, the German restaurant in Greek Street, changed its name to the Swiss Cottage, but still their windows were broken.

Even cosmopolitan Soho, where a host of nationalities lived happily side by side, were breaking into aggressive factions. Business had certainly dropped off at the Portofino and Alex sensed a change in Ricardo. Normally ebullient and cheery, he had become withdrawn and moody. None the less it came as a huge surprise when he informed my grandfather that he and Maria were going to return to Italy. It appeared he had been influenced by his landlord who ran a catering supplies business in Carnaby Street. He had a cousin who worked in the Italian Embassy who predicted that with the onset of war London would be bombed into oblivion. In addition Ricardo had become increasingly disenchanted with the way his customers were reacting. He had received a number of threatening letters and he was worried for their safety. Whilst Alex tried to dissuade him, there was more that concerned Ricardo and Maria. It was likely he had been told that Italy might enter the war in which case Italians living in Britain would be detained. Finally, and confirming that their plans were already well advanced, Ricardo informed Alex that they were going to run a restaurant in Abano Terme, next to Maria's brother's butcher shop.

Alex was really saddened by the news and felt sure that his

friends were over reacting. Their change of plans also had implications for his ability to retain his studio, but he was advised to visit the landlord in Carnaby Street who was also planning to return to Italy. With the prospect of war the price of property in London had plummeted, allowing Alex to purchase the freehold on Archer Street, the final paperwork being completed two weeks before the outbreak of war. Before that, with the shutters closed on the Portofino, the three of them settled down for a last meal together. Alex had also done a deal to buy all the produce left. So for the length of the war he was able to enjoy endless meals of pasta. There were also tins of tomatoes, fruit, bottles of olive oil and importantly dozens of bottles of wine. It became obvious that Maria was less keen on the move but believed it her duty to support her husband. Alex did not want to spoil their last meal together but was surprised by Ricardo's support for Mussolini. He emphasised that he was not a Fascist, but a proud nationalist. He had obviously been bruised by casual racist remarks which had increasingly been directed at them over the past months. They drank bottles of Barolo long into the night before staggering off to bed. The following afternoon the removal van arrived and there was an emotional farewell. Waving goodbye outside his newly acquired home, Alex could not help pondering what the future held for them all. Surely they would never truly be enemies. Whatever, their departure marked one of those defining moments in his life. Unusually he felt alone and vulnerable.

There was a sense of unreality as on September 3rd 1939 the nation crowded round their wireless sets. Despite the volume being turned up, Alex sat close to the radio as if he might miss what was being said. Miss much of it he did, unable to focus but aware that war was being declared. Forcing himself to concentrate on Chamberlain's reedy voice, he heard him conclude: 'Now may God bless you and may he defend the right, for it is evil that we will be fighting, brute force, bad faith, injustice, oppression and persecution and against them I am certain we will prevail.' Alex was not so sure It had hardly been an address to inspire confidence. Outside the street was empty. No one to share his thoughts with. With petrol rationing already forecast Alex had decided to sell his car. It really was not needed in London and he would use the train when visiting his parents. With the streets so deserted it seemed a good time to take a spin round London. He had hardly ventured outside Soho for months. He garaged his car in a stable yard in Ham Yard, just off Great Windmill Street. Many of the yards in Soho were still used for stabling horses used by costermongers and those trading in Covent Garden. Four horses looked up expectantly as he entered. They were not disappointed as he gave each of them a carrot. Alex loved these gentle giants, their warmth and the smell of hay. He carefully reversed the car out, turning right on to Shaftesbury Avenue. There were only a few people wandering towards Piccadilly Circus. No crowds had gathered round and there was no sense that this day was any different. He was not really sure what he had been expecting.

As he drove towards Hyde Park Corner there were sandbags piled up outside banks and public buildings, but otherwise all was normal. There was a smattering of people listening to the soap-box orators at Speakers' Corner. Part of

Hyde Park was being dug up for cultivation, which was different. So were the anti-aircraft guns positioned opposite the entrance to the Dorchester Hotel. Two huge barrage balloons hovered above, presumably in an effort to dissuade the Luftwaffe. Was this really the extent of the defences for central London? Alex decided he needed a drink. Driving past Buckingham Palace where a sizeable crowd had gathered, he continued on down the Mall to Trafalgar Square and on to the Strand.

Parking the car opposite the entrance of the Savoy, he wandered into reception and on into the American Bar. The barman greeted him, 'Good morning Mr. Beck. Your usual?' Alex always marvelled at the barman's ability to remember customers, particularly as he had not been to the Savoy for months. Irish whiskey poured, a lonely day stretched out before him. For weeks he had experienced the artists' equivalent of writers' block. He was hoping that the war might stir him from his lethargy. As he brooded, a swishing of expensive fabric and a whiff of perfume engulfed him. A young woman held out her hand, 'Alice' she said. Clambering down from his stool, 'Alex' he replied. 'Alex?' she queried, 'Not Alec?' 'No, Alex' he confirmed. 'Good.' She spoke with a pronounced lisp, 'I will call you Alexander. Bob, mix me one of your wonderful cocktails.' 'M'Lady.' And while the barman busied himself Alex tried to take in this confident young woman who had just entered his life. Again, feeling clumsy, he lit her cigarette positioned on the end of a long black lacquered holder. She was tiny in stature, with straight blonde hair that had been savagely cut, surely not by a hair stylist. She was one of those fascinating women he had noticed over the years who teeter between beauty and ugliness. Her eyes were close to turquoise blue, watery and sparkling. They chatted over their drinks and then this unusual young woman said, 'Come on Alexander, you can take me to lunch.' Turning to the barman she called, 'I don't normally pick men up at bars, do I, Bob?' 'Absolutely not M'Lady.'

Settled in the grill room, Alex realised on reflection that she had managed to extract his life story from him by the time they had eaten their Dover sole. By contrast he had learnt nothing about her except she was off to the country the next day. Presumably the country was cover for some country estate. She was difficult to age. He reckoned late twenties or possibly early thirties. With a bottle of Montrachet tucked away with the fish, they enjoyed a good vintage port with their cheese. Alice was fascinated to hear Alexander was an artist, although she confessed she had never heard of him. His enquiries into her background were graciously deflected, although he did glean that her reference of going off to the country was to enlist, not to visit some country pile. Where she was enlisting she would not say, only confirming that she would be joining up as a ordinary private. Very strange, but Alex loved a mystery, particularly one as attractive as this.

She shocked him again with her directness. 'I suppose normally at this stage you invite a girl back to your studio to see your paintings.' Alex started to protest, but was stopped in his tracks when she said with a naughty grin, 'I have some etchings upstairs you might like to see.' She handed him a bedroom key, assuring him that it was a spare. 'Sorry to be a bore' she continued, 'Do you mind using the service lift, they are a bit funny about chaps roaming the corridors.'

With that she was gone. Alex sat for a moment. Was this some sort of sting? Would an angry husband arrive demanding. Demanding what? Money? What the hell, Alex thought, you only live once and besides Lady Alice fascinated him. No angry husband appeared. Instead they made love. They were not passionate, rather gentle and caring. Sad almost. She was a waif, almost boy like. She was at pains to assure him that this was not how she normally behaved and he believed her. It was as if the outbreak of war was going to change all their lives in so many ways. A need to experiment, throw caution to the wind just as he had in the Great War. Dressed again, they sat for hours talking. He really wanted to see her again, but she continued to be evasive. He felt hurt, for here at last he felt he had met someone who would fill a yawning gap in his life. Stroking his hair, she said it would be crazy to get too involved with all hell about to break out. 'I will remember you though.' Reluctantly he left her, but he returned the following day to the hotel. Neither reception nor the concierge were able to give him any forwarding address or even the full name of Lady Alice. He felt sure the barman would help, but he too only knew her as Lady Alice.

She never did contact him after the war, although he did remember that strange afternoon for many years. It was actually some thirty years later that she did come crashing back into his life. Alex was browsing through the new releases at Hatchards when he saw her face staring down at him from the top rack. It was a book devoted to women who had lived extraordinary lives, operating behind enemy lines in occupied France. It featured six young women, one of whom was Lady Alice Frobisher.

Unable to wait until he got home, Alex settled himself on a settee in the bookshop and started reading. Alice Frobisher had been brought up in France after her parents divorced. A fluent French speaker, she was recruited by British Intelligence, initially employed on clerical duties in London. She was transferred to the Special Operation Executive in 1941. After impressing during her gruelling and dangerous training, she was dropped into occupied France early in 1942. For the next couple of years she was a constant thorn in the side of the Nazis. Captured once, she managed to escape liaising with local fractious groups, organising escape routes for British pilots. She gained a reputation for ruthlessness, even executing two resistance fighters whom she suspected of treachery. Feared by friend and foe alike, she was known as 'the little wasp'. She was finally captured leading a group of airman over the Alps towards Switzerland, a route she had completed several times before, even in the depths of winter. She was executed by firing squad on New Year's Eve in 1943.

Alex felt sick. How strange that he could have been so affected after all those years, but in a life where he tried yet constantly failed to find love, he was close to tears. As often in times of real stress in his life, he longed for peace and to be alone. By the time he reached Dean Street he realised that his leg hurt too much to make it to St. Patrick's, his normal refuge. Instead he veered into the French pub and got hopelessly drunk. It was only when he arrived back at Archer Street that he realised he had left the book on the bar. Collapsing fully clothed onto his bed, he sobbed like a child.

Chapter 18

The waiting game

A lex was woken by the noise of slamming doors and raised voices. Looking down from his bedroom window, it was barely light and a thick frost lined the road. Gloria was issuing orders to a taxi driver as he struggled to heave heavy suitcases from the cab. Alex had not seen or heard from Gloria since before Christmas. Opening the front door, she brushed past leaving Alex to lug her cases in and pay the cabbie. Alex had acted quickly on finalising the purchase of Archer Street. Realising there would soon be a shortage of material and labour he organised plumbers, carpenters and decorators to transform the Portofino in to a comfortable town house. With many of the grand houses decamping to the country, he had been a regular visitor to the auction rooms, picking up superb eighteenth century furniture for a few pounds. Modern sculptures and some of his paintings created an unusual blend of ancient and modern which he was really proud of.

Gloria's arrival marked a unique period of their complex relationship. For the best part of two years they lived the life of a married couple when Gloria was in London. She had grandly declared that London's hotels were turning into little more than refugee camps. Gloria never ceased to amaze Alex. She was a comfortable companion and astonishingly really domesticated. Despite Mrs. Morgan from the dairy in Brewer Street coming in daily to clean, Gloria still dusted and hoovered even though the house looked spotless. She also cooked for them, performing miracles with the produce available since rationing was introduced, confining their pasta suppers to just once a week.

Subsequent historians have written about 'the phoney war' as if nothing had changed, at least on the surface. Certainly there had been warnings of mass bombings and imminent invasion that did not happen, but the character of London had changed. After Dunkirk the streets were thronged with troops from around the world. Australians with their slouch hats standing out amongst their British cousins. There were French too who congregated around the York Minster, sometimes known as the French pub. There were Commonwealth troops from Canada and New Zealand, whilst the Dutch met at 'De Hems' in Macclesfield Street. Add in the rather dashing Polish pilots and London was a volatile brew of nationalities waiting anxiously to see what was going to happen next. In June Italy declared war on Britain. Following instructions from Churchill to 'collar the lot', Italians were rounded up, many of them being sent to a camp on the Isle of Man. Darby Sabini was incensed as his son was serving in the RAF, but no exceptions were made with even the most distinguished Italians being interned.

Whilst Gloria fed off the devotion and applause on stage she preferred to be left alone in her private life, sometimes becoming short tempered and grumpy with autograph hunters. Luckily Soho had any numbers of celebrities living locally and after a few weeks Gloria could walk round unmolested, having been accepted as part of the community. Alex noticed a profound change in her. She was more serious and less flippant. She talked of helping with the war effort, but did not know how. Alex also felt a need to contribute, contacting the authorities to see he if could become an official war artist. He received no response and assumed they had more important matters to attend to. He did join a local group of firewatchers but the skies remained empty. The sense of anti-climax continued with increasingly few people bothering to carry their gasmasks. Alex was contacted by the Air Ministry who informed him that his house in Bushey was to be requisitioned. He was told that it was required as an overflow facility for officers stationed at RAF Stanmore. Subsequently he learnt that it was used at various times as a safe house for defecting Germans, but also as an interrogation centre. Senior enemy officers were housed there, with rooms bugged in the hope of gaining useful information for the Allies.

Monica was still making bookings for Gloria, mostly at London nightspots that remained open. In August Gloria made her first venture into helping the national morale by appearing in a works canteen in an armaments factory in Derby. She became a regular top of the bill in the popular wireless programme *Workers' Playtime*, normally broadcast from factories around the country. Once again, adapting to her audience, she was seeing a huge increase in her popularity with her recording of 'A nightingale sang in Berkeley Square' out selling the version released by Anne Shelton.

Those early months of 1940 were probably the nearest the couple ever achieved in establishing a stable relationship. It really was quite touching, as told to me by my grandfather. On the nights when Gloria was performing he would stay up for her, making her a hot milk and whiskey as a nightcap. When she was not working after supper they would either read or listen to the radio. A tenderness developed between them that never really left, even in many of the traumatic times that were to follow. During this time he also made numerous sketches of her and a number of oil studies. The painting she loved most was the time he accompanied her to a Bristol aircraft factory and he sketched her as she performed, again for an edition of 'Workers Playtime'. He transformed this into a major work, which has either been lost or is lurking somewhere with the owner being unaware of its importance.

Alex made a trip out to Bushey to finalise the handing over of the house to the Air Ministry. First he called at a florist in the High Street and spent ten minutes at Helen's grave. Memories came flooding back, particularly when he returned to the house. It is a feeling we all tend to get if revisiting a place where we have previously lived. In typically military fashion all the contents of the house had been meticulously listed, even down to the last teaspoon. I still have this list in the archive, each room photographed with the list of contents attached. Looking at the photos today it is like viewing a time warp from the 1930s. The kitchen with a single sink and draining board. The wooden units are serviceable rather than stylish and there are two plate racks. The dining room must have been quite cutting edge at the time. The table still looks modern, mounted on curved stainless steel legs, whilst the zebra fabric of the dining chairs certainly makes a statement.

The living room seems rather gloomy by comparison, not helped by the wooden panelling and accentuated by the black and white photo. The settee and armchairs look really comfortable and the couple obviously spent many hours here. Either side of the brick fireplace is a radiogram and a wind-up record player. Helen had been a collector of Parian Ware and assorted Victorian scantily dressed maidens were spread throughout the house. My grandfather spoke to me of the nostalgia his visit prompted, particularly revisiting their bedroom and the room overlooking the garden that had been Helen's studio.

With the paperwork duly signed, the RAF Corporal left Alex to have one final wander round the house. Moving outside he went to the garden shed and pulled out a deckchair. It was a glorious August day with scarcely a cloud in the sky. Perhaps he was being mawkish sitting in exactly the same place as he had found Helen that dreadful afternoon, but rather than cause a wave of sadness he sensed a nearness, as if at any moment she would appear through the French windows bringing a pot of tea and some of the delicious cakes she baked. The garden stretched out before him. The lawn still neatly trimmed and the roses in full bloom. The swallows had not yet left, like the swifts and cuckoos. He could hear a tractor in the distance preparing to take in the harvest. It was an idyllic scene and yet it was already obvious that the war was closing in. For over a month the Luftwaffe had been attacking British ports, but it was still a huge surprise for Alex as several planes came into view bearing German markings. Clambering from his chair they were followed by two Spitfires. They pirouetted across the sky as if being choreographed by an outside force. Walking out onto the street he joined neighbours staring skywards. He joined in the cheering as the Spitfires engaged the *Messerschmitt*s before disappearing over the horizon.

The next few weeks would decide if Britain was going to be invaded. Back in Archer Street Alex brooded on the fact that some of those British pilots he had witnessed were probably not much older than his son who had just started training to become a pilot. Alex knew that many failed to complete the strenuous course. He felt guilty thinking it, but he hoped with all of his heart that Paddy was one of them as the life expectancy of these brave young men was only a matter of a few weeks. The mood at supper that night was muted. Both Gloria and Alex understood that the phoney war was over and they were not alone in fearing for the future.

Chapter 19

Feeling the heat

Each night as darkness fell Alex slowly climbed the iron fire escape stairs of the Windmill Theatre. From its flat roof he had a panoramic view of London, stretching as far as the eye could see. The aerial Battle of Britain merged with the increased offensive by the Luftwaffe, which became known as 'the blitz'. For over fifty consecutive nights London was bombarded from above. Alex had still not heard any news about his request to become an official war artist and was further frustrated when he was rejected as a volunteer ambulance driver. He was unable to fit into the driving seat because of his extended leg. Although for much of his fire watch duties he was just an observer of the carnage being heaped on London, he knew that eventually he would be called into action and he was right. Initially he looked helplessly to the east as the Docks became the first target and overall it was the East-Enders who soon bore the brunt of the destruction with terraced houses close to the Docks consumed in a frightening fire storm. Just days after the initial attacks, the West End sustained its first major damage when Oxford Street was hit. It was astonishing to see the gutted John Lewis store still trading the following day from departments open to the elements, as customers were served through gaping holes where windows had been.

Alex stood guard with his buckets of sand and water, watching flares being dropped to be followed by the drone of the bombers as they dropped their lethal loads. At any other time the view might have been thought beautiful. Dramatic certainly. Almost like Guy Fawkes night, only to be followed by ominous thuds as explosions ripped through buildings, many of them historic landmarks. It was March in 1941 before he was actively involved. He remembered pouring himself a cup of tea from his thermos when he was rocked back from an explosion very nearby. Cursing his injured leg he descended the staircase as fast as he could to be confronted with a horrific scene. Prone bodies were lying in the street. A woman with her leg ripped open was shrieking in pain. This unnerved those first on the scene and there was a degree of panic. Alex took command, organising blankets to be brought from the theatre for those still alive. Ambulances arrived within ten minutes taking the injured away, leaving the onlookers to cover the twelve dead, one of whom was a young electrician who worked at the theatre. He was to be their only fatality during the conflict, whilst bombs and incendiaries continued to pepper the area.

This was a prelude to one of the worst nights of Alex's life a couple of weeks later. One where he was convinced that Gloria had been killed. Monica had secured a booking for her at the fashionable night club, the *Café* de Paris on Coventry Street. Unusually she was sharing top billing with another black entertainer 'Snakehips Johnson'. He was doubling up on another booking at the Embassy Club, creating an opportunity for Gloria. She had appeared at the Café de Paris five years previously and had been introduced to the Prince of Wales who regularly attended the night spot.

Considered to be the safest place in town, it was situated below ground in a two tiered basement. Approached through double glass doors, the decor represented an exact replica of the Palm Court on the doomed liner the Lusitania. Entering 'the bridge' there was a central lobby which gave a dramatic view of the whole restaurant. Twin staircases, each of twenty one steps, swept down to the dance floor. Diners instinctively looked to view every newcomer, adding to the air of theatre. Before the war formal dress was required, but now lounge suits were grudgingly allowed, although many attending that night were wearing uniform. The explosion as the bomb hit was heard for miles around. Alex knew instinctively from his viewpoint on the roof that it was uncomfortably close to where Gloria was performing. Cursing his lack of agility, he stumbled down the slippery staircase. All around the sky was lit with flares that had been dropped. Some had fallen on adjoining buildings and a breeze was fanning the flames. The cafe often used by the Windmill girls was ablaze, but as Alex hobbled along towards Shaftesbury Avenue he heard cries for help coming from Ham Yard where he had garaged his car.

There were frightened snorts and neighs from the horses stabled there. As he entered the yard he was met by a girl he recognised from the Windmill. She was struggling with a horse, trying to attach a head collar. Another girl appeared leading two horses who just had ropes round their necks. The roof to the stables was ablaze and the remaining horse was bucking and rearing in fright. With rafters falling around him Alex plunged, grabbing the horse by its mane. Unable to restrain it, the horse rushed out onto the street galloping up past the theatre. Alex took hold of two of the prancing horses whilst one of the girls ran off in an attempt to catch the traumatised grey who had so nearly been killed. Eventually he was brought back and amidst the blazing buildings they all saw the funny side as they stared at each other with blackened faces. Thanking Alex, the girls went off with the horses, calmer now, singing at the top of their voices. Alex marvelled at the undimmed exuberance of youth as he made his way with some trepidation towards the Café de Paris.

His progress towards Coventry Street was slow and painful. In the confusion at the stable he had dropped his walking stick and it had been too dangerous for him to attempt to retrieve it. As he approached the cafe, ambulances and fire engines were already arriving. The safest basement in London had been devastated by a freak bomb which had descended straight down the ventilator shaft before exploding on the dance floor. The odds on this happening must have been millions to one.

In alarm Alex pushed his way downstairs to be met for the second time in a matter of days by a scene of death and devastation. Much was made later of the fact that 'Snakehips Johnson' lay on the floor as if asleep without a scratch on him. This was not true of others. Body parts had found their way onto the shattered piano. The band's instruments lay twisted, strewn across the dance floor. With smoke clouding the room Alex rushed as fast as he could, identifying that blood strewn bodies were not those of Gloria. Looking up he glimpsed something so shocking that it was seared in his mind, and eventually formed the second of his iconic war paintings that can still be found in the Imperial War Museum. As he crunched across the broken glass and debris, Alex saw a man wearing a helmet, removing rings from a corpse spread-eagled like a rag doll but with one leg missing. Alex made a lunge for the creature but he squirmed out of Alex's grasp. 'The Rat' completed later that year was the work that he remained most proud of. The image, so fixed in his mind, led to the eventual arrest of the culprit. He was part of a gang who roamed the streets in a mocked up ambulance. It was often first on the scene, keeping the public back before disappearing with their haul before the authorities arrived.

His eyes streaming from smoke, Alex stumbled out into the cold night air to be greeted by a familiar voice shouting above the mayhem. ;Alex, what are you doing here?; Running over, he crushed her in his arms, realising just how much he loved her. They stayed until all the injured and the bodies had been taken away. Slowly arm in arm they made their way home. Gloria had been saved as she was in her dressing room when the bomb exploded. Blown over, her only injury was a nasty bump on her forehead which over the next few days developed into two spectacular black eyes. Back home they allowed themselves the luxury of drinking a bottle of red wine. It was a night that neither of them would ever forget and one that for a time changed the course of Gloria's life and one that was about to propel Alex to international acclaim.

Alex was half expecting Gloria to decamp to one of London's swanky hotels after the trauma at the Café de Paris. As ever her reaction surprised him. Rather than be intimidated she declared she was bored entertaining the wealthy and influential. It was ordinary people who were suffering and she intended reaching out to them. She persuaded Alex to go with her to Piccadilly tube station. People had been sheltering on the platforms of tube stations since the bombing started. None the less they were astonished to find an international star performing for them on the stationary escalator.

She sang her latest recordings before ending with a sing-song of Cockney tunes. News of her concerts swept through London as she alternated between Leicester Square and Piccadilly stations, before the police banned her from performing any more because of safety considerations. Her popularity soared, with sales of her records and sheet music surging. With the wind of popularity in her sails and determined to serve a still wider audience, she next went to a rather grand building in Upper Grosvenor Street, the home of the Entertainments National Service Association (ENSA). This had been formed in 1939 to organise entertainment for serving troops. A rather startled Major in charge of the office took her details and advised that they would be back in contact. So started a four year association with entertaining troops around the world, although her initial engagements were visiting camps throughout Britain where she cut her teeth performing for rowdy soldiers in Catterick, Oswestry and Rhyl. What really appealed to her was her officer status. She loved uniforms.

So ended a settled and domesticated part of their relationship, although Gloria continued to stay in Archer Street between engagements. The visits to underground stations also led to the creation of another important work by my grandfather. He produced a major painting of the crowds sleeping on the platform at Leicester Square. Although it did not have the instant impact of 'The Rat' it was an important work which was exhibited at the Royal Academy in 1942.

Whilst Gloria was away entertaining troops in Aldershot, Paddy came to stay at Archer Street on a forty-eight hour leave. With the imminent threat from the Luftwaffe reduced, the rush to get pilots fully trained was slightly relaxed. Previously some young men had seen active service with as little as six months' training. This had now been extended to about a year. Paddy had passed the induction process, progressing to a elementary training school. Here they learnt how to fly, with Paddy having his first solo spin in a Tiger Moth. He showed a real aptitude for the practical side, but struggled with the mathematics required. On return from his leave he was to join up at an advanced training school where he would be introduced to more powerful aircraft and simulated flying. Alex saw very little of the young man that weekend. He had not realised that Paddy had been seeing a young Windmill girl before joining up. He was not introduced to her, although he had seen them walking hand in hand leaving the theatre. She was quite tall, dark haired and willowy, with the poise of a professional dancer. With Paddy back at camp, life returned to its normal pattern, less stressful now with far fewer raids. Alex threw himself into his work, his enthusiasm rekindled. Gloria joined him over Christmas. He managed to get a chicken in Berwick Street market and their Christmas lunch was finished off with the luxury of tinned pineapple. It was early in the new year that Alex received a phone call from Paddy informing him that his girlfriend was pregnant. With his easy access to the theatre Alex went and introduced himself to the young woman and invited her to meet him back at the house. Angela Perks was beautiful and very worried and tearful. She was too frightened to tell her parents and was convinced her father would kill her. Calming her down Alex suggested in Paddy's absence the alternatives available, none of which were straight forward. She insisted she loved Paddy but they hardly knew each other. Paddy was prepared to marry her, but Alex felt that was a matter of duty rather than love. His son was due to pass out within weeks before being posted, but had no idea where. Whilst not noticeable to most, the piercing eye of Vivian Van Damm had already made remarks about the girl's girth. It was all a bit of a mess. After much discussion Alex agreed to speak to her parents. He also told her he would speak to his mother, as some sort of provision would have to be made for looking after the baby, but Angela was not about to decamp to some grand home up north. She was a Londoner and proud of it.

The following day Alex made a trip over the Thames to a modest semi-detached bungalow in Penge. It was a difficult meeting with Angela's parents. As she had feared her father was incensed, accusing Paddy of being irresponsible and a disgrace. He also railed against his wife who had encouraged their daughter to join the Windmill. Alex could understand the father's anger, the girl was obviously the apple of his eye. Mrs. Perks was altogether more rational, saying that the child's welfare was the prime concern. They agreed that the couple should be married and that Angela should go back and live with her parents. Alex was not so sure. Orla had suggested that the family should buy the couple a small house so that they could be independent, but Alex did not mention it at the time. At home in Archer Street he mused on the problem. It was one that was being played out all over the country. He liked Angela. She was bright and intelligent, although it was no use ignoring the fact that the couple came from different sides of the tracks. In England class or perceived class differences were seldom far below the surface. Gloria could just not understand this about the British and Alex agreed with her. Whilst not the best start for any young couple, there was no reason why an initial attraction should not develop into a lasting love.

Paddy completed his advanced service flying training in early February and was proud to be awarded his wings, signifying he was now a fully fledged pilot. He was assigned to 92 Squadron who were due to depart for Egypt on his return from a week's leave. This was a hectic period into which were squeezed a wedding and a honeymoon. The wedding day passed off far better than Alex had feared. His parents travelled down from the Midlands and Angela's father was persuaded to come along with two aunts and uncles. Gloria was not about to be left out of the celebrations, distributing signed photographs of herself to the Perks family, despite none of them requesting one. The marriage service was simple with readings from Alex and Angela's uncle Arthur. The bride looked stunning in a classic cream satin dress. Alex was very worried by his mother's appearance, but Orla was in great form determined to enjoy the day.

After the service they walked round the corner to Kettner's in Romilly Street. Alex knew the head waiter there and managed to prise a few bottles of champagne from him for them to be able to toast the happy couple. And happy they both looked. Paddy certainly cut a dash in his newly acquired uniform, whilst his bride had a willowy natural grace. Alex could well understand his son falling for this girl, but wished the circumstances were different. Vivian Van Damm joined them at Kettner's. Renowned for getting extremely grumpy with any of his girls who became pregnant, he was outwardly at least all charm and congratulations. Gradually the party broke up and they waved the couple off in a borrowed car full of petrol with spare cans in the boot. Whilst petrol was rationed you could get anything if you knew who to approach, particularly in Soho. Angela and Paddy spent their honeymoon at a small hotel in Sussex at Cooden Beach. They spent much of the time walking along the beach which had unfortunately been festooned with barbed wire, whilst above them were concrete bunkers with guns pointing seaward in preparation for a still possible invasion.

I never discovered that Paddy was my father until I was a teenager and it was only then that my mother began to talk about him. It was Alex, my grandfather, who was eventually able to describe him in detail about his childhood, his easy going character and unusual ability at sports, a small percentage of which I hope I inherited. It must have been desperately hard for a young couple to be parted after such a short but intense relationship. Later that month Paddy set sail for the long and uncomfortable voyage to Egypt. 92 Squadron had won an enviable reputation, having seen action over Dunkirk and claimed record numbers of enemy aircraft in the Battle of Britain. For a newly qualified pilot it set a formidable precedent, but one he was determined to emulate as the troop ship made its snail like progress, eventually meeting up with Air Headquarters in the Western Desert.

Within a month of the wedding Alex received a call from his father urging him to come home as Orla's condition had suddenly worsened. Unable to hire a car, it proved difficult to get a train as many were reserved for troop movements. He arrived in the early hours and was relieved to learn that his mother was still alive. 'I think she has waited for you', a nurse who was attending her informed him. 'Hello mum' he said quietly. At first he thought she had not heard him, but slowly without opening her eyes she took his hand. It was barely warm but he felt a slight increase in pressure. He sat by her bed listening to her breathing that came irregularly. Several times he thought she had gone only for her to draw in a breath once more. Although George was devastated by her decline he just could not bear to hear her as she fought for breath. Instead he stationed himself on a chair behind the door. Alex assured him this was not cowardly, he had seen so many different reactions to death in the trenches. There was no right way, it was something that everyone confronted differently. Alex drowsed off only to be woken by a rattle of breath, and the nurse had assured him that Orla was in no pain. At about three in the morning his mother suddenly sat bolt upright in bed and said quite clearly, 'Bloody hell!' This made Alex smile. How in character, he thought. He drowsed off again, waking with a start. This time there was not a sound. He went over to her. Now there were no tortured gasps. She was quiet at peace. He went and woke George. In death she had reclaimed much of her beauty. Standing by her bed they hugged each other with the intensity of lovers.

Chapter 20

The dark side

The bond between mother and son is invariably deep but complex. Orla remained an enigma. Remote when he was a child, tantalisingly out of reach emotionally. Yet she would sit with him spinning these strange stories of fantasy and bygone times. Then quite suddenly she would be galvanised, becoming extrovert and funny. Looking back she was often almost ethereal and yet he loved her so and longed for her approval that seldom came. Latterly their relationship had changed and they had become much closer. Viewing her now from an adult's standpoint, he sensed that for much of her life she had been unhappy. Perhaps unfulfilled would be a better description. He had never noticed her heavy drinking when he was young, but it may have accounted for her vagueness as if she inhabited some parallel universe. He also realised that many of these traits had emerged in his own personality. A sense of not belonging which had increased since Helen's death. Of dissatisfaction despite his growing reputation and success. He was lonely now that Gloria was seldom in London, and although he loved her he knew that she would never bring him a sense of stability he needed.

His mother's funeral was a sad affair. The church was packed and Alex gave the eulogy. Although he had worked hard to convey his mother's unique character he felt that he had not done her justice. Marcus, to his credit had joined up and was on leave from serving in the army with R.E.M.E, and lightened the mood with a witty yet moving address. Poor George looked physically smaller. It was as if the air from his lungs had been sucked out. Stretton House had been requisitioned by the army and he was about to move into an Edwardian town house in Kettering. Although his business was booming it was now largely being run by professional managers appointed by the board. He was talking of selling but both sons advised him to hang on until the war was over.

Back in Archer Street Alex had little time to reflect on his mother's death. The house was in turmoil as Gloria prepared to leave for her first foreign posting with E.N.S.A. She had become increasingly pretentious, informing him she was unable to tell him where she was bound due to security issues. All she would say was that wherever she was going it was hot. In her new guise she really did see herself as 'a woman of the people', increasingly being referred to as 'the forces' girlfriend'.

A staff car came to collect her. Proudly dressed in khaki she blew him a kiss. Closing the door he felt a profound loneliness descend, one he always felt on first parting from her. He was also depressed by what he felt was a distinct change in the atmosphere in Soho. What had largely been a harmonious neighbourhood now appeared tense and on edge, perhaps caused in part by the incarceration of those nationalities deemed to be aliens by the government. They had been increasingly replaced by deserters and small time crooks avoiding call-up. The arrival of the first American forces was also adding to the mix. There was a resentment from British troops as these newcomers had money to burn and were attracting legions of British girls who had also descended on the area. Rainbow Corner on Shaftesbury Avenue was the Red Cross club for GIs and it continued to be a magnet for young women throughout the war.

Tension was raised further with a series of gruesome murders taking place in the surrounding streets. A prostitute was found strangled in a ground level air raid shelter, to be followed the next day by another street worker being killed. She had also been strangled but then savagely mutilated. She had been discovered in her flat on Wardour Street which was notorious with lines of girls lurking in doorways. For a few days news of the war was banished to the inner pages as lurid headlines shrieked of a new ripper on the loose. Girls whose pitch was near to Alex's house started confiding in him. They were really scared, but he found it interesting talking to them, inviting four of them to join him in Archer Street for coffee. He had considered creating a latter day series of Hogarth's *The Harlot's Progress* but had never found the time to develop the idea. Following his chats with the girls he realised that they required skills other than just attracting punters. It was important for them to be able to spot weirdos who posed dangers. It was a skill they developed, but there was also a kind of camaraderie between them when they warned each other of worrying men trawling the area.

The murders continued in a series of gruesome discoveries. Three more girls strangled and butchered. The girls retreated, seriously concerned now. Only those desperate for money ventured out. The police could only suggest that the killer was left-handed, not something the street girls would normally take much notice of. Then the killer's luck began to unravel. It appeared he was totally out of control, taking crazy risks. A young prostitute was approached by a serviceman who invited her for a drink at the Trocadero. On leaving he grabbed her and dragged her into a side alley. She fought like an alley cat and her screams caused him to run away. The following day another girl had an even luckier escape. Her punter had managed to get a ligature round her neck when luckily there was a power cut. In the confusion the assailant panicked, running off and leaving his service belt behind. The sadistic rampage was ended. Gordon Cummins, a 29 year old officer cadet was arrested. It did not take the jury at the Old Bailey long to find him guilty and he was hanged at Wandsworth jail in June 1942.

Later that month I was born. There is a photograph of my mother holding me, presumably in the nursing home. Even so soon after the birth she managed to look glamorous. My relationship with her was far less complicated than Alex's had been with Orla. For as long as I can remember I adored her. She was different from my friends' mums. She was cheeky, funny and often outrageous. She had the graceful look of an aristocrat and often the mouth of a fisherwoman, but overall she was an irresistible life force, bolshy yet always optimistic. She never lost her Cockney accent, if anything accentuating it particularly when debunking pretentiousness. Later when attending Oundle school she became something of a legend when kissing the rather stuffy headmaster on their first meeting. Rather than offend it disarmed him. Some frumpy and lumpy mums were upset by this dreadfully common woman, an opinion not usually endorsed by their husbands.

Following the birth Alex was determined to honour his promise of buying Angela and Paddy a house. He was trying to balance the need for his grandson to have somewhere decent to live without being over generous. He did realise it was important for the young couple to make their own way in life, but these were strange times and he had money sitting in the bank. Angela wanted to live in London but not too near to her parents. Her grandparents lived in Islington and it was an area she knew well. She chose a terraced house in Colebrooke Row. Now extremely fashionable, back in 1942 Alex was able to acquire the house built in the eighteenth century for just a few hundred pounds. There is a letter in the archive from Paddy thanking his father and promising to pay the purchase price back when he was demobbed. There are also a couple of letters from Paddy to my mother. These are not those written by a lovelorn husband torn away from his wife by war. They are rather awkward, written by someone either unable or unwilling to express his undying love. There is also a photograph of him standing in front of a Spitfire as the sun burns down on some desert airfield.

Alex only ever loved three women, apart from his mother. His love for Helen was obviously deep and long lasting, but he continued to think that it was never completely reciprocated. His relationship with Gloria was chaotic, veering between extremes and yet enduring. She fascinated, intrigued frustrated and irritated. She was a presence that came into his life at a time that she dictated, again leaving him emotionally unfulfilled. Then there was my mother. What of Angela? I witnessed a growing and profound love between them. But what kind of love? Certainly the most complicated.

Chapter 21

A matter of life and death

Ever since her marriage to Paddy, Angela had addressed Alex as dad which he really did not like. Despite gentle promptings requesting that she call him Alex, she persisted. Answering the phone that November morning he failed to register the tension in her voice. 'Dad!' 'Hello my dear' he replied. 'Dad...' she hesitated, 'Dad, I have some terrible news' she continued, but he put the phone down before she had finished telling him about Paddy's death. Although in shock later he was ashamed at his reaction, having been more concerned with his own feelings rather than than those of his daughter-in-law. Naively he had thought that being posted away from Europe, Paddy would be in less danger.

Alex remembered he had just finished listening to the weather forecast when Angela phoned, and rain was predicted to fall all morning. In a daze he pulled on his raincoat and stepped outside. He needed air. Suddenly the house seemed like a prison. Soho also was claustrophobic. He started walking without knowing where he was heading. He felt sick. Waves of nausea had him retching into a rubbish bin. Passers-by assumed he was getting rid of the previous night's excess. His tongue was coated and his leg was already beginning to ache. He quickened his step, welcoming the additional pain as if he needed to suffer some penance for his son's death. Memories of Paddy refused to be banished from his thoughts. The first landmark he remembered that morning was passing Euston station. The streets were packed with servicemen. He saw a couple of RAF pilots with their wings proudly displayed. He felt an urge to tell them of his loss but he restrained himself, hobbling now along the Euston Road towards St. Pancras. Was it a sub-conscious reaction that was heading him towards Islington? With the rain falling his walk had slowed to a shuffle and the pain in his knee shot down to his ankle. He struggled on uphill along Pentonville Road, pausing as the pain took his breath away. Wet and bedraggled, he stood outside Angela's house in Colebrooke Row. Although the distance he had walked was barely four miles, it had taken him almost three hours.

Neither spoke when she opened the door, they just embraced as if their own lives depended upon it. She helped him out of his sodden raincoat and went and made a cup of tea. The house was sparsely furnished and the settee Alex perched on needed re-springing. Normally Alex hated sugar in tea but today it was comforting. He started to apologise for his appalling behaviour by cutting her off on the telephone. She interrupted him 'Oh dad, don't be silly!' 'For Christ's sake stop calling me dad, my name is Alex!' He looked so furious that despite herself she started laughing. 'Right, Alex it will be.' Then her laughter turned to tears, her whole body was racked and shaking. Alex was unsure how to react but rising he held her, pleased that she had broken down before him as he resolved to stay strong, at least in company. Angela was still just nineteen and Alex, in his early forties, was old enough to be her father, but whilst wanting to be a mentor for her he had no wish to become a father figure. To ease the tension Angela suggested they went to have a look at the one thing that bound them together at that time – me. Apparently I slept soundly unaware of the trauma they were experiencing.

Downstairs again Angela told my grandfather all she had learnt about Paddy's death. She did not spare him any of the more distressing details. Paddy had arrived in Egypt in April to join Air Headquarters in the Western Desert. Typically there were no planes to fly. For four months the crews sweated and waited before taking some leave in Cairo. The Spitfires finally arrived in August and the squadron was transferred to RAF Heliopolis, just in time to take part in the final throws of the battle of El Alamein.

For months the battle had raged with first the Italians being defeated, until the Germans went on the offensive. Desert war was uniquely difficult as lack of water supplies or petrol forced retreats. Finally the British were gaining control as Paddy's squadron provided air cover for the advancing troops. Bizarrely, although Paddy's plane was hit, he was able to make a tidy crash landing with his aircraft, initially not appearing to be badly damaged. Unfortunately the impact of the crash made it impossible for him to release the cockpit which was made of toughened plexiglass. The fire from the engine had started slowly and seeing he was in trouble some lads jumped from their tank armed with hammers to release him. Eventually they managed to haul him out, getting burnt themselves from their frantic efforts. Paddy was conscious and was able to thank them whilst an ambulance came to collect him. At the field hospital his burns did not appear to be life threatening, but his condition worsened and he was transferred to the general hospital in Alexandria where he died three days later.

By now their initial shock was over to be replaced by the recognition that neither of their lives was ever going to be the same again. Alex was becoming rather irritated by Angela's reaction. The problem was that she was probably just too honest. She spoke of not really even knowing Paddy. She had worked out that they had only spent less than a couple of weeks in each other's company. This was not what Alex needed to hear at that time. He thought she was inconsiderate to his feelings, just as much as he had been to hers earlier in the day. She walked with my grandfather to the taxi rank on Islington Green, wheeling a large cumbersome pram whilst I slept soundly, unaware of all the drama.

Alex pecked my mother on the cheek before clambering into the cab. Both had a sense of disappointment at the other's reaction to the tragedy. As the cab pulled up outside Archer Street the air raid siren wailed. One of the local street girls gave him a friendly wave. Inside he sat at the kitchen table with a bottle of whiskey. It was in the early hours before he fell fully clothed onto his bed. It had been one of the worst days of his life. First the loss of his mother and now his son. He was consumed with grief. The following day he visited the prostitute who had waved at him. With the business done she really did not have time to listen to his problems or sympathise. He felt helpless in his sorrow. He wanted to shout and rage at the unfairness of it all. Instead he returned to the whiskey bottle.

Reg Duggan was an armourer serving in 462 Squadron in

Libya. Following the second battle of El Alamein thousands of Italians had been captured and the Germans were in retreat, having been defeated in the battle for Tripoli. Reg was ordered to fly in a Halifax to Cairo to pick up much needed spares. As General Montgomery had decided to hold a victory parade in Tripoli, Reg reckoned it would be a good idea to pick up some booze to help lubricate the celebrations. He had managed to arrange for crates of beer and cases of Muscat de Samos wine to be collected. What he had not realised was that he was also to pick up a small E.N.S.A concert party. This was due to be Gloria's last appearance before returning home. She was being supported by four girls who sang and acted as a backing group. Reg was a great fan of Gloria and she was very gracious as she handed him a signed photograph of her appearing in Paris. She had spent hours signing hundreds of photos, guessing correctly that those who survived would be fans for life. Reg was obviously very persuasive on the long noisy flight back to Libya as Gloria agreed to put on a special show for the squadron that night. A makeshift stage was erected, microphones magicked from thin air, a battered piano transported in from Tripoli and they were ready to go. To raucous applause and constant wolf whistles, Gloria and the girls managed to get the roughly eight hundred men singing and dancing along with them. Not waiting for the victory parade, the beer and wine flowed.

As always after a performance Gloria found it difficult to sleep. She opened the entrance flap to her tent staring up at the desert sky. How strange it was from her normal five star accommodation, but wonderfully memorable. She had performed dozens of concerts in Egypt but now after Tripoli it was time to go home. She had received a gloomy letter from Monica urging her to return to paid performances as she reckoned Gloria's finances were beginning to look a little stretched.

Next morning after a breakfast of corned beef covered in sand and a hot liquid pretending to be coffee, they were on their way into Tripoli in an extended Land Rover. It did not take long for the effects of recent battles to appear. Burnt out tanks, abandoned staff cars and damaged and discarded weapons were strewn on the roadside. As they entered the outskirts of the town one of the girls screamed for the driver to stop. Rushing across the road she returned with a bundle. Wrapped in a shawl was a baby no more than a few days old. There was a label attached to its arm. Written in Arabic and English was the name Maya. The baby had obviously been abandoned and as they continued their way towards headquarters the girls fussed and cooed at the little tot, who was hardly old enough to open her eyes. Gloria's voice cut through the excited jabber of conversation. 'I will adopt her' she proclaimed. Her maternal instinct moved into overdrive. Having shown a criminal neglect of her own son she was now set on acquiring a daughter, and when Gloria decided on a course of action it was almost impossible to distract her.

Her first action was to take the baby to the general hospital to get her checked out. She was apparently rather dehydrated and under weight, but otherwise totally healthy. An Indian attendant at the hospital told her that Maya meant 'magical'. 'Magical Maya', she mused, 'just perfect.' With two concerts completed her task now was to get permission to take the baby back to Cairo. She started with the top brass, even trying to get an appointment with General Montgomery. Instead she was passed to a succession of officers, each having a slightly lower rank. Despite her fame they were all far too busy with battle plans to help. Eventually she ended up with a padre, Captain Hugh Thackery. To her delight he thought it would be an excellent idea for Gloria to adopt the poor little thing. He signed a docket authorising her to take the baby to Cairo, although he really did not have the authority, but who cared in the heat of battle. Cairo would doubtless be a more difficult hurdle to clear.

Back in Cairo Gloria started the same process of trying to persuade senior officers of the acceptability of her adopting Maya. These though were not fighting men. They were basically administrators who spent a lifetime 'going by the book'. They too referred her to more junior colleagues who stalled and prevaricated. She was beginning to despair until she met a war correspondent for the Daily Express. He could sense a scoop. What a headline, 'Gloria saves abandoned baby from war zone.' Mark Lawrence might be an old hack but he knew a good story when he saw one. He was also canny. He had already telegrammed his editor for help with the top brass. It would be a good news story that the British public were crying out for. He also understood that Gloria was desperate for his help and might be prepared to give something in return. Mark Lawrence was not an attractive man, either in looks or character. Short and wiry with thinning ginger hair, Cairo had been an eye-opener for him. For a few shillings he had enjoyed more sex in a month than he had managed in his lifetime. Live shows, some so disgusting that it even turned his stomach. All those girls had been prostitutes, but could he really get the famous Gloria Bird to come across? He need not have worried, Gloria had never been squeamish about trading her body for a favour. Within days a call from Lord Beaverbrook, the proprietor of the Daily Express, had unlocked all the bureaucratic doors and Gloria was on a flight to Britain with her newly acquired daughter.

Monica received a telegram from Cairo in which Gloria requested that Monica should find a house to rent close to London, but not in the centre. The house was to be suitable for a mother and baby and should have easy access to open spaces. Richmond was suggested. Monica had ceased to be surprised by any requests from Gloria. She was also instructed to appoint a children's nurse. Intrigued, but determined not to give Gloria the satisfaction of asking why as even she could not have conceived and given birth in the months she had been away, Monica's response was concise. 'Will do' she replied and she did. Nothing was available in Richmond but she did secure a long lease on Rose Bank Cottage, a substantial house in Hampstead with easy access to the heath. She also interviewed a raft of children's nurses before settling on a rather moon-faced young woman in her early twenties. Muriel Frampton was to become a long term influence in Maya's life. As Gloria's maternal instinct waned as swiftly as it had appeared, Muriel went from nurse to nanny to lifelong friend and mentor.

When Gloria did finally arrive at her new house with the baby she was justifiably exhausted after her long and uncomfortable journey. Having inspected the beautiful converted nursery that had been created, she took to her bed for forty eight hours. Even then she did not thank Monica for her Herculean efforts in arranging the house and a resident nurse. Rose Bank cottage had been vacated by an international banker who had taken his family to the safety of New York for the duration of the war. Gloria showed little interest in the baby whilst conceding that she was cute. This did not stop her from complaining when the baby cried. She did try feeding Maya once but quickly delegated the task to Muriel. Her focus was now concentrated on getting some money into her bank account. She had done her bit for the war effort. Following all the publicity, the sales of her record of *Begin the beguine* had out-sold all her previous recordings. Monica had been busy and organised a nationwide tour starting at the Hippodrome in Brighton. Before she set off on her travels Gloria rang Alex and invited him over to Hampstead. She had written a letter of condolence to Alex on hearing of Paddy's death. She was never comfortable with illness and bereavement and she hoped that Alex would not dwell on it when they met. She was shocked by his appearance, his complexion was grey and he had lost weight.

He showed more interest in Maya than Gloria thought necessary, instantly irritated that he had not asked about her Libyan adventures. Instead he regaled her with news of Angela's baby and how young Rex had given him hope for the future. She was bored with baby talk and although Alex was still recovering from his walk uphill from Hampstead underground station, she insisted that they go and explore the heath. Alex loved the house and the opportunity to breathe in some fresh air. He was finding himself constrained by the narrow streets of Soho, and the increasingly wild atmosphere prompted largely by the influx of GIs on the hunt for a good time. They agreed that Alex should go and stay with Gloria for a week before she left for her tour. This probably marked a subtle change in their relationship. Although they continued to see each other for years to come it was seldom for more than a few days. My grandfather also suggested that it was a time of lessening physical involvement. This was probably caused in part by an ongoing succession of lovers she acquired. This, he insisted, was not because of an inflated sexual appetite, but rather a desperate need for assurance that she was still desirable. She had never been discreet and her romances filled the gossip columns.

In Leslie Hutchinson, the singer 'Hutch', she found a kindred spirit. A West Indian, he had acquired the manner and speech of an English toff. He had a string of lovers including, supposedly, Edwina Mountbatten. His affair with Gloria was second only in length to that of Alex, but it seems likely that her constant involvement with other men rather cooled my grandfather's ardour. Whilst sexually less involved, their long term commitment to each other never wavered. His week in Hampstead did help restore his spirits, but his despair at losing his son felt as raw as ever. The tide of war was gradually turning, at least giving some hope for the future. He made regular visits to Islington to visit his grandson, but in honesty he realised that it was Angela who was restoring his will not only to live, but to enjoy life.

He consciously tried to suppress his attraction to his daughter-in-law. He viewed his thoughts as being almost incestuous. He tried not visiting her, but then she would arrive on his doorstep. She was an irrepressive force of nature, teasing and cajoling him back to a sense of normality. He did try to encourage her to go out and meet people of her own age, but she assured him that she was quite happy as she was, thank you. Of course much later my mother confided in me that even at that early stage she was really attracted to Alex. He was so kind, good company and she thought extremely good looking. She was also fully aware that a romance with one's husband's father, whilst not unheard of, would be generally frowned upon. For the time being they carried on going to the park or shopping together, letting neighbours draw their own conclusions. This was not about the passion and unique connection felt for Gloria. Different also from his complex marriage to Helen. This was to be a slow burner, which I as a child was witness to and one that was the most influential in my life.

Touring now became central to Gloria's life. Living out of a suitcase and staying in a succession of provincial hotels. It was in Liverpool appearing at the Adelphi that she met Hutch and a mutual bond was formed. She galvanised audiences across the country, getting wonderful reviews for her show at the Grand Theatre in Swansea. She did return to Hampstead every few weeks, becoming more attached to Maya as she grew. She had declared to the nurse that she thought babies were disgusting. From Bristol to Blackpool her work rate was phenomenal, made possible by her abstinence from drugs. It was only in Scotland that her reception was rather muted and so, true to type, for years she refused to appear north of the border. With her bank balance by now fully restored and with rumours of an allied landing in Europe, Gloria was already asking Monica to make plans for her continental return, but as ever Gloria was getting ahead of herself.

Chapter 22
Shifting sands

The news was encouraging. The tide of war had surely turned. The Allies were preparing to invade Europe, but there was an ominous twist in the tail. A new form of warfare was about to be unleashed. Unmanned rockets known as 'doodlebugs' or 'buzz bombs' were launched in their thousands, most targeting London. It brought even greater fear than experienced at the height of the blitz. There was something disturbing about an unmanned assault. Pedestrians looked nervously skywards. Eerie black rockets were spotted flying above the roof tops. It was important to listen as well as look for trouble. When the engine cut out it was time to dive for cover. German radio warned that even more powerful rockets were now in production. There was a genuine fear that victory was going to be wrestled away. Anti-aircraft guns had little effect in deflecting these new invaders and RAF fighters were again deployed to defend the capital. Over 5,000 Londoners were killed by these random missiles and over 30,000 casualties nationwide. Again it was the East End that bore the brunt of the attacks, but central London was targeted too. There were dreadful scenes when a V2 fell on Aldwych and Selfridges was damaged when a rocket fell near Speakers Corner. Angela felt the force of the blast as another buzz bomb fell on nearby Goswell Road, to be followed by another hitting Kings Cross station. Shopping in Chapel Street market suddenly felt risky.

Earliest memories vary wildly in age. Somerset Maugham always maintained he could remember being in his mother's womb. Mine is on a visit to my grandfather in Soho. Angela hated little boys with savage, short back and sides haircuts. Despite Alex's objections that I looked like a girl, my hair was long, curly and unruly. I remember being plucked from my pram by one of the friendly ladies that always lined the streets near my grandfather's house. I was engulfed by a mass of peroxide blonde hair and the smell of a cloying perfume. Other ladies gathered around asking how old I was. The blonde lady gave me a shilling before returning me to my pram. Even in adulthood I retained a sentimental liking for street girls. I often wondered what had happened to the friendly blonde. Did she dream of making enough money to enjoy a suburban retirement or had she been happy plying her trade?

Towards the end of June 1945 Alex received an official government letter asking him to present himself the following day to an address in Whitehall. Intrigued, he was led along endless dingy corridors before being shown into a large office overlooking Horse Guards Parade. A weary looking Brigadier glanced up and, without offering Alex a seat, carried on signing a folder of letters on his desk. Alex sat down opposite the desk and was subjected to a baleful stare. Alex smiled blandly. He remembered this type from his time in the army. Disdainful pen-pushers continued to irritate him. Apparently whilst not actually an order it was assumed that he was willing to go to Berlin in the capacity of an official war artist to record the collapse of Germany. It was pretty obvious that the Brigadier had a dim view of what he described as arty types, but he was given to believe that Alex had produced a memorable image from 'the first show' and this was an opportunity to repeat the trick. Alex would shortly be told where to report and a departure time. A tray of tea and biscuits for one only had been brought in by a secretary. Looking up, the staff officer said 'That will be all.' 'Thank you for your hospitality' Alex replied with heavy irony. Pausing at the door they continued to look at each other with mutual dislike.

It was a smell he had never forgotten. The sweet perfume of death. Within a few minutes of their drive into the centre of Berlin it rose and engulfed them from the rotting bodies lying beneath the piles of rubble that lined the streets. The heat of a glorious summer's day only increasing the sickly stench. Alex had been assigned a driver from the Devonshire regiment. They were joined by a taciturn Soviet Major. Alex, armed with just a sketch pad and a selection of pencils, was one of the first Britons to be given access to the centre of Berlin since it was captured by the Red Army. Alex had not been given any brief. He really wanted to feature people rather than buildings, no matter how important. Still over a mile from the centre, Alex was attracted by a chain of women passing buckets full of rubble to each other until each was tipped into a waiting lorry. Alex asked the driver to stop so he could record their activity.

He was aware of the Major standing so close to him that he could feel his breath on his neck. Seemingly impressed with the results the Russian's face broke into a fleshy smile. Jabbing a finger towards his face he indicated that he wanted Alex to sketch him. Alex hoped that he was unable to speak English as the driver said in a stage whisper, 'Better make it good Sir, or I reckon the bugger will shoot us.' Posed by Alex, with one foot raised onto a fallen rafter and to a background of ruined buildings, the Major was every inch a hero of the Soviet Union. The picture refined the soldier's coarse features, an image to impress his family and friends. Upon seeing the result he was transformed from a surly brute into a laughing, delighted schoolboy. Covering Alex with kisses his breath was foul, so bad that for a moment it blocked out the lingering smell of death. They stopped again so that Alex could capture an old man pushing a cart loaded with furniture and a threadbare carpet. They passed a young servicewoman conducting the traffic with two flags. Her hair was tied in a pigtail. She was rather attractive and looked out of place in this desolate landscape. The Major refused to let Alex record dozens of marauding drunken soldiers drinking from wine bottles. He felt uncomfortable with the seeming lawlessness and was pleased to have the Major riding shot-gun for their protection.

Driving down Unter den Linden was not a scene Gloria would have recognised from her visits. No longer the elegant pedestrians, the smart bars and restaurants, just rubble, debris and the meerest shadow of its former glory. Alex recognised the shattered entrance to Hotel Adlon. He asked permission from the Major to venture inside. The entrance was dominated by a huge poster of a benign looking Uncle Joe Stalin. He had noticed others stuck to billboards on their journey. The lavish interior of the hotel had been reduced to ruins, although a few impressive columns and the grand staircase survived. Plaster continued to float down from the ceiling, whilst an ornately carved statue teetered on the edge of an exposed balcony, as if contemplating whether it would be better to fall rather than being left in such an uncompromising position. If statues could commit suicide Alex decided that this marble lady might have opted for it. He was also given access to the Reichstag. An unexpected bonus. Several burnt out vehicles lay outside the main entrance, their tyres flat and tilting as if just about to topple over. Inside soldiers were climbing ladders to add their contribution to the sea of graffiti that lined the surviving walls. The Major, in an act of bravado, dropped his trousers and pissed on the remnants of a torn Swastika flag that lay on the floor, to the cheers of his watching comrades.

Back in the Land Rover, Alex asked the driver to take a side turning. Here the damage was even more devastating. Abandoned wrecks of buildings with no sign of life except a scavenging dog driven half crazy with hunger. More burnt out vehicles as the road became more littered with rubble until finally the road was blocked. As the driver attempted a three point turn to get them back to the main road they heard the most terrible and frightening cry. Two soldiers, one pulling up his trousers, ran from a ruined building laughing and whooping. Alex rushed inside followed by the driver. He had the image he needed but at what a cost. The woman was possibly in her thirties but could have been any age. Her blouse had been ripped and her floral skirt was flecked with blood. Behind her a little boy, probably about the same age as his grandson, was crying hysterically. The laughing Major was not laughing now. His face contorted in rage, he cleared his throat and spat a globule of phlegm at the terrified woman. Before Alex could respond the Russian was performing a number of exaggerated pelvic thrusts and indicating Alex should take his turn. The Major then let out a volley of abuse and left his British comrades to take their fill.

Alex knew all about war but he was stunned. 'They are savages' he said. 'Some of our boys do it as well sir, don't kid yourself" the driver said. Alex reached into his wallet and gave the woman a five pound note which was the only money he had. She threw it on the ground, her eyes burning with hate. The driver gave the child a bar of chocolate that he also threw back. 'Leave it sir, you can't do anything. It's just war sir, that's all.' Outside the Major was beaming again giving the thumbs-up sign. They ignored him. Alex could not wait to leave. To leave Berlin, Germany and a part of war that was to haunt him for years to come.

The war in Europe had ended officially days before Alex set off for Berlin. Weirdly there had been a thunderstorm of Wagnerian proportions in the early hours of May 8th known as VE Day, just as there had been on the morning war was declared in September 1939. Angela rang early that morning to say she was on her way over as she did not want to miss the celebrations. Alex arranged for Mrs. Morgan to babysit for a few hours so that the couple could join the throng making their way along Shaftesbury Avenue towards Piccadilly Circus. The atmosphere was joyous, people kissing or embracing passers-by. A sea of Union Jacks were waved and most of the girls wore scarves or ribbons of red, white and blue. On the far side of the Circus a lone piper skirled away to cheers from the crowd.

There were uniforms from every branch of the services mingled with hundreds of GIs. A French soldier unfurled a giant Tricolour and there were Polish and Canadian flags hoisted too. Eros had been boarded up and there was a young woman standing on top with three or four soldiers sitting looking down on the vast crowds. A sailor grabbed Angela and led her off to join a long line dancing the conga. Alex caught glimpses of her through the crowd, her face flushed with enjoyment. A GI kissed her to cheers and applause. With her back arched she posed long enough for his pals to photograph the clinch. A press photographer was obviously on hand as the photograph appeared in many of the papers the next day. Later it was featured in Life Magazine. From that fleeting moment her image still lives on as representing the joy, relief and exhilaration encapsulating the end of the war.

Watching, Alex was convinced that this lovely girl should be spending more time with people of her own age. The thought provoked a terrible sadness that Paddy was not there rather than lying in some barren desert grave. She wriggled her way through the sea of bodies and threw her arms around him. He had never seen her look so happy, helped no doubt by all the bottles of booze being handed round. There was a brief silence as the familiar voice of the prime minister was projected from microphones installed at strategic points. 'We may allow ourselves a brief period of rejoicing, but let us not forget the toils and efforts that lie ahead.' For the moment the crowds only wanted to celebrate and the street party went on deep into the night.

As they made their way arm in arm to Archer Street an

impromptu band started up and the crowd belted out *Any old iron* followed by *Blue birds over the white cliffs of Dover*. It had been a memorable few hours. For once no moaning, just sheer unrestrained joy and happiness. They walked past the Windmill Theatre where the queues were longer than ever. Vivian Van Damm was letting servicemen in free of charge for that day only. In Archer Street a group of musicians was also playing, and Angela and Alex joined other couples as they danced in the street devoid of traffic. Alex was unsteady on his feet as he tried to keep in step. Angela was holding him too close as she stared up adoringly at him. He assumed she was tipsy. He attempted to break away, aware she was holding him like a lover rather than her father-in-law. Despite himself he was captivated with her clear blue eyes and the feel of her body against his.

Eventually back at the house Alex started cooking supper whilst Angela prepared Rex for bed. She was a dreadful cook but Alex enjoyed trying to create simple but tasty meals. The remnants of the Portofino's larder was just about holding up. He opened a bottle of di Montepulciano, taking a huge gulp as he waited for the water to boil. Wearing a snazzy little apron he announced that tonight he would be serving tagliatelle with a fine pesto sauce. Sitting at the pine kitchen table they toasted each other, Winston Churchill, the King and the future. A second bottle was opened.

Alex then informed Angela that he hated her name as much as he had hated her calling him dad. He solemnly announced he would call her Angel from now on. Jumping up she sat on his lap. 'I will always be your angel!' she breathed in a hammy, sexy voice. She really is drunk, he thought, but he was not sure. He tried to shift her from his lap but she just wriggled making him feel really uncomfortable. Saved by the bell, the telephone rang. It was Gloria. She was appearing at the Winter Garden as top of the bill for the summer season. He found it difficult to concentrate on what Gloria was saying. Eventually she asked him pointedly if anyone was with him. 'Only Angel and Rex' he said, 'We have just got back from....' 'Angel!' Gloria spat the name out accusingly. 'Angela' Alex said, correcting himself. The rest of the conversation was very stilted with Gloria hanging up abruptly. 'Your girlfriend, was it?' He had never kept his relationship with Gloria secret, but now he was aware that one woman in his life was beginning to have less influence on him whilst the other....what of his renamed Angel? They washed up and cleared the dishes away in silence. The job done Alex said it was time for bed. 'I thought you would never ask.' Relieved, he realised that she was joking. So it was with a peck on the cheek that they parted that night. Alex half expected her to turn up in his bedroom, but thankfully she did not. Instead Alex lay awake conflicted and tempted, but resolved to discourage any romantic thoughts the lovely Angel may have. He remembered his mother's favourite saying 'Act in haste, repent at leisure.'

Chapter 23

Looking for a little sunshine

In the immediate aftermath of war London was dingy and sad. The expectation of better times squashed as further restrictions and rationing were introduced. There was still a whiff of glamour, a hint of seedy opulence, but overall London had lost its swagger. Its streets pock-marked with bomb sites, blackened like rotting teeth. The GIs had gone home leaving thousands of broken hearts and hundreds of babies to be explained to parents and returning servicemen. My memories of that dark period after the war were of heavy snowfall in the bitter winter of 1947. Going with my mother and Alex to watch the marathon runners gasping their way towards the finish along the streets approaching Wembley Stadium during the Olympic Games the following year, and being taken to watch my first football match at Stamford Bridge.

Alex titled his shocking painting of the poor German woman and her terrified child 'Defeat'. It too was purchased by the Imperial War Museum and somehow encapsulated the futility of war. A difficult subject, it received a less enthusiastic response from the public who were seeking relief from tragedy in the books they read, the songs they sang and the paintings they viewed. Simon Marks, a critic for *Live Arts Magazine,* penned what was to be the first of a long and bitter assault on my grandfather's work. He wrote: 'Whilst there is some crude vitality in Beck's two wartime supposed masterpieces, what was produced in the intervening years was largely banal and unchallenging. His work is mundane and lazy.' The article continued in a similar vein. On being appointed the art critic for the *London Evening Standard*, his criticism became even more damming and personal, and yet the two never met. Alex never responded publicly to criticism. No matter how waspish the critics were the British public continued to love his work that over the years drove Marks to such extremes that eventually years later it led to him being fired from the Standard.

Within months of the war ending the house in Bushey was returned by the Air Ministry to my grandfather. After some soul searching he decided it was time to make a break from the past. He took anything of sentimental value back to Archer Street and sent the remnants for sale at auction. Although property prices remained depressed he decided to sell the house, which eventually sold after being on the market for months.

His relationship with Angela stabilised. They still saw each other regularly. At this time as I began to take notice of all around me, I saw a fondness and easy familiarity between them. My mother loved dancing and I do remember having babysitters whilst she went out, but I have no memories of men staying or even visiting our house. When I was much older my mother told me that young men were only interested in one thing and they were not any good at that either. I think I can pinpoint the time when her relationship with Alex changed and deepened. Before the war a British industrialist who had moved to Spain bought a number of my grandfather's paintings. They were generally smallish works of the hectic activity backstage at the Windmill. It was his suggestion that the purchase money could be paid into a Spanish bank.

Due to Alex's buoyant financial situation he had left the money sitting in Spain. Now with currency controls severely limiting the amount of money being allowed to leave the country, an idea of a holiday home suddenly appealed. He had never been to Spain and had no idea how to start a search. He vaguely remembered hearing about an artists colony in a Majorcan village called Deia, as he found that as in Newlyn artists working in close proximity to each other did tend to produce a creative energy that helped them all. It was only later that he discovered that the writer and poet Robert Graves lived close by, his poem *When I'm killed* being as powerful as anything produced by either Rupert Brooke or Wilfred Owen.

He booked into the Grand Hotel in Palma in the heart of the old city. None of the agents he visited had any properties available in Deia. They actually tried to discourage him from seeking a property there, trying instead to interest him in flashy apartments in Palma. Frustrated, he hired a taxi for the day and drove the winding coastal road up into the mountains. The views overlooking the sea were worth the cost of the trip alone. The village had just one main street with a number of alleys leading off, but was dominated by the hilltop church of Sant Joan Baptista. It was lunchtime when he arrived and the place was dead, shops shut and the sole bar empty. He left the cab and walked up to the church where he actually found an artist at his easel painting the exterior of the church. The man was Dutch but spoke good English. He did not know of any properties for sale, but suggested he enquired at the sole bar Alex had already spotted. After a welcome beer he managed to understand that the bar owner did in fact have a very modest building that had been uninhabited for seven or eight years. After lunch of a tasty omelette and much sign language, the couple set off down an unmade track. The building was a wreck hidden in a jungle of weeds and fallen trees. It was surrounded by an olive grove and from a rickety upstairs balcony it was possible to glimpse the sea. As ever with Alex he made a snap decision. He also had the capacity to imagine the property fully restored. He loved it. They agreed a price on the spot with Manuel, the bar owner, spitting on his hand to seal the deal. Later, of course, Alex was to learn he had paid far too much for the wreck but he did not care. Now he had something to look forward to and a project that he would enjoy overseeing.

The end of the war marked a change in Alex's relationship with both Gloria and my mother. He was a constant presence in my growing up. Looking back on my early years as a child he was a regular visitor to Islington. They appeared at ease in each other's company and there was no inkling of any romantic involvement. The greatest influence he had on my mother at that time was to introduce her to reading. She had very little formal education but his advice to read authors like Ernest Hemingway and *Émile* Zola had her making increasingly regular visits to the public lending library. The first book he recommended was *Gone with the wind*, after that she was hooked. She always had a book in her hand whilst hoovering, cooking and even locking herself in the lavatory to read a few pages without interruption. Her interests expanded to non-fiction and her quest for knowledge remained with her for all her life. To her own astonishment she was able to retain vast tracts of facts she had gleaned. She could quote poetry that she had only read once. Her mind was like a sponge. Living in today's world she would have undoubtedly gone to university and possibly become an academic. Back in those dark days after the war very few women attended university, and most women would not go out to work unless forced to for economic reasons. Against her better judgment she tended to defer to men less well versed than she was. It was still a period where clever women were treated with suspicion. The news that Alex had bought a house in Majorca had her enrolling in evening classes to learn Spanish. By the time we all went to Deia for the first time she was already able to make herself understood.

Whilst Alex's relationship with my mother appeared to have settled down to one normally associated with a daughter-in-law, he was renewing his romance with Gloria. She had arranged a three year extension on the Hampstead house and he was a regular visitor in between her touring arrangements which were at the time confined to Britain and France. He admitted that he continued to be physically attracted to Gloria despite her frequent affairs. To Gloria this part of life was simple. If you met someone who you found physically attractive it was stupid not to take advantage of the situation. Alex did not agree. He realised that he was a hopeless romantic, but whilst true love evaded him it would take a saint to reject Gloria's advances. Their time together during this period was happy enough although Alex was concerned that Gloria spent so little time with Maya, who was growing up to be a beautiful but painfully shy child, far more devoted to her nanny than her mother. These visits seemingly heralded the end of their intimate relationship, with a prolonged absence from each other as Gloria prepared to depart on a world tour being arranged by Monica Wiseman. She was to visit Singapore and Hong Kong, before going on to New Zealand and Australia where she was scheduled to stay for four months.

It had never occurred to Alex that he would ever become considered a member of the establishment, but this doubtful honour was bestowed on him in 1950 much to the rage of critic Simon Marks. To become a member of the Royal Academy often meant stepping into a dead man's shoes. Membership was confined to eighty artists, although vacancies were also created by an existing member reaching their seventy-fifth birthday when they become a senior academician. The arcane procedure of awarding the appointment dates back over two hundred years.

The artist has to be proposed by an existing academician and subsequently endorsed by at least three others. The appointment is then confirmed or rejected by the General Assembly. Alex was completely surprised by his appointment and assumed it had much to do with Alfred Munnings, the president of the Royal Academy. Although Alex was not a close friend he actually rather liked him, despite his reputation for being irascible and a frightful snob. Munnings was also savaged by Marks and many leading critics, but Alex really admired his beautiful paintings, particularly of horses which he reckoned were second only to Stubbs. Another artist who had supported Alex was Stanley Spencer, whom he visited several times at his studio in Cookham where he was completing his masterpiece 'The Resurrection'. Alex, despite himself, was secretly delighted to have been honoured by his peers and that evening he celebrated by taking my mother to eat at L'Etoille in Charlotte Street. With the work proceeding in Deia it was agreed that we should join him as soon as my school broke up. It was in Deia that their love for each other really blossomed. Gloria was not about to be easily sidelined as she always demanded centre stage. She resented competition, both professionally and romantically. Life was about to get complicated.

Chapter 24

Delights and disappointments

G loria was being foul. To Monica despite the successful world tour that she had so meticulously arranged, to Muriel because she was jealous of her closeness to her daughter, but mostly to Maya for being so ordinary. The child was certainly pretty, but despite private lessons for piano and singing she showed little aptitude for either. She had no difficulty learning to read music, but her playing was mechanical and the child sang hopelessly off key. Gloria had imagined the two of them appearing together later in her career, but it was already obvious that Maya was just not musical. Even at school she was considered to be of only average ability. Gloria hated average. Her definition of average was boring. She was now one of the world's highest paid entertainers and she was stuck with a daughter who in turn irritated and infuriated her. She was meek and lacking in confidence, although her precious nanny insisted that she had been full of life whilst Gloria had been away. Monica also warned Gloria that it was wrong to expect the child to be a carbon copy of her mother, particularly when they had no common blood bond.

Gloria's reception on her world tour had been exhilarating,

particularly in Australia, but now she was experiencing a huge sense of anti-climax. She was also angry that Alex was showing her so little attention, talking of nothing but some house he had bought in Majorca. There was something more. Since her return he had rejected any advances she made. This infuriated her further. She was at that awkward age. Was she really less desirable? There was more to it. She had that inbuilt woman's intuition. She convinced herself that he had found himself a woman at last. But who?

Feeling so low, she had resorted to taking sleeping pills again. They did not seem to make her sleep any better, but they had a calming or perhaps a dulling effect. She decided she hated Hampstead with her neighbours being either pseudo intellectuals or ghastly snobs or both. She was beginning to hate England too. Since the arrival of West Indian workers in London she could not fail to notice that people were treating her differently. Driving through London she had seen signs in boarding house windows: 'No dogs, blacks or Irish'. Britain was slowly becoming more like the States. She began contemplating a move to Paris where she had not witnessed any race discrimination.

A letter she sent to the Daily Mail decrying the treatment of immigrants was published. The response shocked her as she received dozens of letters, most of which were abusive and a couple threatening to kill her. All of them were sent anonymously. She issued a statement through Monica deploring racism. Hundreds more abusive letters flooded in. The anti-Semites also targeted Monica. For a time Gloria imagined she had found a cause to pursue, but apathy overwhelmed her as she continued to swallow sleeping pills like children craving sweets. There was one final gripe that was eating away at Gloria.

Although initially pleased for Alex that he had been made a Royal Academician, it did not take long for jealousy to take over. She had assumed that her voluntary work entertaining the troops would be rewarded with a suitable decoration. As each year passed her anger and resentment grew. She convinced herself that this slight was again a racist reaction from an establishment hanging on grimly to its inbuilt privileges.

Stirring herself, she decided to take a trip over to Archer Street to see Alex. He seemed rather taken off guard and she wondered if he had some lover hiding upstairs. He offered to make her some tea, but she had a glass of wine instead. Whilst he went into the kitchen to fetch it she noticed several photographs of my mother and me taken in our Islington garden. There was one taken in a studio of my mother alone. The lighting was very soft and she looked extremely glamorous. Gloria snapped. As Alex came back with the wine she was standing, eyes blazing in fury. 'I knew it!' she shrieked, 'You are shagging your own daughter-in-law. It's disgusting!' She was crying now, quite inconsolable. Alex tried to calm her but she was awash with fury and self pity.

Eventually Alex was able honestly to deny her allegations, explaining that of course he was fond of Angel. Angela, he corrected himself knowing that calling her Angel was likely to set Gloria off again. Suddenly all the fire and anger disappeared. For the first time Alex thought she looked old. Her lifestyle was catching up with her. Where once her skin had been flawless it was now puffy and blotchy. He felt a huge wave of sorrow sweep over him. She seemed quite broken. He took her in his arms comforting her, much as a father would a child. With her calm now he explained that his major concern was his grandson. 'Do you promise that you haven't been to bed with her?' 'Of course I do' he assured her. She really was irrational and behaving like a spoilt child. It did not seem to occur to Gloria that she had always been totally uninhibited, whilst she demanded total loyalty from Alex. Make-up restored, Gloria was calm again as they chatted away until Alex made the mistake of mentioning that he was taking the family to see his new house. 'Family, what family?' He tried to explain that it was all entirely innocent but she was not listening. She stormed out of the door, hailing a taxi which ignored her. She slumped to her haunches. Gently Alex escorted her inside again. That night he undressed her and laid her in his bed. He was worried about her. He still loved her but love was complicated, it had moved on from passion to concern. Had she seen through him? Was the Deia house just a ruse to seduce Angel? If they did get together was it a form of incest by proxy? Alex could not sleep that night and yet after all the upsetting rumpus Gloria was as peaceful as a baby. The next morning they breakfasted together as if nothing had happened, and yet Alex understood that life for both of them would never quite be the same again.

Just as Londoners were looking for a lifting of post war gloom another cloud descended. Well not a cloud exactly, more a fog. To start with few people took much notice as fogs were common in London. By the following morning that October it became obvious this was a super fog soon to be dubbed smog. The weather had been unusually cold resulting in huge numbers of coal fires being lit. The air was quite still with no breeze to shift the smoke. A static anti-cyclone caused the cold sulphurous air to stay trapped under a layer of warm air. Staring through his studio window Alex was fascinated by the strange half light. Grabbing a sketch pad he set off towards Shaftesbury Avenue. Although he knew the area really well it did not take long for him to lose his bearings. It was impossible to see just a couple of yards ahead. He stumbled into an abandoned car seemingly left in the middle of the road. The air was foul and he covered his face with his woollen scarf. Eventually, with the help of a couple of pedestrians, he found himself in Piccadilly Circus. It was here that he sketched what was to become his best known image, produced as a print in thousands and sold worldwide and still in print today. He captured a lone eerie figure wearing a raincoat and trilby, lighting a cigarette to a background of a ghostlike Eros. The lighted match was to provide the only colour against a background of graded greys. Normally it is a bright subject matter that helps sell prints, but Alex caught the strange mood evoked by this unique weather.

By the third day the chimney smoke had merged with exhaust fumes and cloaked London in an all enveloping filthy and smelly embrace. People lurched blindly, coughing and sputtering as they made a vain attempt to carry on with their every day lives. As the smog tightened its grip shops and stores closed. Those brave enough to attend a theatre were unable to see unless seated in the front stalls. Soon the theatres and cinemas closed too. Doors and windows were unable to keep the smog at bay and as Alex lay in bed that night he could not even see across the room. There appeared to be no escape. The smog continued to pursue you, attacking your throat and lungs. By the fourth day twelve thousand people had died and over one hundred thousand taken ill. Catching specific moments was my grandfather's greatest skill. Although only a small painting that was exhibited the following year at the summer exhibition, it received universal acclaim. Even Simon Marks aimed his poisonous barbs at other artists. It remains a wonderful image that draws you in very much as the smog did on that day.

It was the following year that gave the country the lift it had been so desperately seeking. Like thousands of others Alex invested in a television to enable him to watch the coronation of Queen Elizabeth. I remember the day well. I went with my mother to Archer Street and the plan was for us to watch the procession as it rounded Piccadilly Circus on its way to Trafalgar Square and ultimately to Westminster Abbey. We were then to rush home and watch the service on the television. It was a truly memorable occasion, with over twenty thousand troops lining the route where about three million spectators had gathered. I was pushed to the front of those gathered around Piccadilly. I had a view of the Queen Mother in the Irish coach. She wore a crown bearing the extraordinary Koh-i-Noor diamond. Finally we witnessed the gleaming gold and glass state coach carrying the Queen and Duke of Edinburgh. We all cheered ourselves hoarse. As a youngster we were all led to believe that this was the start of a second great Elizabethan era. Unfortunately this dream was unfulfilled, but for that day at least many really believed it. Back in Archer Street we sat glued to proceedings being beamed from Westminster Abbey. Alex had prepared sandwiches and he shared a last bottle of champagne with my mother. It was a happy day and we had an exciting holiday in Deia to look forward to.

Alex was due to leave for Majorca the following week whilst my mother and I were to follow when I broke up from school. Alex had been out a couple of times since buying the house to check on progress. Initially he had been impressed with the builder he had appointed, but on arrival it appeared that progress had ground to a standstill as the temperature rose. Too many siestas and Alex was horrified at how much still needed to be done to make the place habitable. With less than a month before we were due to arrive there were still no window frames or tiles for flooring on site.

He fired the builder and arranged for a gang to come from Palma. Although they did make progress the house was still virtually unfurnished when we arrived. Alex had at least ordered a kitchen table and three beds, but no other furniture and just bare light bulbs. The place still smelt of paint and Alex was rather mortified that he had only two sets of cutlery and no provisions to feed us. He was hopelessly unpractical and should have probably delayed our arrival to the following year. Nothing however was going to dampen my mother's enthusiasm. She organised the builders who flirted with her constantly, but within a few days the work was completed. Alex had bought a small Citroen which was suitable for the narrow village streets, so the following day we set off for Palma to undertake a massive shop. Within a week the place was transformed. As well as crockery, bedding, rugs, lampshades, chairs and settees, Angela decided the whole place needed brightening up. The dark stained beams and doors were painted a variety of pastel shades. Whilst the sun beat down outside my mother organised us with tins of paint, brushes and turps. The effect was staggering. From a dark traditional Majorcan cottage she had created a light airy house. A place where I knew we would spend many memorable weeks. What I didn't know then was that it would form the backdrop to a complicated but lasting love affair.

Chapter 25

You are my sunshine

Many of us experience a holiday romance at some time in our lives. Perhaps it is a change of scenery, a break from our everyday life. Maybe it is helped by the sun and an ability to forget any problems we may have lurking at home. Whatever the reason on arriving in Deia there was a dramatic shift in my mother's behaviour towards Alex and one that he reciprocated. Although I was only about ten at the time it was obvious. Whereas previously they had been affectionate, they were now outwardly flirtatious. I caught them in a passionate embrace. Their response was to draw me to them and we enjoyed a family cuddle. I was pleased any tension that had existed between them was blown away. The guilt that perhaps they had felt was banished under a burning sun and cloudless skies. As an adult now I can understand the emotional hurdle they needed to clear. The ever present shadow of the father I never met, a barrier that I know continued to trouble them but one that was banished on arrival each year in Deia.

Every year until I went to university we made our pilgrimage to Majorca, with Alex and my mother continuing until the late sixties. The house had a comfortable sitting room and a large kitchen where we ate, when not going to one of the growing number of restaurants that sprang up over the years. Upstairs each of the three bedrooms had balconies with views either over the mountains or down to the sea. It is a strange fact that Alex scarcely picked up a brush or completed a painting in the many years he went to Deia. For him it was a time for relaxation. He told me many years later that somehow the vibrant colours found all over Majorca did not suite his style. He was locked professionally into the drab background of post war Britain.

Another disappointment for Alex was his relationship with Robert Graves. Although they had so much in common with their great war experiences and their ability to convey this through verse and paint, there was always a tension between them. My grandfather thought that Graves rather resented Alex's arrival. He had lived in Deia since 1929 and he could see that what he had cherished was slowly going to disappear. He was right, for today Deia is a tourist attraction with swanky hotels and expensive restaurants. My grandfather's arrival did certainly add to people's awareness of this little gem, but for the first few years of our visits Deia remained largely unspoilt. Luckily Graves's house, where he entertained a string of both male and female muses, and our own cottage were at opposite ends of the village. We drank and dined in different bars and when the two men did meet they were polite but distant.

It is strange looking back how the weeks rushed by and yet our pleasures were simple. Most mornings we would take the battered Citroen down a rutted track towards the sea. The car was parked in the shade and the last half mile had to be taken on foot which was difficult and painful for Alex. My mother was interested in the wild life and pointed out the crossbills and blue rock thrushes flying in and out of the caves in the mountainside. Sometimes we saw black vultures circling above. Alex was a keen and strong swimmer. Still conscious of his wounds, he always wore black tights and a T-shirt. The beach was small and often deserted. Two brothers who were fishermen had set up a shack, and we often ate there with fish straight from the sea cooked by one of the brothers' wives. As the years passed they created an informal restaurant overlooking the sea. Wine and beer became available and the kitchen was expanded, although with no electricity they continued to cook with Calor gas. Memories of those wonderful leisurely lunches linger on.

As I grew older I did wonder why my mother and Alex did not get married. They were obviously very much in love, and yet after these wonderful summer breaks they went back to their separate lives. I assume it was because in Majorca they were unknown. There were no explanations needed, we were just a family group whereas in London it was more difficult for them. Life was so different back in the 1950s. People were very judgemental and their relationship was unusual. Alex did tell me that it was my mother who was wary despite her obvious love for him. This is surprising in a way, as her natural instinct was to be outspoken and not worry about what people thought of her. Although I had no proof I did begin to think it was something to do with my grandfather's continuing attachment to Gloria. He did manage to keep the two apart and to my knowledge they never met after my parents' wedding. Their lives were neatly compartmentalised and recharged each year under the heat of a Spanish sun.

Meantime Gloria, with some trepidation, undertook a tour of the United States. She immediately made the headlines by refusing to appear at a Miami night club unless the audience was desegregated. The papers reprinted what she had written to the Daily Mail. To her surprise the owners of the club relented and overnight she gained a whole new set of fans. The show was a great success, followed by her appearing as the queen of jazz in a vast cavalcade in Los Angeles. Despite constant rave reviews, her support for integrated audiences was causing waves in a period when there was a witch hunt for tracking down communists. Despite her having no sympathy for socialism, Monica advised her to come back to Europe before long unless she fancied a spell in an American prison. For once Gloria heeded the advice and she returned home to the plaudits of the British press. She could now claim the support of the gay and black British communities. She basked in the acclaim and of being in the unusual position of claiming the high moral ground, something that Alex was about to lose in a scandal that for days dominated the headlines and saw his reputation shredded.

It all started with an invitation from Vivian Van Damm for Alex to join him for a coffee. It was several months since he had been backstage at the theatre and he paused at the doorway to the audition room. A new applicant was being put through her paces by the dance master. Dressed in a leotard and accompanied by a pianist, she looked very accomplished to Alex's untutored eye, but she was being harangued by the dance master to show more expression. 'Come on darling, you can do better than that.' The Windmill demanded complete dedication and professionalism. The poor girl started her routine again as my grandfather climbed the narrow stairs to the staff canteen on the top floor. Here some scantily dressed dancers enjoyed a cup of tea between acts and they were often joined by members of the troupe who were enjoying a day off. Van Damm was sitting in the corner with a young dark-haired girl who was probably only about seventeen. Waving her aside he told her he would call her back when he was ready. He was always immensely autocratic. 'Well what do you think?' Van Damm asked about the girl. 'Very pretty but why should I be interested?' Van Damm did not laugh or even smile much, but now he had a wicked grin. Van Damm was a great showman, never missing a trick to get publicity. He was a master of P.R even before the term was in general use.

He went on to explain the girl called Anna Newman had joined recently. She had applied whilst still at school and although his performers tended to be in their teens, he felt she had been too young. Subsequently she had left school and had joined with the backing of her parents. Van Damm was convinced that she was unique, having joined straight from a convent. He explained that attendances had been dropping recently due to a number of unlicensed strip clubs opening up in Soho, and here he was convinced was a chance to get the punters rolling in again. Alex could not understand how he could help. 'I want you to paint her' the impresario suggested. 'Why?' Alex reckoned that surely a photograph would be better, but Van Damm was convinced that a painting would create far more publicity. How right he was.

Van Damm called the girl over and introduced her to Alex and explained his plan. It is strange that a girl who was happy to be ogled naked in a theatre was very doubtful about posing for an artist, no matter how well known. Van Damm had obviously not explained his idea to the girl, and neither had he got confirmation from Alex that he would take on the commission. As usual with Van Damm these small hurdles were just minor irritations. He was used to getting his own way and he was determined to convince these two doubters. Anna was cute, almost childish, and spoke with a pronounced lisp. Her main reservation was Alex. She had heard all about artists and their muses and she was not up for anything like that. Alex could not help laughing but he could understand the girl's reluctance. Without thinking he told her he could arrange for his daughter-in-law to sit in on the sessions. 'You agree then, excellent.' Van Damm's face actually broke into a smile. Alex had been railroaded into submission, but Van Damm had been really helpful to him over the years and so perhaps it was payback time. Alex assured the young girl her pose would be almost demure and certainly not in any way sexy. She obviously had a mind of her own and despite her boss's obvious annoyance she told them she needed time to consider. A couple of days later she agreed, providing she was paid an additional model's fee. Alex admired her maturity for one who looked so young, and readily agreed.

It was all Angela's fault, or at least that is what Alex laughingly told her some months later. Alex only required three sessions for him to complete his preliminary sketches. Anna changed behind a screen and allowed Angela to position her in a demure pose. She wore a crucifix round her neck, but there was something missing to bring the pose alive. Firstly Angela tied the girl's hair into two bunches, and then suggested the props which were to propel the painting and the story around it to the front pages. A blazer, gymslip and a straw hat were hired from a local costumiers. They were neatly folded and placed on a chair next to the reclining figure. Alex was guilty of naivety if he did not realise how controversial the picture was going to be. It was surely the props and the crucifix that caused such offence, as a knee was raised here and a hand there so that only the suggestion of a breast was exposed. No matter, on release all hell broke loose and attendances at the Windmill soared. Anna was handed a two song contract by a leading record producer, and Alex gave her both his preliminary sketches which she sold later for thousands of pounds.

Simon Marks led the way in *The Evening Standard* whose headline screamed 'Beck resorts to porn.' That was just the start. Most critics found the painting sleazy, appealing only to those who prey on young girls. The religious leaders piled in with the Archbishops of Canterbury and Westminster joining forces, and even the chief Rabbi delivering a broadside. The leaders of children's charities demanded action from the police. Letters to the press added to the feeding frenzy of condemnation. Alex was genuinely shocked and annoyed by the reaction of what he thought was a good painting.

He was pleased to get a call from Monica Wiseman, who suggested he should not speak to the press and possibly go away until the furore died down. She told him she would handle the criticism and attempt to explain his side of he story. Alex liked and trusted Monica and agreed with her proposal. He rang Angela and told her to pack for an unscheduled holiday. It was no use flying abroad as there would be press photographers at the airports. So they hired a car and headed for Holyhead. As he had suspected, no one recognised them as they boarded the ferry for Dublin. During school term time they already had taken a number of long weekend breaks. A Mr. and Mrs. Beck never raised a problem as they visited Bath, Harrogate or Edinburgh, but now they felt like criminals on the run. Whilst they were touring round Ireland staying in small hotels they kept in touch with Monica who had started a fight back. A host of the more liberal minded had been encouraged by Monica to support Alex. Many were influential, including the poet Ted Hughes, the critic Kenneth Tynan and artists Stanley Spencer and Lucian Freud. The day before they were due to return Alex learnt that the painting had been bought by a Texan oil magnet for a record price by a living British artist. The only part of the whole rumpus to interest Gloria was the fact that he had disappeared with 'that woman'. She was furious.

Chapter 26

Recognition

Within weeks Gloria's mood had somersaulted into one of joy and Alex was the first to learn why. Unfortunately for Alex it was only 6.00 am and he had only been in bed for a couple of hours, having seen in the new year with Angela and a group of their friends. Gloria announced excitedly that she had been awarded the O.B.E. in the New Year's Honours List. Having not spoken to her for weeks, despite his hangover he was touched that he was obviously one of the first people she had told. Angela was asleep at his side and he was worried that she would wake up setting Gloria off in another rant. He tried to sound enthusiastic and luckily Gloria had others whom she just had to ring. She did not contact him again for months, but later her picture was all over the front pages proudly wearing her medal outside Buckingham Palace. Her mood then went into overdrive as she was summonsed to appear in the Royal Command Performance at the London Palladium in November. She was slightly miffed that Mario Lanza had been named as top of the bill, with Gloria closing the first half of the show. Monica was also excited and for the first time in years Gloria put in some serious rehearsal time. The show was produced to run like clockwork and Gloria was determined to give the performance of a lifetime. Unusually she was nervous before going on stage. She was convinced the comedian Arthur Askey was over-running his allotted spot, but like most star performers he was reluctant to leave the stage because of the continued applause.

Gloria received prolonged applause as she started her routine, with the chorus pretending as always to being out of step. Then as the chorus completed their routine she reappeared in a dress made entirely of feathers topped by an extravagant head-dress. Finishing her next dance routine the feathers were discarded to reveal a stunning evening dress. Sitting at the piano she moved seamlessly from Chopin and Liszt to honky-tonk blues. She had the audience cheering and stomping their feet. Standing now, she took the microphone singing a number of her best known songs. Then waiting for the applause to die down she gave a genuinely moving version of 'Where have all the flowers gone'. Did she really genuinely break down then or was she just working the audience? As she sobbed people rose to their feet. Trying to compose herself she took twelve curtain calls.

Back stage Mario Lanza could be heard complaining loudly. He was an even greater diva than Gloria. He had made impossible demands all through rehearsals and made himself thoroughly unpopular with the entire company. He had a superb voice and his performance was also greeted with generous applause, but at the final curtain call it was Gloria who was given a standing ovation. Bouquets were presented and the fixed smile on Lanza's face looked more like a grimace. There are several photos of Gloria that night being introduced to the Queen. One catches her mid-curtsy, not a position she was used to. My grandfather did admit to me that he was slightly hurt that Gloria had not sent him any tickets for the show. Her jealousy of my mother continued to fester, whereas Angela had accepted that Alex continued to be attached to Gloria. Rightly she realised that my grandfather's love for her was solid and ongoing.

Alex had known Vivian Van Damm for almost thirty years and they remained good friends, but Alex was worried about him. The showman's health was declining in tandem with the Windmill. What had been considered daring before the war was now reckoned to be tame and old fashioned. Increasingly explicit strip clubs were opening up like pimples on a teenager's face. Cabaret clubs, like the Talk Of The Town, were offering a night out including a meal, dancing and a top line performer. Van Damm's increasingly jaundiced complexion heralded his admission to hospital. His daughter, the rally driver Sheila Van Damm, joined the theatre in an attempt to arrest the decline, but she was having to learn from scratch. Even from his hospital bed Vivian insisted on knowing every detail of what was happening at the theatre.

A few days after entering hospital he issued a rallying call to all the staff, congratulating them on how well they had supported his daughter. Unfortunately his condition continued to decline and he died in December. Sheila withheld the news from the company until after the final curtain call that night. She posted a message that there was to be no mourning. In the best showbiz tradition she requested that they should go onstage and give it everything that they have got. The funeral was a private family affair. A memorial service was held later at Hampstead synagogue attended by hundreds of friends and former performers, including Alex and my mother. Alex formed a warm friendship with Sheila Van Damm, but realised she was going to find keeping the Windmill afloat extremely tough.

Britain was having trouble addressing the changes of perceived morality, whilst a blind eye was turned to increasingly explicit strip clubs and pornography. The calls to clear the streets of sex-workers was gaining ground. With legislation shortly to pass through Parliament Alex realised that now was the time to capture the last days when girls lining the streets were able to ask any man passing if he was looking for a good time. A thought persisted that he should complete a modern version of 'A Harlot's Progress'. He was, however, fascinated by one particular prostitute he had witnessed over the years when visiting a restaurant in Lisle Street that cooked the best omelettes in London. Lisle Street was very poorly lit and it is where the older and less attractive women tended to ply their trade.

The woman he wanted to record for posterity had recently seen her fortunes blossom. In an inspired moment she had transformed herself from a rather tubby, ageing, sad woman to the lady of the manor. Was her change of identity her own inspired idea or was she controlled by the Messina brothers? Certainly they had introduced modern time and motion study into their operation by only allowing their ladies a maximum of six minutes with a client for a basic service. Alex was fairly certain that this lady had acted on her own account as the Messina boys favoured young girls who would earn them far more money. The Messinas who drove around Soho in their Bentleys were ruthless controllers. They paid their girls a salary and provided them with clothes, but if they stepped out of line their looks were likely to be rearranged with a razor.

The master stroke pulled off by the Lisle Street dowager was to dress in a tweed suit, woollen stockings, flat shoes and a row of pearls. On first sight she would have been welcomed in any country estate ready for a day's shooting. Fantasy obviously plays a major part in sexual attraction, so after years of standing virtually ignored, suddenly she was in constant demand. When Alex approached her she obviously thought he was a punter, but a ten pound note attracted her attention long enough for him to make a detailed sketch. He reckoned she must have been in her sixties and she had added a pseudo posh voice to her repertoire. He would really have liked to learn more about her background, but he knew by speaking to a variety of street girls over the years that all you got was make believe. Over the following weeks he created a painting of the woman with keys in hand. Behind on a misty evening a bowler-hatted man hovers as if plucking up courage to approach her. The painting featured in the following year's summer exhibition prompted Simon Marks to accuse Alex of being sex mad.

Back home after a visit to the Royal Academy, Alex had a phone call from Monica Wiseman informing him that Gloria was getting married. She was not happy. She was convinced that Gloria's groom was a fake. Monica was a great judge of character and was seldom wrong.

Chapter 27

Italian interlude

The cab driver stared at the paper bearing the address Monica had given Alex and shook his head. He handed it to other drivers waiting in line at Naples airport. They gathered round Alex talking excitedly as the sun beat down. He knew the house was several hours drive away but none of them seemed keen to take the job on or did not know how to find it. Another driver was summonsed from the far end of waiting cars. A young man wandered up and introduced himself as George. He spoke with a strange Scottish hybrid accent. His parents apparently ran a fish and chip shop in Glasgow and he had returned to Naples to get married. Alex explained that it would be a long job but he would pay him well. They agreed what Alex realised was a vastly inflated price and so with the meter turned off they headed south. They drove for over two hours through parched countryside where sporadic fires had broken out on the hills.

It turned out that Monica had been right about Gloria's sudden marriage. Initially Alex had not been too concerned. Gloria was a big girl, fairly streetwise and surely able to look after herself. She had a record of reckless love affairs but since her first attempt another marriage had never been considered. This time Gloria had married a peroxide blond man some twenty years her junior. Alex admitted that it was not a good start but he genuinely hoped that she would be happy. They married in the idyllic setting of the Caesar Palace on Capri. Photographs of the happy couple appeared in a couple of Sunday newspapers. Monica had done some digging on the groom who called himself Thomas de Groot. His real name was Keith Noble and he came from Ilford. Before the marriage he had apparently tried to become a joint signatory on Gloria's bank account. Monica, who continued to look after all of Gloria's money and investments, refused but agreed to a meeting on the couple's return from honeymoon. Keith Noble may have been a great seducer of older women but he was not that smart. Rather than wait for the greater gain he wanted the highlife now. Concern from Monica turned to alarm when within a week of the marriage Gloria made a payment of twenty thousand pounds to a financial services company whose sole director was one Keith Noble. By now the couple had moved up the coast to stay at the fabulous Grand Hotel in Amalfi. Monica had put in a number of international calls to speak to Gloria only to be told by Noble that Gloria was resting. It was obvious that he was blocking contact.

Alex had a meeting with Monica at Archer Street. He had rung the hotel and asked to speak to Mrs.de Groot. An Italian woman who spoke no English answered. Gloria was known all over the world, so he rang again asking if she was staying at the hotel and was assured that unfortunately they had never had the honour to welcome Miss Gloria Bird. So where was Gloria? Through contacts in Soho Alex hired an Italian private detective tasked with finding where Gloria was and if she was well. They became increasingly anxious as it was over a week before the private-eye contacted Alex again. There had been one possible sighting, although the information was not conclusive. The detective had almost given up when he received a report from a gardener living in Agropoli which was a four hour drive from the Amalfi coast. He was retained by the owners of an isolated villa that was usually rented out to holiday makers. It was situated in the dramatic Cilento Valley and part of the Cilento and Vallo di Diano National Park. A couple of weeks previously he had been working when a car drew up. A man and a woman got out supporting another figure who appeared to be unconscious. The man was young with blond hair and the woman wore a nurse's uniform. The gardener was told to leave and he would be contacted when needed again. He thought the whole thing suspicious, but the young Englishman gave him a very good tip so he was not that worried. He assumed the woman who was dragged into the house was ill and presumably she was to be looked after by the nurse. Although not conclusive it was enough for Alex to set off to investigate. He thought he might have had difficulty in explaining to my mother his reasons for going, but she just smiled knowingly and said of course he should go and be the white knight.

Even with the car windows open the heat was oppressive and Alex's wound on his back was weeping, sticking his shirt to the car seat. George the taxi driver kept him amused with endless tales of growing up as a foreigner in Glasgow. It was good training for looking after himself in another tough city like Naples. George kept a cosh and a knuckle duster under his front seat in case of emergencies. He was a fast but not reckless driver. Suddenly he screeched to a stop and threw the car into reverse. Looking at the address Alex had given him which was Villa Torre Mangoni, there was a drive leading up to the house which was out of view from the road. They both clambered out of the cab, relieved to be able to stretch their legs. The way was barred by a metal gate secured by a hefty padlock and chain. George wandered up the side of the property. The stone wall which stretched into the distance was too high to scale.

The padlock and chain were rusty but the resourceful George went to the boot of the car, returning with a hammer and chisel. Taking it in turn it took them almost twenty minutes before finally gaining access. Driving up the steep gravel driveway the white house sat commanding wonderful views over the valley. There was no sign of life, with all the windows shut despite the heat. There was a single towel flapping on an upstairs balcony. Alex hammered on the door whilst George went to explore. His wife was a huge fan of Gloria and he could not believe that he could be involved in a possible rescue. Alex sensed movement behind the front door and a female voice started shouting at him in Italian. Moving to the side of the villa Alex could see a woman in a nurse's uniform trying to contact someone on the telephone. George appeared, 'She's there, I've seen her, Gloria bloody Bird laid out on a sofa. She's either dead or out cold.' George went to the car and came back brandishing his cosh. Hammering on the window he shouted at the nurse and drew his hand across his throat. Laughing he informed Alex that he told her he would break in and cut her throat unless she opened the door, which she did. Brushing past her Alex went in search of Gloria. He found her as the driver had said, lying comatose on a sofa. On a table at her side were bottles of tablets and stacks of needles. Alex checked her pulse, but she was just unconscious and not dead as he had half feared.

The ever resourceful George had ripped out the telephone wires and ordered the nurse to organise some lunch. Although plainly terrified she prepared a cheese and bacon salad followed by ice cream. Gloria had still not stirred, but the nurse assured them that she would be fine and she had been instructed to keep Gloria sedated as she had been told that the lady was mentally unstable. George explained that she was now making all kinds of excuses for her behaviour and that she was fearful that the Englishman who had hired her would not pay her. On that they all agreed and she started to cry. Ready to leave, Alex draped a blanket round Gloria who was still dressed in nightclothes. George offered to carry her to the car and as he lifted her up Alex noticed something sticking out from one of the settee's cushions. It was her passport. Presumably she had been conscious enough to stop Keith Noble stealing that as well. Leaving the distraught nurse behind, they drove down the drive and made for Agropoli to fill up with petrol. It had been Alex's intention to drive straight to the airport to get a flight home, but he really wanted to meet Thomas de Groot, alias Keith Noble. He felt a loathing for this small time crook and he wanted to teach him a lesson. When he explained his plan to George, the cabbie could not contain himself. 'This' he declared, 'was better than going to the movies.'

The receptionist at the sumptuous Grand Hotel in Amalfi informed Alex that she had just seen Mr. de Groot go onto the terrace for pre-dinner drinks. The sun was just going down and the views over the glistening sea were spectacular. Pausing, Alex surveyed a collection of bald and grey haired men seated with young women half their age. Alex had always observed how miserable the super rich looked. Presumably if you were able to afford anything you wanted then nothing excited you anymore, not even a young blonde. The one male peroxide blond stood out amongst the sea of paunches and gold chains. Keith Noble was sitting with a beautiful young woman whose cleavage attracted the attention of everyone else around.

Alex rather rudely placed his walking cane on their table. 'Mr. Noble, Gloria asked me to give you this.' Noble had spotted the danger too late and as he struggled to his feet Alex hit him with all the force he could muster. Noble crashed back hitting his head on the balcony rail. Although much younger than my grandfather, despite his deep tan he was flabby and unfit. With blood spurting from his nose Alex gently raised him to his feet before kneeing him in the groin. The squeal of pain could be heard throughout the hotel. Placing the crumpled figure back in a chair he collected his cane, apologised to the young lady with the cleavage and made his way towards reception. He had expected to be seized by waiters, but no one made a move. People either stared at him in amazement or averted their eyes, frightened that perhaps he was some kind of crazed lunatic. Others feared he was connected to the local Mafia, although the assailant looked an unlikely member of that organisation, a feeling underlined as he coolly wished them all a pleasant evening. Outside the taxi's engine was already running. As they sped towards Naples Alex was expecting to hear police sirens at any minute, but they travelled on unheeded. Gloria stirred for the first time, opening her eyes and said, 'Alex darling.' Seemingly reassured she lapsed back into a deep sleep.

Luckily arriving at Heathrow later that night there were no press photographers around to capture Gloria unsteady on her feet and covered in a blanket. Alex had given all the cash he had to George the cab driver on the understanding he would not go to the press with his story. He was as good as his word, apparently satisfied with a signed photograph and a hand written letter of thanks from Gloria. Astonishingly no news of the fracas surfaced, with the hotel obviously anxious not be involved with unwelcome publicity. Weeks later Alex visited Gloria in Hampstead. She was still unwell having been subjected to a cocktail of drugs and sleeping pills over a period of weeks. Already partially dependent on sleeping pills, the Italian experience worryingly appeared to have deepened her addiction. Although drowsy she was able to explain to Alex how she was duped by Keith Noble.

It was Monica who blamed herself of much that was to follow. Rather against her better judgement she had booked a three week stint for Gloria at Murrays, a London night club with a rather dubious reputation. Whilst doubtful about the booking, the owners of the club had been prepared to pay over the odds to secure Gloria's appearance. For three nights a dozen red roses were sent to Gloria's dressing room. She normally avoided 'stage door Johnnies' but on this occasion she agreed to meet her secret admirer. Enter Thomas de Groot. She was not to know that he had form. His usual method was seeking out vulnerable older women enjoying a cruise ship holiday. With his underground connections he had acquired a selection of passports and with them suitable aliases. He had a certain smarmy charm and was an expert at relieving vulnerable ladies of their money. Each success financing a seemingly bona fide and extravagant lifestyle.

Gloria was no fool and she had been round long enough to spot spongers and potential con men and yet she fell for him. She found him physically attractive which was a good starting point. At a time when she felt she was losing her allure she was flattered by the attentions of a younger man. He also went to considerable pains to convince her that her money was the last thing on his mind. Quite the reverse, it was he who was super rich. He set her up with great skill and understanding of her character. He professed to being an avid fan, which helped.

He knew by going out to attract a super star he was moving into a different league, and because potentially the pickings were so huge he was prepared to invest heavily in order to gain access to her undoubted wealth. He invited her to spend a weekend with him down at his house at Bray on the River Thames. He arrived to pick her up in a bright red E-type Jaguar which had only recently been launched by the manufacturer. On a lovely sunny summer's day and with the wind in her hair she felt young again and rejuvenated. The Edwardian mansion was impressive with immaculate lawns stretching towards the river's edge. The staff featured a butler, housekeeper and its own gourmet chef. She later admitted she was blown away. This attractive younger man living in luxury was a powerful aphrodisiac, not that she needed any extra stimulation. He was insatiable to the point where she really felt exhausted. He explained that he was part of an old Dutch East Indian dynasty that still dominated the spice trade and who owned vast tracts of forestry in Indonesia.

Again it was only later that Gloria learned that it was not only the name Thomas de Groot that was a sham. Both the car and the house were rented and the Dutch connection illusory, but she fell for it. He stayed with her in the weeks leading up to the wedding. He explained they were unable to go down to Bray as major reconstruction work had begun. He was clever, leaving bank statements around showing massive deposits. These were created for him by a forger based in Ramsgate. There was more. He hired an out of work actor to ring him and Gloria would listen to bogus deals apparently worth millions being discussed, and still he overwhelmed her with his passion. Life she honestly felt could hardly be better, and half to her surprise she found herself readily accepting his proposal of marriage despite Monica's obvious disapproval. Following the Capri wedding all seemed well, although marriage appeared to have massively reduced his lust for her. He constantly complained of feeling unwell and was irritable and increasingly petulant. He was very insistent on them opening a joint bank account but Monica had warned her against this.

When it was explained to him that Monica controlled Gloria's finances and investments he became really angry, explaining that she would be the one to gain as obviously he had far more money than Gloria. Changing tack he started being affectionate and passionate towards her again. He managed to find out that Gloria still kept a substantial sum in her current account, much to Monica's annoyance.

Changing strategy Noble now opted for short term gain rather than playing the long game. Perhaps she should have spotted warning signs as it was left to her to settle the hotel account for their first week's stay, as he maintained he had to go at short notice to a business meeting in Positano. On his return he was excited about a deal involving a purchase which could make them a fortune. He was investing half a million and suggested she might like to make a small investment. He discovered she had some thirty thousand pounds in her current account and he suggested that she would double her money within weeks. She really had no reason to doubt him and besides she had always enjoyed a bit of a gamble. She wrote the cheque for an investment finance company. Her bank rang and she confirmed that she was happy for the cheque to be cleared. From the moment the money was transferred her memory became vague. The next thing she remembered was seeing Alex in the taxi on the way to Naples airport.

It is difficult to understand what Noble was trying to achieve. Thirty thousand pounds was a huge sum back in the early 1960s. Perhaps he realised that Monica was going to be an on-going problem for him to be able to access all of Gloria's money and investments. Maybe he had decided to bank his gains and move on, although keeping her drugged rather suggested that he would try to cajole or threaten more money out of her. We shall never know. What we do know is that Keith Noble disappeared bandy-legged that night from the Grand Hotel without paying the bill. He was arrested two years later in Cape Town where he was still up to his old tricks. This time the widow of a wealthy diamond merchant tracked him down and for the next three years he languished in a Durban jail. Meanwhile Keith's wife continued living with their two children in Ilford. Having refused to give him a divorce she had arranged a very violent home-coming if he ever set foot in Essex again. Gloria never did get her money back but the fact that Noble was already married guaranteed that Gloria was now free to marry again, but she promised both Monica and Alex that this was never going to happen. This time she was true to her word.

Chapter 28

A final curtain

It difficult to pinpoint decline, both in health and ability. Certainly the Italian experience affected both Gloria and Alex, albeit in different ways. Whilst Gloria had flirted with drugs throughout much of her career, she now became increasingly dependent with a particular addiction to sleeping pills which affected her performances. Monica negotiated an important television series *An evening with Gloria*. This should have been an opportunity for her to expand her popularity, but her appearances were stilted and wooden. She needed a live audience, feeding off their applause. Being in front of a camera seemed to suck the vitality from her. As well as singing, she interviewed guest stars but she showed little spontaneity. It was if she had tried to memorise a set script. It verged on the embarrassing and she was not invited back for a second series. Alex also suffered a setback after the scuffle in Amalfi. On his return home his hand swelled up alarmingly. His knockout punch had broken his hand in several places. He had already witnessed the onset of arthritis and this worsened markedly over the following years. Eventually he could hardly hold a brush, but even in the short term the quality of his work declined.

It was at the very time that he was doubting his ability to continue painting that he received a letter informing him that he was to be knighted. Until the official announcement he had to keep the news to himself, not even informing Angela. I have a number of photographs of the three of us standing outside Buckingham Palace. I had come down from university as they both felt that being photographed together would start tongues wagging and they wanted to avoid publicity. Alex was genuinely shocked by the honour and joked that they obviously thought he was dying. The change in my mother's appearance over a very short period was startling. In less than a year her hair had changed from brown to a silvery grey. She had not experienced any trauma or shock but the change was dramatic. Unlike many women my mother embraced her new look, and rightly so as it heightened rather than diminished her attractiveness. Holiday snaps from Deia show her transformed in a matter of months. They continued to love their summer months together, although like Robert Graves they were also now beginning to regret the march of the tourist industry. Now lines of tourists encouraged the opening of bars, restaurants and gift shops. Hidden gems across Europe were hidden no more.

Earlier they had unusually appeared in public together to mark the closing of the Windmill theatre. Alex had become friendly with Sheila Van Damm since the death of her father. They met regularly for coffee whilst she explained the difficulties she was experiencing keeping the theatre afloat. The swinging sixties had led to a far more liberal climate and queues no longer wound down Great Windmill Street waiting for a glimpse of naked flesh. Now there was plenty on show in the surrounding streets. Despite her heroic efforts the business was losing about a thousand pounds a week, losses that were not sustainable. Quietly she put the theatre on the market, but initially there was little interest. It was too small to survive as a theatre with a seating capacity of only three hundred. Eventually a buyer was found and it seemed likely that the building would revert to being a cinema.

For thirty two years this unique venue had produced non-stop entertainment, but it was time to let go. Once news of the sale was announced the public flocked back in droves. Four performances on that final Saturday were fully booked. Despite their close association with the theatre it was the first time that either Alex or Angela had sat in the auditorium. The final show was slick and one that even the critical Vivian Van Damm would have been proud of. Artistes who had appeared at the Mill and gone onto fame were invited on to the stage. It had proved to be a tough training ground for many comedians who desperately tried to grab the attention of punters only interested in bare flesh. Richard Murdoch and Michael Bentine were cheered to the rafters, to be followed by Harry Secombe and a host of other household names. A gigantic party followed the final curtain call. This was to be a celebration, not a wake. Five hundred bottles of champagne were on hand and the celebrations went on well into the early hours. Alex saw hardly anything of Angela as she plunged into a melee of girls she had danced with all those years ago. Some had changed completely, piling on the weight, whilst others still held themselves like the professional dancers they had been. It was a mad scrum. There are photographs of my mother with Des O'Connor and several of the girls who danced with her some twenty years earlier.

Later that night laying in bed together Alex again asked my mother to marry him. He was fed up with pretence. He was proud of his Angel and wanted to be seen by her side. Gently she turned him down telling him they were fine as they were. He could not understand why. Surely enough time had elapsed and anyway attitudes had changed. 'Not now, Alex' she whispered, 'But maybe some day. You know I really do love you.' He was feeling old and vulnerable. He would have willingly exchanged his knighthood and his wealth just to find permanent happiness with Angela, but as ever true happiness continued to be elusive. As he was drifting off to sleep the phone rang. It was three o'clock in the morning. A befuddled sounding Gloria told him she could not sleep and insisted he came over to Hampstead at once. Eventually he had to put the phone down on her. Angela was sitting up in bed. She had obviously heard the conversation. 'Gloria?' she enquired. Alex started to explain, 'Don't worry.' Angela said, 'I understand.' But Alex was convinced that she did not and that was the crux of their problem.

During the 1960s London was the world centre for fashion, music and creativity. People came from around the world to wander down Carnaby Street, soaking up the excitement that new ideas and enthusiasm had brought. By the early 70s much of this gloss had been consumed in a sea of terrible hair-styles and flared trousers. Perhaps it was a need to reconnect with the past that led to Monica obtaining a booking for Gloria to appear at the Talk Of The Town, London's most popular night spot. Like many international artistes Gloria had been affected by the craze for rock'n'roll, where often singers or groups would take top spot on the back of just one hit record. Work for Gloria became more difficult and her recording contract was not renewed. This had led to her being more needy, constantly ringing Alex for reassurance. Her sleeping pill intake also increased dramatically, and she spent much of her day either asleep or stumbling around in a drowsy half life.

The booking at the Talk Of The Town was important but Monica was worried. The Talk Of The Town had been open since 1958 and was on the site of the former London Hippodrome. For several years it functioned as a circus with a particular emphasis on horses and high-wire acts. Later it became a music hall and then as a theatre specialising in light comedy. A fortune was spent gutting the building and creating a glamorous night spot with a particular appeal to suburbia. Here was a chance to take your family or join your work colleagues for a memorable night out for about twenty pounds a head, which included food, wine and a top line entertainer to conclude the cabaret. It was wholesome, the chorus girls wore exotic costumes but there was not a bare boob in sight. It seated around eight hundred with some tables situated right next to the stage often reserved for celebrities, whilst others fanned out across a vast area with additional tables looking down from a first floor balcony.

During rehearsals Monica searched Gloria's hotel bedroom. She threw all the sleeping pills she could find down the toilet, but like an alcoholic Gloria had squirreled them away in the most unlikely places. Despite a huge row the first night's performance went well. For the first time Monica sensed that Gloria was nervous. Whilst many major performers suffer stage fright all their careers, this had never been a problem for Gloria. She revelled in the response she drew from the audience and on that night they were generous in their applause. If anything the second night was even more assured and Monica began to relax. Satisfied, she did not attend for the following three performances which Gloria assured her had gone well, but Monica had a phone call from the general manager of the club asking her to visit him that afternoon. She was alarmed to hear that Gloria's performances were causing concern. The previous night she had stumbled from her piano stool and luckily the audience thought this was just part of her act. In truth, Gloria being a pro had carried this off with aplomb, but overall she appeared hesitant and on a couple of occasions forgot the lyrics of the numbers she was singing. Monica assured him that Gloria had picked up a minor urinary infection and she should be admired for being such a trooper.

Back at the hotel Monica found Gloria asleep. She stayed with her until it was time for her to prepare for the night's performance. She explained the management's concerns. She expected Gloria to shout and pour out excuses. She normally refused to accept any criticism but that night Gloria's reaction was passive. She smiled explaining that she was feeling good and tonight she would have the audience on their feet. They were but many were booing and demanding their money back. Her act started well enough. She got through the dance routine without any mishaps and at least she made it to the piano stool without falling off, but then the trouble started. She was half way through singing 'It was on the Isle of Capri' when she stopped, closed the piano lid and said, 'I hate that bloody song.' At first there was a stunned silence as she staggered to the front of the stage holding a microphone. Someone at the back shouted out, 'Are you pissed?' Responding to an audience was normally one of Gloria's strengths. At this stage she could have won her audience back, instead she let rip a tirade of abuse. She attempted to start her next number but she was drowned out by a wave of booing. Taking matters into her own hands Monica came on stage whilst Gloria was escorted away. Monica apologised on Gloria's behalf and explained that Gloria had a urinary infection which can cause a change in personality. The booing continued until Monica asked if there was a doctor in the house.

She was saved by a doctor joining her on stage confirming that the condition can bring on changes in personality, including uncharacteristic aggression. The situation was further rescued as the Beverley Sisters had been in the audience to see Gloria. In true showbiz tradition they came on stage and wowed the audience with a stellar impromptu performance.

Early the following morning Alex received a phone call from Monica who explained the disaster of the previous night. Gloria had one final performance to redeem herself, but now she was refusing to appear unless Alex was backstage to support her. By the time Alex arrived at the Piccadilly Hotel Monica had cleverly arranged for Gloria's suite to be changed, leaving any hidden sleeping pills behind. Gloria burst into tears the moment Alex entered her room, telling him the audience the previous night had been cruel and she insisted she would not perform later that night. He was having none of her histrionics and was brutal in his assessment of her. She was being pathetic and not only risking her future but also her legacy. If she wanted to pull out that was her problem. He told her she was a fraud, not a true trooper, someone who had been living off her past reputation for years, adding that she was looking old and that she was a coward who couldn't hack it anymore. He had taken a risk but he knew she would balk at his criticism. She went straight back on the attack telling him he had no right to judge her as he had not painted anything worthwhile for years. Monica was a spectator as they hurled abuse at each other. Finally they could think of no other insults to hurl. Alex took her in his arms and she dissolved into tears again. This time not tears of anger or even self pity. Pulling away from him she shouted, 'I'll show you. I'll show them, you wait.' And she did.

The story of her breakdown in front of a packed audience was too late for the morning press and there was no mention of it in the early editions of the London evening papers, but she was aware that news would have circulated by the time she came on stage. Alex watched her from the wings with renewed awe. Never apologise, never explain has proved a good mantra over the years. Gloria made no mention of the previous evening but started by telling her audience that tonight they were all going to have a ball. She was terrific, flawless, full of verve and vitality and the audience were loath to let her go. She had one final card to play. Eartha Kitt was sitting with a party close to the stage and was invited to join Gloria in a couple of old favourites. People were standing, cheering where twenty fours hours before they had been shouting abuse. As usual with the adrenalin flowing following a triumphant performance, Gloria insisted on them finding a restaurant to round off a perfect evening. Most were already closed so Gloria suggested going back to her hotel for a nightcap. Gloria did her best to reinvent the past, but Alex gently suggested that tonight she really did need to sleep. Rejection, no matter how tactful, was enough to send Gloria into overdrive. He could still hear her shouting as he waited for the lift. The only words he could pick up were 'Bloody Angela!'

Chapter 29

Just call me Angel

Ageing is something we all have to come to terms with eventually. Everyone handles this process differently. There are those who are in denial, who try to defy nature, but ultimately there is only one winner. Others embrace old age with it being a great leveller. Gloria, like most professional dancers, remained physically incredibly fit for her age. Unfortunately a life of drugs, sleeping pills and increasingly a liking for brandy was taking its toll. She continued to work mostly on the continent, but more often now at secondary venues. Monica tried to protect her but Gloria was frequently depressed and confused. Her moods could still change alarmingly from self pity to moments of exhilaration. During these interludes she was back to being her old self, brimming with confidence and fun, talking of plans to make a world tour, only for her to relapse into self inflicted gloom. A suggestion by Monica that perhaps Gloria should think of retirement produced a reaction of rage and abuse.

Alex's problems were entirely physical. Years of not taking exercise and sitting or standing in front of an easel were coming home to roost. As a young man Alex had been a keen sportsman. He had shown great promise at tennis but his injuries, particularly his leg, restricted his participation in active sports. He had attempted golf but he found it impossible to keep his balance, finding himself prone on the ground after attempting to drive the ball off the tee. His interest remained and he spent many happy days at Lords, and he also enjoyed a day out racing often in the company of the artist Alfred Munnings. His diet was also not very healthy. He ate out a great deal either with Angela or when he was alone in Archer Street. It was easier to go to one of dozens of wonderful restaurants close by. He was lucky that he never piled on the weight, but he noticed he was becoming increasingly breathless and he was also subject to occasional giddy spells.

Age is also a key factor in relationships, particularly when one partner is considerably younger than the other. What had not seemed a problem in the first flush of love can fester later when the age difference becomes more apparent. This was not the case with my grandfather and Angela. As the years passed they became even more attached to each other. She was patient as walking became more of a problem to him. She was content just being together. Astonishingly neither could ever remember having a real row. They bickered but always in the knowledge that their love was solid and long lasting. They still led their separate lives enjoying their own space, but increasingly they spent more time together culminating in their continued annual trips to Majorca. It was unfortunate that the house in Deia was the setting where Angela realised that she had a problem.

It had been a particularly hot day and Angela had spent the afternoon tending their small garden. It was in the shower that she first noticed a small lump in her breast. Determined not to be obsessive about it she tried to push it to the back of her mind, but the lump persisted. She made no mention of it to Alex. They still had over a month before they returned home, although Alex did register later that Angela had not been quite her normal breezy and cheerful self. Once home Angela went to see her doctor who referred her to a specialist. After a series of tests it was confirmed that she had cancer. Her specialist did not spare her. At her relatively young age the prognosis was not very encouraging. Having let her down with a bump he then sought to encourage her with the number of new treatments now available. For the next two years Angela endured the roller coaster ride familiar to those who have experienced a similar problem. Radiotherapy, chemotherapy, remissions, hope and despair, all intermingled.

The diagnosis did obviously have a profound effect on Angela and Alex's lives. To his immense relief Angela finally agreed to marriage. The thought of her fighting this illness alone was not an option as far as Alex was concerned. Their first major decision was to sell their two properties and find somewhere to live together. Angela's consultant was based at the Middlesex hospital in Mortimer Street, so it was important to find somewhere in central London so that she would not have to travel far for her treatment. By a strange quirk they found that the hospital was originally situated on Windmill Street in the eighteenth century. Ever since the Windmill closed down a decade before Alex had been thinking of moving, now circumstances demanded it. Soho was always full of gossip and rumours and much of the talk revolved around Paul Raymond. His Revue Bar, which had a whiff of sleaze and surface glamour, had proved an enormous success since opening in 1958. Sex sells and the Revue Bar became a magnet for men from all over the world splashing out on their expense accounts.

The shows produced were professional, but always pushing the boundaries of what was thought acceptable. As Raymond's empire expanded into magazines and casinos, his wealth continued to grow. The word was that he was buying up blocks of property in Soho that were still relatively cheap. Alex had been to the club once with some chums from the Royal Academy and met Raymond on a couple of occasions. Alex visited him at the club in Walkers Court. He was welcomed by Raymond already drinking champagne at eleven o'clock in the morning. Alex found him friendly, charming and certainly interested in acquiring Archer Street. Within days he had sent his team of surveyors and valuers to look over the property and a deal was agreed within the week. Angela's Islington property took longer to sell, but Alex had found what he thought was a suitable apartment for them on Albermarle Street. It was situated above an art gallery where mostly nineteenth century paintings were sold. They were also renowned restorers undertaking work at many of Britain's leading ancestral houses. Restoration was extended to transforming paintings of old dowagers into beautiful young women and dark landscapes into golden meadows pictured in dappled sunlight. The art market continued to astonish him.

The wedding was a happy but low key celebration. After the civil ceremony about a dozen of us including Angela's best friend Ruby went to Frederick's Restaurant in Camden Passage. Champagne toasts and rivers of wine helped mask the worry with Angela starting her treatment the following day. Alex had invited Monica Wiseman but she declined saying that Gloria would blow a fuse if she found out. Gloria was aware of the marriage but there was no telegram of congratulations and for the next two years she made no contact with Alex at all.

For those years Alex endured with Angel the rays of hope only for them to be subsequently dashed. During the whole period of her illness she remained cheerful and optimistic unlike Alex who was often subject to periods of panic and depression, although he tried not to show it. Angela was well enough for them to take a final holiday in Deia which ultimately had to be cut short as her condition declined. The consultant told them as gently as he could that there was no more that could be done other than keeping Angela comfortable and free from pain. Life is precious and she hung on for weeks longer than expected. Either Alex or a nurse sat with her in the wonderful apartment that she had so little time to enjoy. Alerted that the end was close Alex sat by her bedside as she slipped in and out of sleep. He was drowsing when suddenly she sat up, smiled and said quite clearly, 'Alex, you'll be the death of me!' She started laughing and Alex held her in a last embrace. She was desperately thin and he laid her gently back in the bed. She gave him a last smile before lapsing into a coma. Within a couple of hours she was dead. He opened the windows to allow her spirit to slip away. For the second time in his life Alex sat beside the body of a woman he had loved. The strain and pain of her long illness were banished and she looked so beautiful as if restored to health in death.

Angela had insisted on being cremated. None of that mouldering in a grave for her, get it over and done with, she instructed. There was a memorial service at St. Mary's, the local parish church in Islington, and Alex was astonished at the attendance with all the seats in the church taken. At the wake held in the Fox, a pub on Islington Green, Alex marvelled at the number of people she had touched during her time in Colebrooke Row. Market traders, antique dealers, neighbours, even the local policeman. When the final guest had drifted away I escorted my grandfather back to Albermarle Street. We sat into the early hours draining the best part of a bottle of his favourite Irish whiskey. He tried to appear positive, but it was obvious that he was devastated. Over the following months I spent many hours with him.

As he began to tell me about his life it occurred to me that perhaps he wanted his story to be told. Certainly he spent days systematically arranging a detailed archive of letters, photographs, articles and recorded interviews. About three months after Angela's death he suffered a heart attack and was rushed into University College Hospital where gradually he was nursed back to health. It was about this time that Gloria contacted him again. There is a letter saying that she had heard that he had been unwell and suggesting that they should meet up again as she was shortly to appear at the London Palladium. Of course they did have that last date ending that night in the Grosvenor House Hotel. It was later that morning that my grandfather had a second heart attack in the foyer of the hotel. Again he was taken to hospital where once more he staged a recovery. He returned to painting, renting a studio from the gallery below his apartment. I kept in regular contact and he seemed more settled and asked me if I would go with him to Deia as he wanted to meet with his lawyers there so the house could be transferred to me and my wife.

Some days before we were due to leave I had a phone call from his daily help to tell me tearfully that she had found him dead in bed. Although he may not have wanted it, his funeral was far more high profile than his beloved Angel. The great and the good flocked to St. James's, Piccadilly. Not only friends and fellow artists, but also those who always seem to turn up for funerals of the famous. There were politicians including the Arts Minister and celebrities who never miss a chance to be in the public eye. I swear many of them had never met my grandfather. Gloria was obviously an important mourner, still managing to look dramatic swathed in black. She sobbed loudly throughout the service but left immediately after the last hymn, not stopping to talk to anyone. Monica made apologies to me on her behalf insisting that this time Gloria's tears and distress were genuine. Later a few of us went onto Highgate Cemetery for the burial.

Alex had explained to me the eerie feeling he got on going back to Bushey after Helen's death and it was certainly true when I went back to Albermarle Street after the interment. Everything was exactly as my grandfather had left it. It was a beautiful apartment, comfortable rather than ostentatious. The pastel shades of the furnishings doubtless selected by Angela. Many of his paintings lined the walls. It had been left to me to settle his estate, with much of his considerable wealth donated to a variety of charities, including Cancer Research. There was a folder on his desk with a note, 'Rex, please turn on the record player and then look inside the folder.' Alex always liked a little drama. Curious, I did as I was instructed. At first I hardly heard the record. The folder contained two exquisite sepia drawings of my mother done in the style of a Rossetti pastiche. He had almost brought her back to life again. How strange that he had arranged this tribute to my mum for now I was conscious of Merrilee Rush singing:

'Just call me Angel of the morning, Angel
Just touch my cheek before you leave me, baby
Just call me Angel of the morning, Angel
Then slowly turn away from me.'

Chapter 30

Full circle

W hen my grandfather was in his early sixties he appeared in a popular television programme called *Face To Face*. In it the former Labour M.P John Freeman conducted a number of interviews with well known figures, ranging from the pop star Adam Faith to at the other extreme Carl Jung and Evelyn Waugh. Unlike modern day TV inquisitors, Freeman's technique was so gentle as to be almost hypnotic. Gentle but probing and decisive, taking his subjects into areas they would have preferred to avoid. Filmed in black and white, the camera technique was intrusive and unsettling. Freeman is only ever glimpsed from behind, whilst the camera honed in on the face of his subject, picking up every sign of discomfort as beads of sweat appeared under the glare of the studio lights.

Alex looked quite composed as Freeman outlined his career as one of Britain's foremost artists. Delving back to schooldays, he moved on to the influence of Alex's parents and the fact that he had been raised in a privileged position of great comfort. He now gently probed into Alex's war record, asking about his decorations for bravery. Alex maintained he had been awarded the Military Cross for being drunk and disorderly and had no memory of the actual event. Despite the closeness of the camera he remained at ease, deflecting from any area that may have caused him discomfort. His painting of 'Despair' and his subsequent time in Newlyn brought no surprises, but he began to look uncomfortable when discussing his marriage to Helen.

Freeman had a way of letting answers hang in the air and his probing of Helen's death saw a bead of sweat appear and the hint of a tear. 'I understand your wife died of an insulin overdose.' Alex explained that injecting insulin was still in its infancy at the time and her death was a tragic accident. There was a long pause and then Freeman's follow up question had Alex shifting in his seat. 'You have never remarried?' Alex tried to lessen the tension by saying he wasn't sure anyone would take him on. Freeman altered tack. 'Another tragic event was the death of your son.' It was obvious now that Alex was feeling really uncomfortable, his eyes no longer looking straight into the camera. The pressure was building. 'I understand you remain extremely close to your daughter-in-law.' Alex appeared irritated. 'Of course, she is the mother of my son's child. It is only natural that we stay close as a family.' Another pause. 'I see,' said Freeman, somehow raising doubts in the viewer's mind.

Another switch to discuss the art world led Alex to more comfortable ground. Again using humour to reduce the tension, he admitted he had often contemplated refusing to authenticate one of his paintings when contacted by auction houses. Why would a painting authenticated by him fetch thousands and yet that same painting selling for a few pounds if he disclaimed it. He reckoned the whole art market was mad but admitted that he continued to benefit from it. Finally he was thrown by a sudden reference to Gloria. The same gentle maddening voice suggested that he had enjoyed a very close relationship with the famous star. Alex had now fully recovered his composure, asserting confidently that Gloria was an old and valued friend spanning over forty years. His ordeal was over but he was left wondering why he had put himself through such an unnecessary cross examination.

The show produced few subsequent ripples and was generally thought to have been one of the less interesting compared to the interview with the TV personality Gilbert Harding, who had been reduced to tears and had an apparent breakdown in front of the camera. Despite his discomfort Alex came over well as an attractive personality.

Typically Gloria was miffed that she had never been asked to appear with Freeman. Now that Alex was dead she realised that he had been one of the few constants in her life and she was going to miss him terribly. A double blow for her was Monica's decision to retire. They had fought and argued over the years, but suddenly Gloria realised what an important part Monica had played in her life. She was engaged by a leading management company but her star was on the wane and bookings were drying up. She was now regularly forgetting lyrics to the songs she was performing. Even she realised it was time to leave the stage.

Her memory continued to worsen and she was diagnosed with dementia. Monica arranged for her to go to a very good but expensive nursing home. Over a period of four years her condition worsened. It was a cruel illness gradually robbing speech, understanding and mobility. Finally she faded away in her sleep almost six years to the day since Alex died. Their paths had always been linked and remained so even in death. Gloria had lived a life of utmost selfishness and yet he had remained enthralled by her. Gloria's selfishness even extended beyond the grave. There is a modern trend for people to design their own funeral service. Alex was not interested in that but he did give thought to where he would be buried. Initially he thought he could lie next to Helen in Bushey, but by doing so he felt he would be denying Angela. He had an aversion to cremation so following a number of visits to Highgate cemetery he bought himself a plot. The cemetery, which was opened in 1839, is a somewhat wild yet magical oasis in north London. Set amidst trees and undergrowth, despite the work of gardeners it was a refuge from the modern world. I make an annual pilgrimage there. His simple stone reads 'Alexander Beck, artist' and the dates of his birth and death. No mention of his title or wartime decoration. My initial reaction to Gloria's far more ornate grave situated right next to him was one of annoyance. She had elbowed her way in by buying the plot linking them into eternity. I felt upset that she had sidelined my mother, but on reflection I guessed that Angela might have found the situation hilarious. Alex and the three women in his life, and still the connection between them was not all complete. Perhaps it could be resolved in the after life.

It was an incredibly important day. My golden wedding anniversary and the last day of my grandfather's retrospective exhibition at the Royal Academy. My wife and I had been to the opening day, but now I wanted to have a last look at the paintings before they were returned to galleries, museums and private collectors around the world. There was one particular work that continued to fascinate me. Gloria stared at me from a crumpled bed after a night of passion with Alex. It was not difficult to see why he was so infatuated by her. Her facial expression could be interpreted in a dozen ways. Love, amusement, desire, teasing, a woman capable of taking a man to impossible heights only to be let down as something or someone else took her fancy. A sexy temptress but a fickle lover. Monica Wiseman had kept it in store for years and hung it in her south coast house until she died. It was now on its way to the Metropolitan Art Museum in New York.

Making my way across the courtyard to Burlington House I was retracing the walk that Alex had made in 1976. Today it was not hot and humid, but a bright early autumn morning. The traffic in Piccadilly remained gridlocked and now Chinese rather than Japanese tourists thronged the street, and like their Asian cousins continuously taking photographs. The old front entrance to the Ritz was now blocked off so I entered from Arlington Street. I sat on possibly the same chair outside the Palm Court and ordered an Irish whiskey. Maya had been to the hairdresser and like my mother she had allowed her hair to grow grey. Set against her olive skin, even in old age she continued to look sensational. She kissed me on the cheek and linking arms we made our way slowly into the spectacular dining room in London. Unlike Gloria and Alex, nobody took much notice of an old couple as they were shown to that favoured window table overlooking the park. Yet my wife was even more famous than her mother, albeit in a totally different field. As you will have gathered, dear reader, Maya and I were married back in 1972, but that is another story.

The End